The Royal Governess

by

Barbara Lohr

Purple Egret Press

Purple Egret Press
Savannah, Georgia 31411

This book is a work of fiction. The characters, events and places in the book are products of the author's imagination and are either fictitious or used fictitiously. Any similarity of real persons, living or dead, is purely coincidental and not intended by the author.

Cover Designer: Kim Killion – The Killion Group
Editor: Bev Katz Rosenbaum

ISBN: 978-1-945523-22-9

For single women everywhere,

may you find your Marco.

Chapter 1

My mother always told me, "Christina, never get into a car with a strange man." Would that apply to boats too? As I studied the back of Milo's head, nerves tightened in my stomach. Maybe I should have listened to Mom.

Milo, the man who'd picked us up at the airport, needed a shave and a haircut. Still, the sign in his hands had my name. Newhart. Was this where my panicked decision to escape Pittsburgh had led me? Not only had I signed on for this governess gig in a foreign country, I'd dragged my fourteen-year-old daughter with me. Actually, Lexi was the reason we were here.

Spray hit my face when the boat dove into another wave. Clutching my tote, I blinked furiously. Around us stretched dark water and foamy whitecaps. No land in sight. Fear raked my chest.

"Isn't this great?" Lexi shouted, her dripping hair flying with each bounce.

Somehow I managed to nod. No way would I let my daughter know how terrified I was right now. How guilty I felt for uprooting her to this summer on a Mediterranean island—or so the ad had said.

If we ended up in a harem in Algiers, it would be all my fault.

After all, I was the one who'd answered the online ad placed by King Marco Napolitano. But this was not what I'd pictured when I'd printed off the boarding passes for the flight to Naples, Italy. I only knew that he lived in a castle with his son Gregorio.

At the airport a morose man had stood at the end of the ramp holding the sign. Eyes gritty from the long trip, I'd rushed toward him. "Hi, I'm Christina Newhart and this is my daughter Lexi."

My extended hand was ignored. He knifed a thumb into his chest "Milo. Where is the boy?" He scanned a note crumpled in his hand.

Oh, right. There was that. I tried to look concerned. "What boy?"

Muttering something under his breath, he shoved the paper back into a pocket. "Come." Jerking his head toward the sign that said *bagaglio*, he took off, dumping the sign. We hurried to keep up. For a guy wearing run-down slippers and a few extra pounds, he could hustle. Grateful for my sensible tie-shoes, I set off after him.

But I would have appreciated a smile. A quick handshake. Some reassurance.

Stop it, Christina. No more snap judgments.

Lexi's head had swiveled as she took it all in. People babbled around us but no one seemed to be speaking English. I'd followed Milo to the carousel where my suitcase with its red tie had just plopped from the chute. Lexi's bag wore a purple tie that matched her hair. Grabbing our luggage, we scurried after Milo, who was already disappearing through the glass door. A limo waited for us outside.

After a short ride from the airport, we ended up on a dock. Our baggage was stowed and the boat took off.

So here we were. Looking over my shoulder, I attempted a smile. Nodding as he flicked his cigarette ashes over the water, Milo looked comfortable in his cushioned seat. All was right with his world. Mine was feeling a little unsteady.

Shivering, my daughter looked around her. How hard would it be at fourteen to have your mother take you away from your friends for the summer? But Lexi needed that distance. Although she didn't want it, she needed it. And I needed it too. "Are we almost there, Mr. Milo?"

"Soon." Tossing his cigarette butt over the side, Milo lit up another.

I opened my mouth to fill him in on how many sea turtles died from eating debris discarded by humans. Then I reconsidered. Maybe another time. My jaw snapped shut. Up ahead, a man in a knit cap handled the wheel. All kind of instruments blinked on that deck.

This would be a great story to tell my friends back in America. Reena and Maddie would find this hilarious. Well, if we survived.

Tying my scarf tighter around my neck, I turned up the collar of my trench coat. "Isn't this an adventure? Going out on our own?" I chirped to my daughter.

"Where are we?" Lexi's dark eyeliner was running from the corners of her eyes. Was that from the crazy waves or was she crying? Arms folded across her chest, she shivered in her black jean jacket. Her excitement was wearing off.

"I think we're in the Mediterranea Sea. Isn't it great? Well, not in the sea, but on the sea." Mercy, I hoped we wouldn't end up *in* the sea.

I will not look down. I just will not.

Another watery bump. Another jolt to my stomach.

I looked away. Lexi had given me tons of trouble the past year. And I'd cried plenty—the hopeless tears of a single mother. At least I wouldn't have to go into Principal Weston's office one more time to hear what my daughter had been hiding in her locker. The embarrassment was twofold since I taught at the same school Lexi attended.

"When are we going to eat?" Lexi's voice held a plaintive note. "I'm starving."

"I'm sure Mr. Napolitano will have lunch for us. Or dinner."

"What time is it here anyway?"

"Probably about nine. I think."

She squinted up at the gray skies. "In the morning?"

"I think so. We moved ahead five or six hours crossing the Atlantic."

Lexi turned away, flipping up the collar of her jacket.

The last month of school had been a frantic jumble. Paging through a professional magazine during my seventh hour prep period, I'd seen the ad for a governess for a high school junior on an island. My heart had lifted. I could pry my daughter away for the summer. Long ago I'd read about an actress who'd moved to Scotland with her daughter to get her away from peer pressure and bad decisions. The plan had worked. If we were away on our own, I'd have some parental control. At least, that was my plan.

When Mr. Napolitano wrote in response to my inquiry, his requirements had been demanding. And the royal stationary had been intimidating. He might be a king, but nothing was going to stop me. I kind of went overboard with my resume, but what's a desperate mother to do? Lexi was slipping away. My only child. The girl who supposedly would comfort me in my old age.

Behind the boat, gray water churned before peeling back in a white-flecked wake we left far behind. Nothing appeared on the horizon to quiet my fears. Jamming my fingers into my pockets, I found some cellophane packets and pulled them out. "Look, sweetheart. Food."

Biscuits. That's what the flight attendant had called the cookies when she came down the aisle toward the end of the flight. Mr. Napolitano had generously booked us in business class. That had seemed promising. The flight attendants actually paid attention to people in that section, although two packets of biscuits weren't exactly extravagant. Last night's late dinner had consisted of freeze-dried chicken on flattened beds of lettuce with some sort of creamy dressing. I took a pass.

Lexi opened her packet and slid a biscuit out. I did the same and we began to munch. The cookies tasted of cinnamon and nutmeg.

Spying something up ahead, I pointed. "Look." On the edge of the horizon, a blueish gray image had materialized. Turning to Milo, I asked, "Is that the island?"

"Napolitano? Yes, yes." He pulled out a phone.

My spirits lifted. The fog had dissipated, and a weak sun

struggled to break through the clouds. *Sunblock.* I'd forgotten to bring sunblock but certainly there would be stores on the island. As the sun grew stronger, the water took on a pleasing aquamarine tint. My tense muscles eased.

Slipping the scarf from my head, I ran a hand over the hair I'd yanked into a ponytail before the delayed last leg of our three flights. After all, I wanted to make a good impression.

Although I'd searched online, I couldn't find much about King Marco Napolitano and his son Gregorio. They kept a low profile. The family was involved in making wine, but that had been on the fourth page of my search.

Oh, I couldn't wait to meet them. Now I was delighted by the shoreline. Fitting snugly together, pretty pastel buildings peeked from the dark green foliage. My earlier fears faded along with the morning fog. At the dock, men bustled about their boats. Shouting and laughter carried across the water along with the smell of fish.

"Yuk," Lexi muttered.

"Local color, Lexi. Isn't it charming?" Just as I was searching the crowds along the pier, the boat veered to the right. I grabbed the railing with my left hand and Lexi's arm with my right. Lips pursed, she shook me off.

The scenic village receded. Next to me, Lexi sighed. Turning back to Milo, I shouted, "Where are we going?" I wanted to go back to the wharf with the cute little cottages.

Apparently, Milo hadn't heard me. "When will we be there?" I asked in a louder voice.

Studying his phone, he shook his head. "Soon."

A man of few words. But at least we could see a shoreline.

Behind us the town grew smaller and smaller. The sun had strengthened, glancing off the water in sharp rays. Yes, I really should have brought sunblock.

And maybe a handgun. Not that I knew how to use one.

Before too long we approached a boathouse that looked as if it had been there for ages. Some kind of red and green crest adorned the weathered tan stucco.

"Look at that," Lexi breathed beside me. "Just like in the movies."

Right. In murder mysteries, someone was always getting killed in a boathouse. I rubbed my arms to keep warm.

The roar of the motor cut back and the boat glided into an enclosure of silent, dark shadows. A chill snaked down my spine. "Well. I guess we're almost there." My voice echoed from the rafters, where doves sat cooing. Next to our slip sat a larger boat, painted green and red with gold detailing.

Men scrambled to briskly tie up the boat. I couldn't understand a thing they said with Milo as they tossed heavy ropes around. Throwing covert glances our way, they mumbled together. Were they saying, "You take the young one and I'll take the old bat"?

English teachers have wild imaginations. The next few minutes were blurred by activity.

Lexi's eyes widened with wonder. Two burly men dropped a walkway between the boat and the pier with a clatter I felt in my teeth. Getting off with a rolling gait, Milo motioned to us and we marched off behind him. As we walked toward the sunlight

7

pouring through an open doorway, I lifted my eyes to what looked like a crest—the same as the one outside. Two swords crossed beneath an eagle, talons spread. Lots of gilded scrolling. Was the word Napolitano scripted under the crest? When I stumbled, Lexi grabbed me.

Outside, the sun felt warm and reassuring. Our luggage appeared on the dock. Glancing around at the tropical abundance of orange and red flowers, I felt my sanity return. Any uneasy thoughts about that crest were left behind. Probably every island in the Mediterranean sported its own. What had the ad said? "Come to an island in the Mediterranean for your next exciting governess position."

So far, this had been more than exciting. It has been hair-raising. Another limo sat waiting. Milo opened the back door and avoided my eyes. I crawled inside and Lexi followed. We both sighed as we sank into the deep leather seats.

"Are we almost there? I'm starving," Lexi grumbled, all legs as she sat beside me.

"I'm sure there will be food when we get there." But at that point I wasn't sure about anything.

Milo jumped into the front seat and nodded to the male driver, who wore a jaunty cap with gold braid. As the car pulled away from the boathouse, Milo leaned forward and pressed a button. A glass window slid up between us and the front seat. Lexi and I were encased in silence while the two men talked. Some guffawing went on, and I hoped it wasn't at our expense. When I reached for my daughter's hand, she didn't pull away.

As we drove down a winding road dappled with shadows from the trees overhead, I didn't see any buildings. On either side of the road were forests that fell away in deep, green ravines.

Okay, I had a million questions, but rapping on the closed glass felt like a bad idea. So I stayed quiet, taking it all in. We were away from the problems of home and the city. I should content myself with that. But had I gotten us into an even worse situation? As the car swung along the winding road, the scenery became even more lush and beautiful. Certainly nothing bad could happen here.

Lexi dropped my hand. "Look at all the trees."

I drank it in. Back in the states, the dogwood was just starting to bloom. Summer always came late to Pittsburgh. Here? It looked more like midsummer. Maybe that was the influence of the sea breezes, although we'd left the shoreline behind. When I tried to lower my window, I discovered it was locked. The door handle? The same. Fear tied a knot around my chest.

At one point, Lexi yelped and pointed. "Look, Mom. Deer."

The "Mom" was a welcome change. Lately, she'd started calling me Christina. Of course I hated it—especially when she used it in the halls at school. Although I'd tried to have a civil conversation with her about respect, she'd laughed it off. Called me old-fashioned.

Relax, Christina. Relax. Enjoy wherever this journey takes you. Hadn't I read that somewhere when I was going through my divorce? "Life is a journey, not a destination." But I'd never been good at that. This was my one foolish attempt to let fate take its course. And now here we were, locked in the back of a car speeding toward who-knew-where. No map. No GPS. Just Milo and another man in the front seat, laughing about something.

"Look at this." Lexi began fiddling with the knobs and levers. Hidden compartments opened and closed. There was a lot going in that luxurious back seat.

"Lexi, no." I grabbed her hand. "You might break something." And we would owe these people thousands of dollars.

"Oh, for Pete's sake, Christina. Lighten up." She shook me off and curled up next to her window. There, I'd gone and done it again. Eyes damp, I concentrated on the view outside.

Picturesque scenes flew past—so different from our rented bungalow with its small square plot of grass out back. Because the yard was shaded by a large oak tree, having a flower garden back there was useless. But I'd bought a hammock, where I liked to read during the nice weather. Unfortunately, we didn't have a whole lot of great weather in Pittsburgh.

Right now my colleagues were cleaning out their classrooms in rooms that smelled of gum and boys who didn't shower after gym class. Final grades handed in, Reena and Maddie would be packing up their rooms. Usually, it took a month for us to shake off the stress of never-ending papers and deadlines.

Here I was, surrounded by beauty, viewed from a limo.

But this isn't a bloody vacation, Christina.

Well, there was that. I was ready to work my tail off, preparing King Napolitano's son for Harvard. English and math were two things I felt fairly competent about. After all, my BA was from Amherst and my Master's from Boston College. After teaching for seventeen years, I was up to the challenge. Gregorio had to be ready for his SATs—the standard tests juniors took to get a grade that summed up their academic readiness. Mr. Napolitano had ambitions and getting his son into that prestigious American university was at the top of his list.

Was it going to be all up to me? Who had taught the son before? I hoped he already had some background in American and British literature, as well as algebra and geometry.

The limo felt closed in and warm. My head began to bob with the rhythm of the tires. But just as I welcomed a nap, we rounded a bend and Lexi gasped. I sat up as the driver took the curve like a Nascar driver. Down below, the land dipped and rippled with fields of lavender against a backdrop of vineyards undulating into the distance.

It was difficult to pull my attention back to the winding road that led to one place. A castle stretched along a ridge.

"Whoa, is this it?" Lexi was riveted, her green eyes—so like her father's—wide and curious.

"I—I guess so." I could hardly get the words out. The castle was huge.

I rapped at the glass. Slowly the window was lowered. Milo turned and gave me a barely tolerant look. I was not the only one eager to leave this limousine. "Are we there?" I asked.

"Yes." The window slid closed. Milo exchanged a long-suffering look with the driver.

Lexi pressed her nose against the window. "This is like a fairy tale." And she pointed to the castle, probably thinking of *Cinderella* or *Snow White.*

"Um, sweetheart, there's just one thing…"

But there was no time to explain that Marco Napolitano expected a boy, a companion to Americanize his son for Harvard. The car swept through an arch that certainly looked Roman, motored down the road rimmed with tall cypress trees and slowed when we entered a courtyard.

Lexi was beside herself with excitement. "Whoa, look at this."

I winced when she raked one hand through hair that needed washing. The purple hair had happened during a sleepover.

Eyes down, Milo opened the door. Looping my tote over one shoulder, I stepped out into the sunshine. Behind me, Lexi's mouth gaped as she looked around. And yes, there was a lot to see. Stonework. Massive carved doors. Flags flying everywhere.

"Wow." Spinning around, Lexi shrugged out of her jacket. The weather had warmed, and the sun ricocheted off the stonework. I was burning up and quickly unzipped my raincoat. Birds twittered from the olive trees planted around the courtyard. In the center was a fountain. The splashing water brought some warmth to a castle that spoke of antiquity and strength.

Easing himself from behind the wheel, the driver lumbered out. His eyes went to Lexi's t-shirt from one of her many rock concerts, the ones she had been forbidden to attend.

Milo hitched up his sagging pants and snapped his fingers. "Vitas." The driver popped the trunk open.

"Here, I'll just grab those." I reached for my bag. Lexi was still taking in the castle. Two men in claret red livery appeared. Gold buttons and braiding gleamed in the sun. I blinked. Milo rattled off something. The men in red nodded and our luggage disappeared.

"No, let me..." I hurried after them.

But my daughter pulled me back. "Mom. Let 'em go. They're probably the bell hops. Do you have a tip ready?"

When did my daughter become a world traveler? "Honey, this isn't a hotel."

Throwing my head back, I studied this massive structure that extended as far as my eyes could see. Rubbing my neck, I threw Milo a cautious look.

An older woman appeared in one of the arches. Swathed in midnight blue folds, she glided toward us. When she didn't offer to shake my hand, I clutched my tote tighter. She regarded us with hooded eyes. Did she speak English? Was she the head of housekeeping, like in *Downton Abbey*? Time to take the reins and assert myself. "Hello, my name is Christina Newhart. The k-king is expecting us." Okay, I was having trouble getting the word "king" out. "Is he around?"

Lips pursed, she appeared to digest my question. "No." she finally said.

This was like pulling teeth. How many strangers did they have arriving at this door? "I'm the new governess. And this is my daughter Lexi."

"I see." Her eyes widened as she took in Lexi's purple hair.

Hmm. She spoke English, framed with a mysterious accent. "Come." Before I could ask any questions, she turned, her delicate gold earrings glinting in the sunlight. Looking over at me, Lexi raised her brows. We followed the stranger into the castle. And oh, yes. The stonework, the marble, the paintings and wall hangings— this sure as heck had all the trappings of a castle.

"Will you just look at this?" Head back, Lexi took in the stained-glass windows. I followed her gaze. The arches supported a ceiling that could have been in a Gothic church. Covered with cherubs, the vaulted ceiling was probably painted centuries ago. Sunlight fell through the high windows, bathing huge pots of ferns with muted sunlight.

Digging around in her backpack, Lexi produced her phone. The older woman threw her a sharp look. I got the message. Before my daughter could snap a photo for Facebook, I grabbed the phone that had cost me a small fortune and stuck it in my pocket. "First we have to learn the rules," I murmured.

"What rules?" she sputtered.

"Shh." I pressed a finger to my lips.

Our guide got moving. For an older woman, she set a fast pace. Several doors led from this main hall and I didn't want to lose her. In the center of the cavernous hall a staircase rose—one that made the stairs in *Gone with the Wind* look like a step stool. Lifting the folds of her skirt that rustled like silk, the woman made her way up the stairs as if she'd done this a time or two. The stone banister was cold under my hand as I struggled to keep up, motioning to Lexi to follow. It only took twenty steps or so before my chest was burning.

This will be great for my thighs. Trying to appear confident, I kept climbing. But my mind kept up a busy chatter that had nothing to do with this unexpected workout.

What had I gotten us into? If I'd pictured a warm welcome, this sure wasn't it.

By the time we reached the landing, I was gasping and Lexi lagged behind. For a second I considered collapsing on a convenient bench, but they all looked hand carved and ancient. Meanwhile, our power-walker swept into the hallway to the left. We traipsed behind, our footsteps silenced by the longest Persian runner ever made, all dusky taupe and turquoise. Oversized vases stood against the walls and fresh tropical flowers provided bursts of orange and pink on long side tables. Wall sconces complemented the crystal chandeliers, creating a medieval air.

My neck began to ache from trying to take it all in. For the first time in her life, Lexi was silenced. More digging in her backpack and she took out a stick of gum and unwrapped it. Before she could drop the wrapper in one of the vases, I scooped it from her hands. "Not here," I mouthed. An exasperated sigh was her response.

Our guide traversed the hall with authority. But I wanted to dawdle and take it all in, especially the sizeable portraits. Impressive looking men stood tall, crowns heavy on proud heads. Some held scepters, while furs outlawed in the States edged royal cloaks. The only women pictured were standing behind the men or seated meekly at their side. From their clothing, the paintings probably went back centuries. Our guide had slowed and I pulled my attention from the portraits to the deep doorways tucked inside wide gilded moldings.

"Here." She swept a hand toward an open door.

"This is our room?" I pointed, wanting everything to be clear.

She crooked a finger at Lexi. "Come."

Were we going to be separated? Relief did battle with my usual maternal worrying. Not that I wanted us to be together all the time. But I had to make sure there were no fire escapes or trellises. Lexi would be out the window before I could blink an eye. I'd never be able to sleep.

They'd disappeared into the deep doorway next to mine. "You got to see this, Mom," Lexi called out.

Her incredulous tone picked up my speed and her "Mom" nearly brought tears to my eyes. After all, we were in this together. I followed her into a room dominated by a gilded four-poster bed. Everything was swathed in claret brocade, from the windows to the bed. A mini staircase led to the mattress.

Excitement lit up Lexi's eyes. "Mom, remember the story about the princess and the pea?"

While I stood there horrified, Lexi catapulted onto the bed and bounced, as if searching for that pea. "Lexi."

The one word was all she needed. Now, that was a switch. Back home we'd bickered about everything from why aspartame in soda was bad for you to how much gas to put in the car.

Our guide frowned as Lexi slid from the comforter and ran to the french doors.

I peeked around her shoulder, well aware that the woman

behind us was taking in our reactions. "Oh, my. How gorgeous." I squeezed Lexi's shoulders.

"Do these open?" With no hesitation, Lexi yanked the french doors open. Fresh air bathed us as she stepped out onto a balcony.

"Oh, my." In the terraced gardens below, a series of fountains cooled the summer air, surrounded by beds of red, pink and orange blossoms. Their perfume brought to mind exotic places I'd always wanted to visit.

Stone paths wound through the gardens below. The topiaries had been trimmed with an eye to pleasing shapes. On either side of the fountains and gardens stood tall hedges. "Are those mazes?"

Behind us, the woman had fallen silent, straightening an embroidered linen cloth on one of the tables that sat between two boudoir chairs.

"What's a maze?" Lexi turned. "I'm hungry." With that, she pointed to her mouth with one finger as if she were one of the sea lions at the Pittsburgh zoo, hoping to be fed.

Did the woman's upper lip lift? I was probably just being sensitive. "Snack trays will be brought."

Snack trays? My stomach growled. "That would be lovely. Thank you."

A man appeared with Lexi's luggage. "Thank you," I said. Lexi set her suitcase on the leather rack at the foot of the bed and got busy. The top drawer of an ornately carved chest of drawers gave a dry groan when Lexi pulled on it. "This thing's stuck."

"Gentle, gentle." Stepping over, I eased the drawer open and met the smell of dry wood. This drawer had not been opened in quite a while. At the door stood the silent woman, whose eyes missed nothing.

"Don't go anywhere," I warned Lexi as I headed for the door.

"Maybe it would be better if we shared a room." How would I ever keep an eye on her?

"Oh, Mom. Don't worry so much." Scooping up an armful of concert T-shirts, she dumped them into the drawer.

"You are ready?" Weariness laced the woman's voice as if the last few minutes had taxed her strength...or her patience.

"Yes, of course." The warmth in the hallway smelled stale as I reluctantly left Lexi's room. My clothes felt wrinkled and worn after the long flight. "When will I meet King Marco?"

A tiny line etched itself between her deep-set eyes. She played with a necklace I hadn't noticed. The stone suspended from a gold chain looked like a huge sapphire. "At his convenience."

Oh, my. Really? "Of course."

As she swirled away from me. I was tempted to call out, "Don't forget the snack trays." But I was too exhausted. She disappeared.

"Did you tip her?" Lexi had crept up behind me.

"Honey, I don't think this is a tipping situation."

But what were the rules here? And where were we? "Are you finished with your unpacking?"

"Not really. Be right back."

Head throbbing, I started putting my things away. The plush carpet was thicker than anything I'd ever walked on before. Like Lexi's room, my bed was accessible by a small staircase. Rich gold brocade draperies accented the tall, arched windows, matching the spread and bolsters. The french doors opened onto a balcony. I pulled the paned glass doors open, drinking in the fresh air.

Lexi's balcony was just to the right of mine, but far enough to be private. Thick vines crept up the wall. Looking down, I released my breath. The vines might be strong but we were a long way up. Going back inside, I began to put away my clothes, not that it took long. When I opened a dresser drawer, I found a soft green blanket and tossed it on the bed. The armoire worked for anything that needed a hanger, and I hung up my coat and some dresses. Although I'd hoped the one door between the windows and my bed led to Lexi's room, it opened into the fanciest bathroom I'd ever seen. The dark marble floor accented the white marble counters with gold faucets. The deep clawfoot tub would have pleased Charlemagne. How I longed to slip into a pool of warm water. But not now.

The huge mirror told me that this had been a rough trip. Forty-two and I looked like fifty. My hair felt stiff and I ran a hand over my dry skin. I rarely wore makeup. Going back into the bedroom area, I eyed the bed.

After pulling up the soft blanket, I fell asleep on the bed. Sometime later, I heard a discreet knock on the door before it opened. The chatter of crystal made me smile. Someone dressed in red slid a tray onto one of the circular tables. The snack tray? The door whispered shut. Was eating in bed allowed? Hopping down, I carried the tray to the bed and settled back again. Lexi was right. This sure felt like a fairy tale.

I devoured the triangular quarters of a ham sandwich on rye with a soft white cheese. The soda refreshed me but not enough to keep me from slipping back into sleep. In my dreams, I was in a fountain, trying to breathe while the water took me under.

Chapter 2

Next thing I knew, I was drooling onto gold brocade. This
definitely wasn't my blue and green comforter at home on Willard
Street. Feeling around on the bedside table, I couldn't find a tissue
to wipe my damp cheek. My neck had a crick from the plump
pillows. Getting out of bed was a little like going down the water
slide at Sandcastle Water Park. My feet still felt a little swollen from
the plane ride, so I padded around the room in my socks, flexing
my toes. I sniffed. Shrouded in late afternoon shadows, the room
of antique furniture smelled of a recent waxing.

And I felt hungry, but hadn't I eaten earlier? The snack tray.
The faint taste of salt from the ham lingered on my lips. When I'd
fallen asleep, my balcony windows had been open. Now they were
closed. The tray was nowhere to be seen.

A weird feeling rippled down my neck. Someone had been in
my room while I slept. And my bets were on the creepy woman
who was dressed in the silk bedsheets. Going to the windows, I
opened them and drank in the cool air. The sun was not as high in
the sky and the scene below beckoned. I may have signed a
contract, but no one seemed to need me right now.

Pushing my swollen feet into my tennis shoes, I grabbed a

quilted jacket from the drawer and was out the door. Later I would have to ask for a key to my room. As nice as it was to have food delivered, the fact that someone had slid in while I was sleeping didn't sit well. The long hallway sat in semi-darkness, lit only by an overhead chandelier. As much as I wanted to get this adventure going, I had to check on Lexi. After all, I was a mother with responsibilities. Creeping to her door, I knocked softly. When she didn't answer, I pushed the door open. All five foot ten of my little girl was sound asleep, curled up on her tummy.

My heart melted, smoothing away the irritation she'd caused me in recent weeks. Right now, she was just a teenager sleeping with her mouth open. Scanning the room, I saw no snack tray. After tiptoeing out of the room, I stood in the hallway and considered my options.

If I took the thousand stairs down to the major hall, I might run into people— including that woman. Or Milo. Of the two of them, I'd take Milo in a heartbeat. Obviously, Marco Napolitano wasn't eager to meet me, not right now anyway. But I wanted to explore. Somewhere there had to be an exit. Heading in the opposite direction from the main staircase, I eventually found a door that opened into a set of stone stairs. Instead of a handrail, a leather strap was fastened along the wall, secured by pegs. Grasping the worn leather, I started down, being extra careful on the uneven stone steps.

The circular design of the stairs suggested that I was in a tower. Later I'd poke around more. Right now, I wanted to get out into the sun. The forbidding stones gave off a chill. I clutched my jacket tighter around me. The first door I passed wasn't any help. When I pushed it open, I was on another floor, furnished much like the one where Lexi and I were roomed.

Closing the door, I kept going, hanging on to that leather strap. The next door brought me better luck. A blast of fresh air met me when I pushed the door open. I blinked in the bright light, wishing I'd brought my sunglasses. Somewhere nearby, a fountain splashed, and I followed a path of flat stones until I reached the source. Some sort of sea god frolicked in the center—half man and half sea creature.

How glorious was this? Up above, birds chattered in the trees, flitting into the fountain for short, splashy dips. Flower beds perfumed the air. Despite the shade in my backyard at home, I filled the planters on my deck with multi-colored impatiens every summer. This year, they would sit empty. But this was no time to get maudlin and I hurried past the fountain. I wasn't going to think about what I'd always done in the past. Right now, the future was an exciting mystery, waiting for Lexi and me to explore.

At least, that was what I was telling myself.

A geometrical garden lay just ahead, and I hurried down the stone path. Inhaling all the greenery around me, I was stunned by the beauty. A giggle tickled my throat as I pictured the reaction of Reena and Maddie back in Pittsburgh. They would call me lucky, but all three of us agreed that you had to make your own luck.

In the garden of neatly trimmed bushes, a narrow corridor appeared to my left. The maze. I'd seen it earlier from my balcony. Why not? Wasn't I an adventurous woman? Taking a chance had led me here. This step into the unknown felt like opening a new lesson plan book at the beginning of the school year. This time I could write my own lesson, unfettered by curriculum guidelines. And I was making more money than any teacher I knew—funds that could enroll Lexi in any university, if she kept her grades up.

Which brought me to Gregorio. Preparing a young man for Harvard was no small task. When I'd studied for my Master's degree at Boston College, I'd taken the T up to Harvard many times. The staid, historic campus had filled me with awe. More than forty thousand students applied every year, but they accepted a little more than four percent. I had my work cut out for me.

I trailed a hand over bushes that were neatly trimmed into a formidable wall. What would my student be like? He was only a couple years older than Lexi. Would Gregorio be an athlete, a boy who got up to run every morning down the roads we'd taken to get here? Or would he be more like the sullen, snide boys Lexi had fallen in with lately? In my online search, I couldn't find any photos of either the father or the son. My stomach tightened.

Well, I had to hope for the best. If Marco Napolitano's son had his sights set on Harvard, he must have some academic background. Daylight was fading. Deep shadows fell over the path and I shivered. The tall green shrubs looked impenetrable. When I tried to stick a hand through, it came out scraped and bloody. My steps slowed. Where was I? Since I'd left my phone in the room, I couldn't pull up a map.

Perspiration tickled along my hairline. My pink Lands End shirt clung to my body. Unbuttoning the jacket, I wondered if anyone had ever become lost in this maze. Maybe I'd be found here in two weeks, a mere skeleton trying to eat the thorny bushes. Standing still, I listened, my ears straining for the bubbling fountain. But the only sound was the eerie sigh of the wind in the trees and the screech of some bird. Was that a hawk circling overhead? Or a carrion crow?

Man, I was thirsty. And hot. And lost. Was I headed east or west? I had no clue. Fighting panic, I took a couple more turns. Was there some sort of logic to a maze? I'd heard about churches sponsoring mazes to keep people focused. Yet, here I was, feeling very scattered. And frightened. How ridiculous. I batted down my fears. I was an adult woman, here to perform a job. And I'd gotten lost on the first day.

Wait. Was that the sound of a horse? The riding lessons I'd given Lexi after her eighth-grade graduation made me somewhat familiar with the horse world. I blushed, remembering how I'd phrased my equine expertise in my resume. But I wouldn't think about that now. The sound of hooves came again. But how to get to it? Coming to another dead end, I tried to figure out if the left or right path would take me toward the sounds I was hearing.

Coming to a halt, I listened. On the other side of the hedge, men were talking. Of course, I didn't understand a word they were saying, just heard the rumble of voices. Should I call out? But this didn't sound like Milo. Finally, I found an area where the branches seemed less dense. *It's now or never, Christina.*

I plunged my hands into the mess, trying to part the branches. Of course, there were brambles and my hands would be a mess.

The voices seemed to be moving away. How would I get out of here? After yanking a thorn from the palm of my hand, I called out, "Please don't leave!"

Did they hear me? Okay, this called for action. Getting down on my knees, I yanked my jacket over my head and rammed myself through the bushes. Let me tell you, it wasn't easy. I ended up doing a somersault onto my side. Sticks in my hair and hands stinging, I wiped dirt from my mouth.

I was staring at two pairs of dusty boots. "Sorry. I was kind of lost." Heart pounding, I stumbled to my feet.

Different in age, the men both looked startled. From the looks of their clothes, they must have worked in the stables. "What are you doing?" asked the younger man, choosing his words carefully in a swoony accent. He held the reins of a beautiful horse that made me think of *Black Beauty*.

I pulled a prickly stick from my hair. "Going for a walk."

Bringing a gnarled hand to his lips, the older man looked as if he was trying not to laugh. Arms folded over a broad chest, the other man, who might be in his forties, whisked a hand over a stubbled chin. "Walking. Through the bushes?"

What was that smile about? This wasn't funny. Peering over his shoulder, I could see what looked like a stable. Curious horses hung their heads over the stall doors. The earthy smell of the stable drifted to me on the breeze.

My hair had escaped from the ponytail, and I raked my fingers through it. I was quite a mess. "Can you show me the main road?" I asked as if we were standing on a street back home.

The stable boy's shirt was open halfway down his chest. Not that I noticed. Hair tossed into unruly curls, he smelled as if he'd been mucking out stalls. At least, I thought that was what they called it. On the flight over, I'd tried to do some serious horse research to back up my claims of equestrian expertise.

"Which road?" he asked in English, flavored with an accent.

"To the c-castle. That big building. Over there." How many castles were there around here?

A chilly breeze made me pull on my jacket. "Castle." I said again, making all kinds of motions with my hands to indicate the height and breadth of the building. Time to get a move on. Lexi would be looking for me.

Were these two laughing at me? The dark horse nuzzled one of my hands and I jumped, backing away.

"Diablo thinks you have food." The younger man patted the horse's neck. The horse was huge, all powerful muscles and strong legs—kind of like the stable boy.

Shrugging, I chuckled. "No food. Just bugs."

The men exchanged a look. Then, with a low chuckle, the stable boy mounted the horse in one liquid movement that made it look so easy. Maybe this horse thing wouldn't be that hard after all. "Up. Yes?"

When he extended an arm, my eyes went to the corded muscles on his forearm. Yep, he'd definitely been doing lots of mucking out stalls.

"Well, all right. Thank you." What choice did I have? He seemed to know where he was going.

"Your arm," he said again. No time to ponder. I had to get back to the castle. When I gripped his arm, he somehow swept me up.

"Ooof." I landed on my stomach across the rear end of the beast. This felt like my first belly flop at the Gordon Park pool. As if this were happening in slow motion, I slid off the horse's rump. My stomach hurt with a dull ache and I felt nauseated. Diablo snuffled and the stable boy seemed to think this was funny.

"No, no," he said between chortles at my expense. "You must put your legs like…this." And he sketched a horseshoe in the air.

Well, now I felt like a total numbskull. Thank goodness Lexi wasn't here to see this debacle.

From his towering height, he seemed to reconsider, looking at the back of the horse. "A better way." Sliding back, he patted the seat in front of him.

Ohno—ohno—ohno.

The arm came down again. What could I do? I extended my left arm and somehow he swirled me up, swinging my legs to the left. Facing the front, I didn't miss the crooked grin on the older man's face. His left arm around me, the stable boy held the reins in his other hand. One tightening of those legs and Diablo took off.

Not knowing where to put my own hands, I grabbed the pommel at the front of the saddle and hoped for the best. "Do you know the way?"

"Oh, yes." He clucked to the horse.

I was starting to relax until I felt him sniffing my hair.

"What are you doing?" I tried to turn around but the horse picked up speed.

"Your shampoo is very nice."

"Target. I got it on sale."

"The target," he murmured.

"In the States. Target. It's a big box store."

"Big box, huh?" His body was warm on my back and I could feel his breath on my neck. I probably hadn't been this close to a man since my divorce. Was I going to be running into this guy often? Well, I did have to check out the stable and soon.

Thank goodness, we weren't that far from the castle. From where I sat, I could see it towering above the trees. Diablo's hooves clattered on the stones as we rode up. Those men in red appeared again. I guess they quickly sized things up because one of them ran for a little stool. But by the time it arrived, I'd somehow slid down.

"Thank you," I called out as my rescuer headed off, probably going back to the stables.

When I reached my room, a note on the table told me that dinner would be served at eight. To my relief an ancient clock above the mantle of the fireplace seemed to work. Somehow I'd lost my phone. Not even here a day and I could not find it.

After checking with Lexi, I delighted in a hot shower and passed out on the bed for a short nap. When I woke up, I glanced at the clock and froze. Ten minutes past eight! How had this happened? Sweeping my hair into a bun, I quickly dressed and went to get Lexi.

"My phone is gone," she announced when she opened the door.

"Are you sure?" I didn't want to admit that mine was missing too. "We're late. Why didn't you wake me up?" One glance above her fireplace told me Lexi also had an antique clock which seemed to be working.

"Of course I'm sure. I left it on the side table and now it isn't there. I slept all afternoon and when I woke up, the food tray was gone and so was my phone."

"Don't worry. I'll take care of it." But my hands shook on the way down to dinner. I didn't want to begin our relationship on an adversarial note, but some things had to be cleared up. My new employer might feel the same. Behind me, Lexi grumbled all the way down the gazillion steps.

Was my lavender peasant top embroidered with purple flowers too casual? My mother had given it to me for my birthday one year, along with a full purple skirt with practical side pockets. How I wished she were still around to talk over my problems with Lexi. But Mom had been gone for two years. The loss had been sudden, and I missed her every day. No quick conversations. No surprise packages of my favorite snickerdoodles. I smoothed one hand over the skirt. Right now, the outfit gave me some reassurance, as if my mother were there.

Behind me, Lexi was dragging her feet, wearing the only dress she'd brought with her. Of course, it was black and white with a ragged handkerchief hem she found stylish. "I'm tired," she said on our way down the stairs. "Do we have to stay a long time?"

"I hope not." We'd reached the first floor. Which way now? The note left in my room said to take a right at the bottom of the stairs and follow the lights.

"Here we go." I kept my voice low so it wouldn't echo against the stone walls. "I'm sure that we can make the dinner short, Lexi. All I want to do is meet Mr. Napolitano and his son. Then we can excuse ourselves until we see him tomorrow in class."

"Class!" The word broke against the walls.

Stopping, I turned. Even though we were late, I wasn't going into a dining room bickering with my daughter. That's not how this was going to start. "Please keep your voice down."

Her pretty features twisted. "But it's summer. Who goes to school during the summer? I'm not stupid."

"As we both know, you're very bright, although your grades don't always show it. We're going to be studying books you've already read, so this should be easy for you. Plus a little math. Won't hurt to be ready for next year."

"If it's a class, it's not fun." Was this the sulky face Lexi presented to her teachers, my colleagues at Providence High School? Probably. I had a lot of work before me this summer, and it had little to do with the teaching on my contract.

We left the staircase behind, our footsteps falling softly on the carpet. "There's a light." Like the hallway upstairs, this corridor was hung with historical treasures—a collection probably worth millions. Everything was presented tastefully against the ochre walls. Up ahead, double doors were flung wide and light spilled into the passageway. But I couldn't hear a thing. No conversation. No clatter of plates.

Oh, give me strength. I took a deep breath before stepping through the doorway, Lexi's hand firmly in mind. "Good evening. Sorry we're late. I'm Christina Newhart."

My voice faltered on the last syllable. I tried to keep the surprise from my tone. At one end of the long table that could seat ten sat the stable boy. The unruly hair had been tamed, but those deep dark eyes were the same. And right now they were flashing.

At the other end sat the woman who had been our guide earlier that day. Neither one was smiling. In fact, it seemed that we had walked into the middle of an argument. Between them sat a teenage boy, looking miserable. His hair was long, maybe an attempt to hide his acne. The blue shirt was a style not often seen, and he fumbled with the buttons on the cuffs of the wide sleeves.

Chair screeching as he stood, the stable boy gave me a curt nod. "You are, as you say in America, tardy."

Behind me, Lexi giggled. I squeezed her hand tighter. "Tardy is usually used when a student is late for class. If we're late, I'm very sorry. It's been a long day." The words came out in a rush that left me breathless.

With a ridiculous flourish, he motioned to two place settings across from his unfortunate son. "Please." And with that he snapped his fingers. A young man in claret livery sprang forward to edge out my chair and then Lexi's.

This was not at all what I'd expected stepping onto the plane this morning. You could have cut the tension with one of their heavy silver knives, embellished with a scripted N.

When I looked up, our host was skewering Lexi with an intense gaze. "And this is…?"

Here it was. "My daughter Lexi." I hadn't seen Lexi blush in a long time.

"Daughter?" He turned the word over as if he were tasting it. "But I thought you had a son."

Now, for the past week I'd worked on my innocent expression in the mirror. The one where I would not know what my employer was talking about. I hoped my forehead was wrinkling appropriately. "Really? I don't know why."

The king's dark eyes zapped me.

Reaching over, I squeezed Lexi's arm. "Lexi is fourteen, almost a sophomore. She'll join in the classes."

Father and son did not look pleased. The older woman stared at Lexi's hair as if a thousand snakes had sprung from it. Her purple hair was no big deal, although Lexi would choke to hear me admit that.

The chest that had felt so warm behind me puffed out, his wide shoulders expanding. "We are happy to meet you, Christina Newhart and Lexi. I am Marco Giovanni Pietro di Napolitano." The name spilled out in a torrent of syllables. My face broke into a hot flush, thinking of the afternoon. Was this the man who'd cradled me playfully in his arms on that massive horse? Sitting there was an enormous ego I would have to deal with all summer. He reminded me of Chet Daggert, our varsity football coach, after a winning season.

Finally, Marco whoever-he-was came to the end of his introduction. "And this is my son Gregorio."

"His Royal Highness." Finally, the mystery woman spoke,

making things clear.

After holding my breath for the last two minutes, exhaling brought relief. "Very nice to meet you, Mr., ah Napolitano. And you, Gregorio. Your Royal…whatever." My voice warmed as I nodded to his son across the table. The poor boy. Having a father like this couldn't be easy.

"Very good," Marco said with an officious nod.

At the other end of the table, the woman cleared her throat, a delicate reminder.

The royal hand swept down the length of the white linen cloth. "Yes, of course. And this is my mother, formerly the Queen of…" Here he went into another long name that I'd never be able to remember, except that it ended in Napolitano.

Queen. Ah, that explained the jewelry.

"So pleased to meet all of you." Why hadn't his mother introduced herself when she showed us to our rooms? Instead she'd hustled us around as if she were a chambermaid—and a very disapproving one at that.

"I am Ama, the Queen Mother." She sat back, hands resting regally on the arms of her chair, as if she were used to reigning. Nodding to her son, she said, "Thank you, Your Majesty."

An enormous amethyst winked from the ring on her left hand. The chandelier cast deep shadows over her eyes. I'd seen eyes like that in "The Exorcist" on late night TV. Lexi was leaning into me, as if for protection.

More finger snapping from Marco and servers paraded from side doors, the smell of food almost making me faint. Lexi licked her lips as she took a huge wedge of bread, offered on a silver salver.

My throat dry, I sipped from the water glass.

His Majesty—my word, would I have to call him that?—turned to the young man. "More wine, please."

Not a bad idea. But I wasn't a big drinker and I sensed I'd have to watch it tonight. "None for my daughter," I told the waiter when he came to us.

Platters appeared and the tantalizing smell of garlic and tomatoes made me ready to pick up my fork. Men in livery carried one platter after another around the table. I recognized the paella and it smelled wonderful. After His Majesty began eating—must take a lot of food to keep those muscles in tip top shape—I started.

Like any growing boy, Gregorio was shoveling his way through dinner. But when he motioned to the server for another helping of the paella, his grandmother caught his eye. "Gregorio."

One word seemed enough. Face falling, the boy backed off.

When the next dish appeared—mussels were one of my favorites—we'd lapsed into the polite conversation of people who'd just met.

"Your flight was pleasant?" my employer asked, patting his full lips with a linen napkin.

"Oh, yes. Thank you for the business class tickets. Very generous and we appreciated it. Didn't we, Lexi?"

My daughter stiffened and shifted as if she were stretching her legs out beneath the table. "That plane trip was so long. I've got leg cramps."

Across from us Gregorio gave a little snuffle.

Under the table I pulled at her skirt.

But she twisted away. "Mom."

My own face aflame, I picked at a mussel.

"Did you play games?" Gregorio asked, slathering butter on a hunk of bread. "On your flight, I mean? I always like the games."

"Of course," Lexi said, as if she flew across the Atlantic every day. "Planets vs Zombies."

"Wow." Gregorio looked impressed.

"And word games, of course," I added. "Spelltower, that kind of thing. Very good for increasing your vocabulary." The SAT had a vocabulary section and I hoped Gregorio was up to the challenge.

"I didn't play Spelltower," Lexi told Gregorio, as if they were the only people at the table. "But Mom did."

Gregorio nodded. His Majesty had been watching the exchange.

"I was hoping we might talk about our studies, Gregorio," I said. "Are you eager to begin?"

But King Marco took the lead on this. "Tomorrow we will talk about the teaching." He circled the table with a fork.

Okay, I'd been silenced. Gregorio went back to his dinner and so did I. All I wanted was to collapse on that high comfortable bed. Thank goodness Marco never mentioned our earlier meeting. Remembering how I'd been pressed against that very firm chest brought heat to my face. All evening, I hoped the scratches on my hands weren't too noticeable.

Sitting there, I had the surreal feeling that I'd been transported to another world, another time. The paintings on the walls could have hung in art museums. Bucolic landscapes were interspersed among Biblical scenes, along with a few portraits. Very Renaissance. Beyond the dining room table, the enormous salon held clusters of conversational groupings. The furniture could easily have dated back to the eighteenth century, or earlier. Since I watched *Antiques Roadshow*, I knew a thing or two about all those graceful arches and delicate spindles.

Tomorrow I would explore more when I had time. Right now, I was about to fall into a food coma. The stilted conversation continued, and I deflected questions as best I could. After the pasta came the salad. Finally, we worked our way to cheese and fruit, followed by pastries with accompanying parfaits of lemon ice drizzled with port. If I ate like this every day, my clothes wouldn't fit. But I had to set things straight. "King Marco…" I began.

"Your Majesty." His mother cut in, her voice sharp as a knife.

"Your Majesty." My eyes felt as if they had cotton balls pressed against them. "While we were out of our rooms this afternoon it seems that our phones disappeared."

The mother continued to spoon lemon ice through her thin lips.

"No cell phones." His words fell like a sentence.

"But we need our phones." Lexi spoke up.

Thank goodness for the tablecloth. Reaching over under the deep linen drape I squeezed her hand. "Perhaps we can talk about this tomorrow, Your Excellency. Majesty," I added, hoping one of those was right.

Tossing his napkin onto the table, Marco studied me as if I

were a hungry peasant who'd wandered in off the street.

"Tomorrow."

The word sounded like a threat. "Yes sir."

That slight quirk of Gregorio's lips seemed sympathetic.

Looking pleased, King Marco's mother fingered her sapphire. The king rose. I hadn't realized how tall he was. This must be some sort of signal because his mother also got up.

"Lovely to meet you," I managed, pulling myself to all five foot four inches.

Giving me a curt nod, Marco left, his mother taking the arm he offered. She seemed to have some magic force that allowed her to skim the floors without touching them.

When Gregorio circled the table, I was surprised. Why, he was even taller than Lexi and well on his way to match his father's height. "Good night, Profesora," he said with a short nod.

"Good night, Gregorio. Hope to see you tomorrow."

Hi brows lifted a bit at the "hope" part. But what did I know? Marco might give me the boot the following day. Next to me, Lexi executed a stiff curtsy.

"What the heck are you doing," I whispered when Gregorio was out of ear shot.

"Hey, I saw this in a movie. You do that with royalty."

"Over my dead body." Then we looked at each other and laughed. Would it come to that? The silent castle felt forbidding as we dragged ourselves up the steps that night.

"One hundred and thirty," Lexi said when we reached the top.

"I need a minute." Bending over, I tried to catch my breath.

"One hundred and thirty what?"

"Stairs." With her long-legged stride, Lexi headed toward her room.

As I got ready for bed that night, I heard a quiet knock on my door. Was the Queen Mother coming to turn down my bed and offer a chocolate? I chuckled at the thought. If so, she was going to love my Pittsburgh Steelers night shirt. When I cracked open the door, Lexi stood outside, clutching a comforter. Without all that makeup she looked about ten years old. "Is it all right if I sleep with you? That room gives me the creeps."

"Of course, sweetheart."

Long after we were settled in bed and Lexi had fallen asleep, my mind worked overtime. Tomorrow I would straighten everything out.

Chapter 3

When I woke up the following morning, a hazy light filled the room. The warm golden tone made the antiques look like pieces from a movie set. And I was in it. This didn't feel bad at all. I settled back into the silky, multi-hundred thread count sheets.

Dreams had disturbed my sleep. Nightmares involving men in red livery and wild horses. Maybe this whole trip was just a bad dream. But no. Beside me, Lexi slept, her nose buried in a pillow, lips parted and her purple hair a bright contrast to the bedding.

The fancy clock on the mantel told me it was not quite six. Perfect. Sliding carefully from the bed, I tiptoed into the bathroom. After slipping into slacks and a pink knit top, I scrawled a note for Lexi. I wanted to do some exploring on my own and my daughter might not wake up for a long time. Careful not to make any noise, I quietly shut the door behind me and stepped down the hall.

Confidence surged through me, probably the result of a night's sleep. Hand gripping the banister, I made my way down the eternal staircase. By the time I reached the bottom, I knew that yes, Lexi was right. There were one hundred and thirty blasted stairs. The hallway where we'd had dinner might be a good place to start my expedition. I wanted to know more about this castle and the family.

40

The dining room sat empty. Now that I wasn't concentrating on the people seated at the table, I could scan the walls more closely. Holy macaroni, this place could be a museum. Although I loved art museums and visited them whenever Lexi and I did travel outside Pittsburgh, which wasn't frequent, I'd never seen any of these paintings.

But I didn't have time to study them. I had to make good use of my time while no one was around. Unfortunately, some of the rooms were locked. Traveling down the hallway, I tried every one. Finally, I came to a door that opened with a noisy creaking. Frozen, I scanned the hall. No one. Quickly, I stepped inside. Walls of books met me, their musty smell tickling my nose. Looked like I'd found the library. The books were housed to the ceiling. A very tall ladder on wheels made reaching the top levels possible, not that I would ever try it.

Across the back, stretched a long table with spindle backed chairs and reading lamps. The studious atmosphere was broken up by pairs of comfortable chairs. Picturing Marco sitting here reading one of these books stretched my imagination. Did the man ever smile? But the stable boy had, and laughter had warmed his eyes. Had I imagined all that?

As in the dining room, the windows were long and deep and rose to a pointed arch. Despite the comfortable chairs and side tables, this was not a cozy place. And after I'd sneezed the third time, definitely not a place for our classes.

Leaving the library, I proceeded down the hall. Luckily, more of the rooms opened to me when I twisted the large, heavily enscripted knob. Each room had a gigantic fireplace where you could practically roast a pig or a person. Now, that last thought conjured up a medieval picture I had to shut down fast. How modern was Marco Napolitano? His clothing suggested another era, the sleeves ballooning, caught in tight cuffs. And poor Gregorio seemed to wear the same antiquated garb. My heart went out to the teenager growing up in what basically felt like a time warp.

After peeking into four or five rooms which looked the same, I had a feel for the place. The furniture might be different but the décor was mostly creams, ochres and rusty browns—peaceful but not energizing. In addition to priceless antique furniture, each room was hung with paintings—the kind found in history books.

Then I bumbled into a room with a pool table like none I'd ever seen before. My employer probably called this game billiards. Running my fingers over the weathered green surface, I pictured men in period dress, puffing on cigars as they wielded cues racked along the wall. I took one from the rack. The cue was inlaid, much like some of the tables. Feeling the weight, I put the cue back.

If Gregorio and I could spend some time here, I might get to know him better. The stilted meal last night had given me a neck ache. I'd never get to know him under the eyes of his father and grandmother. The poor kid was probably kept on a short leash. Chuckling under my breath, I twirled out of the billiard room and ran smack into His Greatness.

I gasped. Marco frowned, his dark eyes making my empty stomach spiral. "Did you find what you were looking for,

Profesora?"

"Yes—yes, thank you." I'd become a stuttering fool. "I'm really not looking for anything. Just trying to get the lay of the land."

His frown deepened. "Lay of the land," he repeated with suspicion, as if I'd just suggested something illicit.

I was snooping. "Your home—that is, your castle—is so beautiful. I hope you don't mind my looking around. You know, so I can decide on the best room to hold class."

"I've instructed the staff to lock up the silver." Said without even the hint of a smile.

"Oh, I wouldn't…" Then I caught it. The golden glint deep in his brown eyes. It took my breath away. So he was teasing?

With that he took off down the hall. And yes, he looked very nice in those breeches. His period wardrobe could stay. "Have you eaten?"

The mere mention of food set my stomach growling. "Not yet." I stumbled after him.

"Breakfast is served between seven and eight. Didn't my mother give you that information?" He threw me a sidelong glance. I nearly tripped on the Oriental rug.

This wasn't the time to throw his mother under the bus. "Maybe I missed it. Yesterday is a blur in my mind." But not the part about the stable. No, that was firmly embedded in my memory. I ran a hand over my wayward bangs and demure ponytail.

By this time, we'd reached the dining room. Shy sunlight fell into the chamber from the long windows. So much for a home that looked out onto a pleasant scene. These rooms were designed to withstand a siege. The french doors swathed in sheers were probably a later addition.

His Greatness swept a hand toward a buffet that would have fed Attila and his entire army. "Let me know if this does not...meet your expectations."

I could hardly wait to begin.

Taking a plate, he began working his way down the buffet. I did the same. Bacon was heaped onto grilled tomatoes. Potatoes had been replaced by what looked like orzo. The fresh greens were a must. Had to get my vitamin D. Eggs were done in multiple ways. I chose the soft-boiled egg cup just for the novelty of it. The cup was porcelain, painted with delicate blue forget-me-knots.

By the time I turned from the feast, Marco had seated himself and snapped open his linen napkin. At his elbow was a copy of the *Wall Street Journal.* The paper crackled when he folded it into a neat, easily read column. "So, this morning you will start the lessons, no?"

"Yes." I tapped my egg with a spoon until I could lift off the top. My mother would have been proud of me. "Do you have a room that is a little, um, cozier than the library? I found it by accident this morning."

Marco was munching on bacon. A bit of oil at the corner of his lips distracted me. I nearly drove a fork through my left hand. "After breakfast, I will show you the nursery."

"This castle has a nursery?"

He blotted his lips. Sanity returned. "Of course. After all, we

44

had children. I am proof, no?" That naughty twinkle sparked again in his eyes. And this time there was no mistake. Good thing I was eating a soft-boiled egg. Any other food would have caught in my throat.

So he was going to become my guide. I wasn't exactly thrilled, except his mother had obviously left out things. "Wonderful. Terrific."

I was cutting broccoli into edible bites when he said, "Am I mistaken? Did you not tell me you had a son?"

My knife skidded across the plate. "Oh, I don't think so."

Marco's intense gaze studied me like an x-ray machine. This felt like being locked in the mammography machine for my baseline view last year. But that was silly. And so were the many mixed images trampling through my mind.

Thank goodness he returned his attention to his plate. "Usually I am not wrong."

"That doesn't surprise me." *Edit, edit.*

He hadn't missed my mischievous tone. Thank goodness the corners of his lips tipped up.

Time to change the subject. "Your mother speaks excellent English."

"My mother graduated from Wellesley. You know, over in your country." Wearing a satisfied grin, he scooped up a Roma tomato topped with melted cheese.

My fork clattered to the plate, narrowly missing the egg cup. I was relieved to see that it hadn't shattered the precious china that had no doubt been passed down through generations. "Wellesley

---

College?"

"Yes, of course." He kept munching.

So the woman who moved through the halls as if she were an aged retainer was actually a learned former queen. Disbelief swept through my body followed by a chaser of anxiety. Smart women could be dangerous.

A piece of bacon caught in my throat, and I coughed.

Hands on the table, Marco looked ready to push up. But I waved him back. Tears forming in my eyes, I pressed my tongue up into the roof of my mouth—a little trick I'd learned. The concern melted from his face when I finally relaxed. I took a sip of water, considering how to couch my next request, which was really a demand.

"They're just one or two things I'd like to clear up, Your…Highness." Okay, I was struggling with all these titles. "Now, about the cell phone…."

Those handsome features settled into stone. "Not negotiable. Phones are not allowed."

"You would keep your son in the dark like that?" That appeared to get him thinking. "As we study, he's going to need access to information."

"We have a library. Hundreds, perhaps thousands of books."

"Print books quickly become outdated. The Internet is flooded with millions of books. Harvard will require each student to have a laptop."

"This is true?" He set down his knife.

"Absolutely." I might get muscle spasms from crossing my

fingers. "Most certainly. He will need to access history, literature and probably his SAT scores. We need access to wi-fi."

Marco seemed to be considering this. "This was good enough for my father and good enough for me."

"But they probably didn't have computers or iPhones during your father's time, did they?"

Marco's eyes rolled to the frescoed ceiling. "No. Of course not."

"By not allowing phones or the Internet, you are making an island of Gregorio. And yet you expect him to get into Harvard?" I let my incredulity show. But there was a danger here. I was setting a very high bar that I would have to leap over.

Tapping his full lips with a forefinger, he studied me. My own lips tingled and my fingers were twisted into a death grip in my lap. When he swept a hand over his chin, the rasp sent a shiver down my spine. Must be fatigue. "I'll consider this then."

"Good. Wonderful." Releasing my knotted hands, I folded my napkin with satisfaction. Score one for the governess.

"Your phones? Did you lose them?" That broad forehead wrinkled.

"They seem to have disappeared from our rooms."

Nostrils flaring he looked away. "It shall be done."

I pictured Marco as Moses, willing the waters to part. He had that air about him.

Just as we were rising from the table, his mother entered. She seemed surprised to see me. "Good morning…" For the life of me, I couldn't recall her title.

Passing me with a set smile, she headed for the buffet. As the three of us sat there, my mind wandered. Who had scooped up our phones? In a castle like this, servants would not take such liberties. So that left Ama, who was cutting her bacon into small pieces before lifting it to her mouth with a fork. I would have to be very careful with her.

Marco was leaving and I followed him, relieved to leave his mother and her obvious disapproval behind.

"We'll go up to the nursery," he said on his way out the door.

"Great." But when I turned left in the hallway, he turned right.

"Aren't you coming?" he asked.

"Yes, right behind you." I motioned toward the main hall.

Marco looked at me as if I were insane. "No one uses those stairs. You could kill yourself."

"Really? But I thought..."

With a quick turn, he marched in the opposite direction. I got in step behind him. By the time he reached a door I didn't even know was there, my brain was scrambled by those distracting breeches and shiny boots.

Behind the cream-colored door with the wainscoting and gilded framing was an old-fashioned elevator. What was this? The inner golden cage rattled as he pushed it open. "Please. After you."

I'd always been a sucker for a man with manners. My ex-husband Wallace had always walked on the outside on the sidewalk. Maybe just another archaic tradition, but nice.

"This is surprising." I stepped inside. The contraption was probably old but not as ancient as the castle. Metal and knobs gleaming, it seemed well-maintained. As it glided to the third floor with a tasteful rattle, I wondered what they had chiseled out to install it. I also wondered what kind of pomade Marco used on his shiny hair. He smelled spicy and wonderful.

Dropping my eyes to my sensible shoes, I fumed. His mother had purposely made us climb all those stairs. How she must've been laughing. But Her Royal Pain in the Neck had taken them without any strain. Respect evaporated my anger. "Very nice elevator."

Half turning, he grinned. "I put it in after my father's death. You know when I…"

"…became king?" I supplied. Funny how this revelation came to me so easily.

"Precisely." But Marco averted his eyes, a muscle twitching in his cheek. When had he taken the reins of his kingdom? Once I had access to wi-fi, I would definitely do more serious sleuthing.

The elevator stopped and the outer door glided open. I followed Marco out. The third-floor hallway resembled the second floor, done in peaceful shades of ochre and cream. Marching into one of the rooms, he threw his arms out with pleased satisfaction. "A perfect classroom. Do you not think so?"

I looked around. Possibly at one time this had been a nursery where children played. Carved toys were stacked on built-in shelves below a row of cream-colored cabinets. A huge chalkboard covered the side wall. One long table was obviously sized for children, but two others were regular height. But they definitely were not a modern design. Fisher Price needed to do an intervention in this nursery.

"This is quite a setup." A podium was tucked in a corner. Somehow I had to get Majesty to advance into the high tech world. Checking the wall, I found two outlets. "Only two places to plug in computers or other equipment?"

"Other equipment?" He seemed puzzled. After all, I was questioning what he obviously saw as a perfect classroom.

"Yes, teaching equipment. DVD players, a screen." Going to one of the chalkboards, I pulled on a map. The darn thing began to tear and I quickly loosened my grip. But I'd gotten a glimpse of it. "This hasn't been used in a long time. Things have changed." I dusted off my hands.

His eyes swung to the map. "Yes, and so has the world."

Okay, now we were getting someplace. "The other teachers didn't use a laptop or screen?"

"No, I think Professor Rinaldo preferred to lecture."

Lecturing might work in college. But now learning could be enhanced with the right YouTube video. "Poor guy," I said in an undertone, thinking of Gregorio but maybe Rinaldo was the one I should pity. He could have been a competent teacher, hampered by a lack of modern equipment.

"Pardon me?"

"Nothing." My eyes flicked down the length of the nursery. I was dying to open one of the cream-colored cabinets. Someday soon I would.

But right now, I had to make this room a place where we all would succeed, both teacher and students. I couldn't fail. Too much was riding on this. So I needed information. When I swung around, I found him studying my shoes. What the heck? Marco's eyes flew up to meet mine. For a second, our blushes had a race. Which shade of red could reach our cheeks first?

Total nonsense. Keep on track, Christina. "I should ask you what your expectations are of me?"

His eyes narrowed. "Expectations?"

"What do you want Gregorio to get out of this?"

Marco's eyes turned as expressionless as the castle walls. "Ms. Newhart, I thought I made myself clear. Gregorio must attend Harvard University in the United States. He must pass the entrance exam so that he studies there."

His inflexibility stunned me. Not just an Ivy League college, but Harvard. Part of success is adapting to the environment around you. I needed this job and no matter what, I would succeed. So I had to adapt. My daughter's future was at stake. Maybe not Harvard but I did want Lexi to get into a good school. "I see."

I would have to email Mary Carmichael in the guidance department at Providence High School about Harvard requirements, as well as doing my own online research.

My mind cranking ahead, I almost missed his next question. "Sorry, what did you just say?"

He drew closer until he towered over me. "So, you know Brad Pitt...right?"

Chapter 4

What was he talking about? "No. Of course not." The words had a sharper edge than I'd intended. Eyes shuttering, Marco pulled back.

Great. Now I'd offended him. Not a good idea to insult your boss on the first day of work. "I mean, why do you ask?"

He tossed his head as if this were of no consequence. "You come from his town. Pittsburgh. No?" Back to puzzlement again.

Hmm. Tricky. "I don't think Brad Pitt lives in Pittsburgh, Pennsylvania. I think I would know about that."

Then it hit me. "In America, our names do not indicate where we were born, where we live. Not like Catherine of Aragon. Not Like Marco Giovanni..." Here I blundered through a butchered version of his name. When he flinched, I stopped.

"Di Napolitano," he offered, those brown eyes soft as suede. "I see." But his puzzled frown remained.

Thank goodness at that moment Gregorio appeared in the doorway.

"Are you ready for the day?" Marco asked with gusto.

Gregorio nodded. "Yes, sir. I guess."

Sir? And he guessed? Such enthusiasm. You would've thought that I was about to run him through with a sword. Although there weren't any in the nursery, plenty of them patterned the walls.

The tension between them made me sad. Oh, sure, I'd felt the same with Lexi many times. But seeing it here with my student? No, this felt worse than sad.

Time to take care of business. "I shipped a box of books ahead. Mostly teaching supplies and anthologies." And they'd cost a fortune to send. Had they found their way to the island?

Marco was playing with the map, seeing if he could ease it down. "I wondered what that box was. The staff brought it to me. I thought the box had clothing or something like that. The type of things women have."

Dismissal tinged his words. "Yes, things like research books and valuable anthologies."

"Research." He turned and the map ripped away in his hand. Frustrated, he tossed it on the nearest desk. "I will have it brought up."

"Fine." I turned toward my pupil. How I hoped he didn't have the same attitude as his father. "So, I'll see you here tomorrow, Gregorio. Okay?"

"Tomorrow?" Was that disappointment clouding Gregorio's face? The unexpected ego boost made me feel great. But I needed to get my feet on the ground first.

"Tomorrow it is then." And with that, Marco shepherded his son from the room. I was left to study the dust motes floating on the air. Would he allow us access to wi-fi and would our phones be returned?

I didn't want to get our hopes up. Or Lexi's.

After they'd left, I did some more poking around upstairs but there was nothing much to see. Finally, I took the elevator to the second floor, enjoying every minute of it. I found Lexi in her room. Somehow she'd found her way down to the kitchen and snared some food. My daughter had always been resourceful. Seated in one of the chairs, she was pulling on her boots.

"What do you think you're doing?"

"Going riding. Remember when you told me this place had a stable?"

Guilty as charged. I had shamelessly dangled that carrot in front of my daughter. The stable had been mentioned in Marco's ad. I wondered how many tutors had responded because of the stables.

"I ran into Gregorio in the kitchen. He reminded me about it." She twisted her hair into a neat braid. Zipping up her boots, she stood up. Energy radiated from her. Lexi was eager to leave and no doubt would have been on her way without checking with me.

"While we're here, I have to know where you are."

The bottom lip came out. "Why? I'm not a child."

"No, you aren't." I had to be very careful here. "But you are my daughter and I'm responsible for you."

"What does that mean?"

It means I don't want you getting into trouble. "Exactly what I just said. We have to treat things with respect. You can't just pile onto one of their horses."

Standing with one hand on her hip, my little girl looked as if she could be eighteen. With her father's height, she looked mature. But she wasn't. The tears trembling in her eyes told me that this situation was difficult. And I'd gotten her into this. Maybe I should have left her home with Reena. My good-hearted best friend had offered to take Lexi for the summer. But then she'd had an emergency call from her aunt in England. Her summer plans now included nursing her Aunt Penelope.

And in all honesty how could I leave Lexi with anyone? Her friends would still be there, along with the problems they presented. Sending her off to her father's, as Lexi had suggested, was totally out of the question. Wallace wasn't great on discipline— something he'd never known himself. And then there was his closet drinking problem. That hadn't changed.

"Okay, fine." I threw up my hands in surrender. "But I'm coming with you. I just have to change."

"Oh, Mom. Make it quick."

Tromping over to my room, I wished again that we had a connecting door. The stables had been on my list for today. But I hadn't wanted Lexi around when I scoped it out. The boots I'd found at a second-hand shop couldn't compare with the ones I'd bought Lexi two years ago. But they would have to do. Two minutes later, I was ready and we took off. Lexi was amazed when I showed her the elevator that whisked us to the first floor.

"Why didn't Gregorio's grandmother tell us about this cool elevator?" She ran a hand over the wooden paneling.

"Lexi let's not leave fingerprints."

She dropped her hand. "Mom, please don't talk to me like I'm a little kid."

I bit my lip. She had a point. Lexi was growing up so fast. From my years of teaching, I knew that girls matured faster than the boys. When I'd run into boys in the mall after graduation, they always amazed me.

Once on the first floor, we did a little exploring. Eventually we came across the door that opened to the outside. But we scooted around the central courtyard. I did not want to run into the royal grandmother.

"Gee, Mom, you really know your way around," Lexi commented as I led her into the park-like area that we could see from our rooms. No way was I taking the maze today. There were probably shorter ways to get there. Eventually I found the road Marco had taken with me only yesterday. Walking down the gravel road, I couldn't help but remember the feel of him behind me, the earthy smell of the stable boy.

Fifteen minutes later we were standing in the stable that housed quite a few horses. Some hung their heads out of their stall, looking at us with large, liquid eyes. A man's voice drifted over one of the stalls. Of course, we couldn't understand a thing he was saying. Lexi had chosen to take Italian in school but she'd only finished her first year. Still, she listened. "That isn't Italian," she whispered. "But it's close."

The horse in the stall behind us must have heard her voice because the animal lowered its head over the stall. Speaking to him in halting language, Lexi seemed to hit it off with the beautiful tan horse with a blonde mane.

"Good morning." With a smile that creased his entire face, the older gentleman who'd been with Marco yesterday pushed the stall door open. Lexi walked in. Wearing a pleased smile, the man handed her a carrot. Whatever they were saying as they fed the horse, they seemed to understand each other. I hadn't seen her look this happy in a long time, and my heart melted.

"What is the horse's name?" I asked him.

"Nombre?" Lexi threw in.

"Rudolfo." He pointed to himself and then the horse, stroking her neck. "Cara. Sweet, no?"

"She sure is sweet." And Lexi went back to murmuring baby talk to the horse.

Rudolfo's eyes flitted between the horse and this young American girl. Was he sizing her up? The two of them had a quick conversation, straining a bit to understand each other.

Before I knew it, Rudolfo was throwing a blanket over the horse. A saddle soon followed. "What are you doing?" I gripped the top of the stall tight enough to cause slivers. "What's going on?"

"Rudolfo's going to let me ride out on this horse. Isn't that cool?" Her hands clasped in front of her, Lexi was beside herself.

"No, it's not cool." Fear clutched in my throat. I could hardly get the words out. "You're in a strange country. We haven't seen a hospital anywhere."

My daughter's face drew a blank. "Why would we need a hospital?"

Rudolfo handed Cara's reins to Lexi. The horse seemed ready to go along with this. Lexi led her out into the cobblestone corridor between the two rows of stalls.

Worry quickened my heart. "What if you fall off? What then? There is no doctor to take care of you."

Lexi's lips tightened. Rudolfo may not understand what we were saying, but he knew panic when he heard it. Was I sounding like a crazed mother?

Lexi laid a hand on my arm. "Mom, it's all right. I'm a big girl now."

"Barely fourteen," I sputtered.

For a change, she didn't whine or scream. Instead, she turned those cool green eyes to me accusingly. "What do you expect me to do all summer? You told me about the horses. Was that just a teaser?"

Now it was my turn to bite my tongue. Yes, I'd dangled that possibility to make this trip to a foreign land more acceptable. Now I had to deal with the consequences. I'd watched her ride in the beginner's competition last year. Tom VanMeter, her riding coach, had said she was remarkably skilled for her age. As a child, her favorite book was *Misty of Chincoteague*. Riding made sense for her and now I had to trust her.

I had to cut her loose and it was killing me.

While I stood there agonizing, Gregorio appeared. He gave Lexi a quick wave. Slouching as usual, he looked so much younger than my tall, confident daughter. My heart went out to him. The boy needed more than a little exercise. Now he exchanged a few words with Rudolfo and disappeared into a stall. The conversation Gregorio had with the horse was more than I'd heard him say since we'd arrived.

When Lexi walked Cara outside. I scurried after her. "Did you bring any sunblock?" I glanced up at the unforgiving sun.

Lexi laughed. Rudolfo threw me a questioning glance. After Lexi translated my comment, he ran a gnarled hand over a weathered cheek. Okay, maybe he didn't realize that the incidence of melanoma was off the charts and climbing.

Give it a rest, Christina. I could almost hear my friend Reena's voice in my head.

When Lexi mounted the horse with an elastic grace, I felt a rush of pride. *She is competent. She can do this.* Gregorio came up behind us with a caramel-colored horse with a corn silk mane. Shifting from one hoof to the other, this horse was ready to go. Lexi launched into a stilted but determined conversation with Rudolfo and Gregorio.

Bending from the saddle, Lexi said, "Rudolfo will give you a lesson, if you like."

Did she know that was the reason for my early morning visit? "All right, fine. But I want you back here in an hour." I stabbed a finger at my watch, which seemed to have stopped. I shook my wrist. I had to get my phone back.

While I stood there fussing, Lexi and Gregorio took off, heading toward the edges of the field. My breath froze in my throat as they entered the forest and disappeared.

A soft nose nudged my elbow and I jumped. But it was just another horse with Rudolfo, who handed me the reins. "Tesoro," he said, patting the horse's neck fondly. She was a beauty.

"Are we going to be buddies?" I murmured. Okay, those huge

teeth were a little frightening. Standing there inhaling the horse, hay and other things I didn't want to name, I worked up my courage. Didn't I want some adventure in my life?

Heck no. Not right now.

But Reena was in my head again. *Aren't you glad to have some time to yourself?*

Yes, of course I was. I kept drawing deep breaths. The year before I'd taken yoga with Reena and Maddie. What mantra might work here?

May I be one with the horse.

May I be one with the horse.

Tesoro stamped an impatient hoof and I jumped. Rudolfo, who'd been saddling another horse, turned around with more soothing words for Tesoro.

I went back to work on my state of mind. Back home, I would have to pay plenty for these lessons. The summer Lexi learned to ride, almost all of my summer school salary went for the lessons. This would be free. Wasn't I lucky?

Rudolfo had returned and I turned to him. "Are we ready?" I glanced out to where Gregorio and my daughter had disappeared.

Edging closer, Rudolfo patted Tesoro's flanks and set a small step stool below me. *Oh mercy.* A crook of his thumb in an upward motion was all I needed. Grabbing the pommel with my left hand, I stumbled onto the stool. Once I had my balance, I somehow got my left boot into the stirrup and lifted myself into the saddle. The ground seemed very far away but I was up.

With an appreciative smile, Rudolfo led me out to the enclosed area. So we wouldn't be riding through the fields? Relief flooded through me. I couldn't tell if Rudolfo was more worried about the horse or me. It would probably look bad if the governess killed herself while riding one of His Majesty's horses. The sun beat down and perspiration trickled along my forehead.

While I sat there, sweating in the blazing sun on a horse that was way too smelly, Rudolfo returned with his own mount. The old man had probably grown up riding a horse. A few clucks under his breath and we took off at a measured pace around the corral. My body settled into the slow, rocking motion.

This dear old man had taken pity on me. And he might help me fulfill part of my contract—the part where I'd presented myself as an expert equestrian. Who had a son. Well, Rudolfo couldn't help me with that last part.

Chapter 5

Today was the first official day of class, and I was stiff and sore from my ride on Tesoro yesterday. Thinking that some exercise might loosen me up, I ignored the elevator and took the stairs to the third-floor nursery. Nervous excitement jittered in my stomach. My students had always given me good reviews at the end of the semester. But these two students? They might be the most critical yet. And the most important.

I'd left Lexi in the dining room, still sipping coffee—a first for her. Gregorio sat across from her. These two might be a dangerous combination. Ama had shown up for breakfast. She made me nervous, and I didn't miss her hooded eyes shifting between Lexi and Gregorio. Although I didn't always approve of my daughter's actions, I didn't want anyone else disapproving of her. And that included the royal mother. Every time her eyes studied Lexi's hair, she gave an audible sniff. Gregorio lowered his head, but not before I saw his sly grin.

As I gripped the leather rope along the stairs, I smiled. Right now I could be home, teaching summer school. But that wouldn't pay nearly as well as this position. Besides, if I were honest with myself, this governess position had its moments. Every time I remembered Marco's comment about Brad Pitt, I had to chuckle. For a seemingly educated and sophisticated guy, he had surprised me. Maybe this island was more remote than I had expected.

The nursery felt closed in and dusty when I entered. The torn map was still lying across one of the desks. Setting my books down, I pushed the map to one side. Then I slid my notes into the podium, along with a copy of *The Great Gatsby*. The case of books and other materials I'd sent sat in a corner, so I got busy and unpacked them. Then I hobbled over to the tall, narrow windows that were meant more for security than to offer a view. At some point maybe guns or bows had been positioned in these slits—way before the glass was added.

Still, I could see glimpses of the leafy green foliage outside. The island was unbelievably beautiful and I intended to explore more. I just hadn't figured out how. Once I knew how to ride, Tesoro might make things easier. Lexi had turned into a sphinx when I asked her about her ride yesterday. They just "rode around," which told me nothing.

I glanced at my watch. Not quite time to begin, and I drifted out into the hall. Back at my school, most of the teachers stood in the hall between classes. We checked with each other and shared stories. But this hall was very different from the beige tiles and green lockers of Providence High School. If only Reena and Maddie could see this. Later I might snap a picture. Both phones had mysteriously reappeared in our rooms.

Today I had time to appreciate the colorful tapestries accenting the walls along with historical paintings. The floors were burnished bright in the usual deep gold and brown. For some reason there was no rug running down the center of this hall, perhaps because children had once played here. Had Marco once ridden a tricycle over these tiles? The thought brought a warm rush.

Returning to the classroom, I opened one of the cupboards. The hinges squealed as if they had not been used for a while. The shelves were deep and seemed to hold an assortment of paintings. Maybe they rotated out to the walls. These framed works were way too large for me to wrestle out into the open.

"Mom, what are you doing?" Lexi stood in the doorway. The gentle sunlight turned her purple hair to a deep shade of maroon. My daughter was attractive. Possibly beautiful. Then she cracked her gum.

"Lose the gum, Lexi. You know it's not allowed in class." Dusting off my hands, I closed the cupboard. "Just getting my bearings."

Dropping her notebook on one of the desks, she ripped off a corner of one sheet and rolled up her gum. But we didn't have a wastebasket here and she ended up tucking it into her fringed shoulder bag. Wandering over to the window, she peered down. "Will you just look at all that land? The King must be richer than all get out."

Behind us a throat cleared and I wheeled around.

"Good morning." In the space of two words, Gregorio's voice screeched from husky into another octave. So that's how it was. Poor guy. Puberty was never kind to boys. His father's dark unruly hair framed Gregorio's round face. The rumpled shirt must've been made of linen. Didn't Marco believe in permanent press fabrics? It looked as if it should be in a historical museum. His pants were more like breeches, which looked great on his father but uncomfortable on Gregorio. Shuffling forward, he slumped into a seat.

Eyes wary, Lexi took the chair at the table next to him.

Showtime. "Let's get to it. Gregorio, why don't you tell me what you know about American literature. Or literature of any kind."

"Um, not much." Like his dad, his English held a pleasant accent. He rambled through some modern day works, mostly adventure or sci-fi.

"Where did you find those books?" Was Marco letting Gregorio order from Amazon? And how had he gained access? I chuckled at the thought of an Amazon van making its way up the road that we'd taken from the boathouse.

Gregorio's eyes dropped, his fingers picking at the spine of a notebook. "My father took me to London last year. They had many books in London." His eyes flicked up to mine, asking for agreement.

"Yes, they do," I said with a smile. "A couple of years ago, I visited London with some of the other teachers. The bookstores were amazing. Charing Cross Road was lined with them." How nice that Marco had taken the time to introduce his son to London.

Picking up an erasable pen, I began to write on the board. "Have you read any of these?" And I mapped out some of the basic American literature. Sliding lower in her chair, Lexi sighed until I narrowed my eyes at her. Then she sat up a little straighter.

Although she'd had some of these works freshman year, I wanted her to go through them again with Gregorio.

At one point, Gregorio raised one hand. "Pardon me, but what is this Puritan thing?"

Taking a deep breath, I briefly talked about the start of America and the lack of tolerance. He especially liked my stories about the women who were dunked in the river, suspected of being witches.

"Oh no." He shook his head. "That is terrible."

Lexi snorted. "They should have moved to another town."

I looked at her in amazement. "Things were different back then. A woman couldn't just pick up and move. People lived in groups for safety. For a woman to leave was unthinkable."

To my surprise and delight, Gregorio had other questions about the early days of the country where he hoped to study. But after an explanation of Puritanism, Hawthorne and Melville, both Lexi and Gregorio looked as if they might nod off. "Why don't we go outside for a break? The fresh air will be good for our brains."

Gregorio's eyes brightened. I'd dealt with a lot of sophomores and juniors so his quiet introspection and thoughtful questions were welcome. This time we took the elevator. As we whirred to the first floor, Gregorio said, "Lexi told me about my grandmother and the staircase. She can be, how do you say in America, 'something else.' But she is really a very sweet woman."

Now, "sweet" was not a word I would apply to Her Royal Pain in the Neck. Once on the first floor, Gregorio led us to another secret door. Lexi and I exchanged a glance. The boy was proving very helpful in showing us how to navigate the twisting corridors and endless floors.

Outside, the sunlight banished my second thoughts about the summer. Summer had come to Napolitano and I breathed in the warm air. "This sure feels different than Pittsburgh."

"You got that right." Lexi slipped out of her hoodie and tied it around her waist. "Our city doesn't begin to warm up until July."

"I hope you can get my father to open up the wi-fi." He shook his head. "Sometimes he treats me like a child."

The strange thing was, I knew just how Marco felt. "Parents often feel their children are younger than they really are."

"But why?" Gregorio spoke up.

"Yeah, why," Lexi chimed in. "It's stupid. Kids grow up."

"It's our job to protect you. Keep you safe."

Well, they obviously didn't believe me and it was time to change the subject. The soft summer sun fell over the garden, enriching the greenery and bringing out lush colors in the flowers around us. As we walked down the stone path, Gregorio pointed to bushes and trees, giving them names in his language.

"What a beautiful countryside."

"Yes, yes it is." But Gregorio sighed as he looked around. A young man of sixteen shouldn't seem so troubled. Did all this beauty fill him with a sense of responsibility? He was far too young to worry about that.

After twenty minutes or so, we went back to class. I gave Gregorio one of the anthologies I'd sent ahead. "For some background. I've marked the early American literature trends. Let me know if you have any questions. We'll look at that next week."

At least he seemed to have a good background in algebra and geometry. Passing out sheets with simple problems, I asked them to have the homework ready for tomorrow. Lexi glowered at me. "Also, for tomorrow I'd like you to read chapter one of *The Great Gatsby.*" I'd made sure that Lexi packed her own copy and I'd brought a copy for Gregorio.

"So small." He turned the slim book over in his hand. "Are pages missing?"

I laughed. "This small book has a lot in it. And it's historical, capturing the years known as the 'roaring twenties' in America. I think you'll find it interesting."

"Until the guy dies," Lexie said from the corner of her mouth.

I sent my daughter a searing look. Maybe it would be easier to teach Gregorio alone. But leaving Lexi to her own devices wasn't an option.

Just as I was wrapping up class, a knock came on the door. Milo stuck his head in, waving a crisp white envelope.

"Good morning. Is that for me?" I stepped toward him.

With barely a grunt, he delivered the envelope and disappeared.

What could this be? My name was scrawled across the envelope with authority. "I guess class is dismissed."

Gregorio and Lexi didn't move. Their eyes were riveted to what I had in hand. Turning my back, I opened the envelope. Marco wanted to meet with me in his first floor office following class. Fine, I had some issues I wanted to discuss. But my hands shook as I shoved the note back into the envelope, cutting a finger on the heavy vellum.

After Gregorio and Lexi took off, I packed up my books and notes and headed for the elevator. Slowly descending, the gilded cage rattled, and my thoughts clattered right along with it. After what felt like an eternity, the elevator whooshed to a stop. The outer door felt heavy as I pushed it open. Silence met me on the first floor.

Passing the library and dining room, I headed for the next open door. Standing in the recessed opening, I heard the rattle of dry pages turning. "Hello?" I stepped forward.

At the far end of the room, Marco lounged, his feet up on a massive desk. Glancing up from his newspaper, he whisked a pair of glasses from his nose and his boots hit the floor. "Come in, Profesora. Please."

Would a time come when I'd get used to this accent? When the intonation wouldn't sound like some foreign movie star in a film I shouldn't be watching?

My flats slid on the stone floor as I walked forward. My tennis shoes might be a better bet in this castle, but they were so informal. The first class had gone well, and maybe I was feeling a little cocky. Suddenly it hit me that I should be curtsying. That royal dip that I'd seen in movies that the staff executed so effortlessly and that Lexi had tried—how hard could that be? Sliding my left foot behind me, I took a stab at it. However, my left foot kept going. Books flew everywhere, along with notes.

In an instant Marco was on his feet and I was on the floor. Had I ever felt this embarrassed in my life? With his hand under one elbow, I managed to stand up. "Sorry, M—Your Majesty. I'm usually not this clumsy."

My nose should have grown a mile. The fact was, I'd had a lot of awkward moments in my life. Lexi could attest to that. But I'd never curtsied before and it probably showed. My right elbow was killing me.

"Are you all right?" Those deep brown eyes seemed to melt over me, like the chocolate on a hot fudge sundae. Right now I wanted one in the worst way.

"Oh, yes, I'm—I'm fine and dandy." I managed to shove off from his firm chest.

Dandy? Had I really said that? At least I hadn't broken anything. I flexed my right arm, wondering where I'd wind up if I broke a bone here. The idea of an ER located among the pastel houses seemed ludicrous.

"This is not necessary with me, Profesora." One final assessing glance and Marco returned to the desk. I managed to walk forward the rest of the way without falling.

"Please." He motioned to one of the ornate high back chairs.

Did dust poof up as I sat? Must have been my imagination. I folded my hands over the stack of notes in my lap.

"So, did your class go well?" Flicking his eyes from my notes to my ponytail, he leaned across the desk.

"Yes, very well. At least I thought so." How much should I tell him? One class and already I was feeling protective of my student. His math homework would tell me where Gregorio stood in that area.

"So you are still…interested?" Those intense eyes bored into me.

"What?" I squirmed in my seat. "Am I still interested?" Was this a test? If I didn't make the grade, would he have us packed up and returned on the next boat? *Oh no you don't.*

Getting rid of me wouldn't be that easy.

Tapping the papers in my lap, I faced off. "We have a contract. And that contract applies to more than one day, more than one month." Good heavens, if I went back home in June, it would be too late to get my summer school position back. My heart raced with panic.

Feeling like a serf brought in to defend the crops I wanted to plant for the summer season, I licked my dry lips.

His eyes followed. Marco had fallen back into his kingly chair. I'd had enough of his overbearing attitude.

Time to jump to another topic. "It's about the wireless."

"Wire less," he said, breaking it into two words.

"The wi-fi." I spiraled one hand into the air. "We need to be hooked up to the Internet so that we can …order books from Amazon."

There. That sounded a lot better than admitting that I wanted to be able to dig up more information about his family and this island.

The back of his chair was probably as stiff as his spine. "What kind of books?"

My mind scurried ahead like one of the squirrels foraging through the trees. Outside was a beautiful day. I had to keep my mind focused on that prize. I hoped to enjoy many days like this here this summer. If I got my act together. "History books. They are very big. Too heavy to be bring on the plane. Too heavy to send here in that box."

Hands steepled in front of his lips, he seemed to turn my words over in his mind.

"Yes. I suppose so."

"Definitely." I seemed to be gaining credibility.

"And Harvard would expect this?" Dropping his hands, Marco drummed his fingers on the arms of his chair.

"Yes. Most certainly." My throat was so dry it was almost painful. "And there's something else."

His brows rose. "There is more?"

"Yes, there is more. I need to be able to email a guidance counselor, a friend of mine who works in placing students in universities." Mary Carmichael, one of our guidance counselors, had been such a help in placing my students in the right academic environment. "I cannot do that unless I have access to wi-fi."

Now that caught his attention. Marco's expression became very, very serious. "You know such a person?"

"Yes, I work with such a person." Good grief, I was beginning to phrase my sentences like his. If I didn't watch it, my students wouldn't be able to understand me when I returned.

"I would pay her much money for such information."

My mouth fell open. "What?" Let my thoughts wander for just a minute and it was all over. "Forgive me, but I don't believe I heard you correctly."

"I do forgive you. Although I don't know for what." He

nodded with understanding, as if he were accustomed to forgiving people on a daily basis. As if every day he held their lives in the balance, and maybe he did. "Back to your friend. If you have such a connection, I'm glad to pay for this information. Anything to further my son's education."

Oh, wow. Thinking back to recent legal cases, I carefully considered my next words. "In America there is no need to pay for such information." Yep, I was still talking like him.

"This is a woman I work with at the high school where I teach. A guidance counselor who helps students make wise choices. She would be happy to help me with this as a professional courtesy. But I need access to the Internet to contact Mary Carmichael."

And I also want to text my girlfriends about just how hot you are.

What was wrong with me?

"I see." But I wasn't sure he actually saw at all. "Your library doesn't have many books dealing with American literary history."

He pursed his lips. His very full lips with that cute little tuck in the corners. "Probably correct."

"So we need access to wi-fi."

When he slammed one fist on the desk, I jerked. "It will be done."

I struggled not to smile.

"I will have Milo take care of it. He has the password."

"Thank you." Afraid he might change his mind, I hustled out of there. Were people supposed to curtsy when they left his presence? My elbow throbbed. I couldn't risk it.

That night when I returned from dinner, a note was shoved

under my door with a password of symbols that did not make sense. I opened my laptop and signed on. To my astonishment the Internet opened up. I exhaled. This access meant I was no longer stranded. Everything would be fine.

How little I knew then.

Chapter 6

The days settled into a schedule. My phone alarm rang just as the
sun rose over the misty fields. After a quick breakfast, I went to the
stables for my lesson with Rudolfo. Lexi preferred to sleep late.
Fine with me. All these meals together were beginning to wear on
me. While I agonized over what Lexi might say, I had to watch my
own tongue. Ama's visible disapproval was sometimes heavier than
the pasta sauce.

The new schedule also had its high notes. To my delight,
Gregorio finished *The Great Gatsby* within a couple of days.

"What did you think?" This book was one of my very favorites.
Usually my students loved it too. Lexi, of course, would never
admit she loved anything that I appreciated.

"So why didn't Nick go to Jay Gatsby's parties if he lived next
door?" Gregorio's innocent question almost made me laugh.

"Nick was Daisy's cousin, which is why Jay cultivates a
friendship with him. Gatsby wants Nick to speak highly of him." I
could see that Gregorio was mulling this over.

"But why didn't this Jay Gatsby marry Daisy in the first place?
Why did she marry that terrible man instead?"

"Is Tom Buchanan terrible?" I wanted to hear this from

Gregorio's lips.

"Oh, I think so." He looked to Lexi for agreement. "He has money and he brags about it."

"And he's mean to Myrtle," Lexi threw in.

How could I structure this so that Gregorio would understand the class differences? "In the beginning, Jay can't marry Daisy because he has no money. All the men wore military uniforms because of the war so Daisy doesn't get that. But she's used to living in…a castle." Now that was a bit of a stretch.

"Oh, he was like a serf?" Gregorio's eyes deepened with understanding. Sometimes the similarity between father and son was creepy. "Now I get it."

He "got it"? Were Lexi's modern phrases making their way into Gregorio's speech? "Jay Gatsby becomes very wealthy, hoping to win Daisy's heart again."

"But Daisy is married now," Lexi joined in. "And this Tom Buchanan is mean. He isn't even nice to that puppy he gives Myrtle."

"Good point, Lexi. On the other hand, Gatsby will do anything for Daisy. He adores her."

"But Tom is not faithful to his wife," Lexi grumbled.

"No, he is not. And that is terrible." Gregorio shook his head. Although I wasn't here to teach morality, I was glad to hear him say that. "Yes, it was. In America we usually marry for life." With a fifty percent divorce rate? My words made me cringe. My own marriage hadn't worked out that way. "In most cases," I added.

Gregorio hadn't missed that last part and he did an eye check with Lexi seated next to him.

"Unless your father drinks too much," she said, with such loss in her voice. My heart knotted in my chest. Suddenly the room felt too small. This little book might hold a whole world of heartache.

"I guess that's all for today." While Gregorio and Lexi packed up, I went to the window. "Gregorio, are we at the highest point of the castle?"

"Yes, except for the towers."

"You have towers? Really?" Lexi's voice rose with excitement.

"Want to see?" He was already on his feet.

Of course I wanted to see. After stuffing my notes and book into my tote, I was ready for a tour. Gregorio moved with the bumbling motions of a growing boy. When he caught his foot on the chair, it scraped across the floor. I pretended not to notice and so did Lexi. Maybe she was learning.

We followed Gregorio down the hall.

"Were you born here?" I asked as he opened a door leading to a stairway.

"Of course." He started up the winding stairs and I was right behind him.

"In the town hospital, you mean?" Lexi asked.

"Oh, no. We are always born in our castle. The doctors come."

I smiled at the "we," which must refer to royalty.

"How cool." Lexi's voice bubbled with excitement.

"Trust me, not if you're the mother." The idea of bringing a child into the world in this bone-chilling castle made my stomach heave and other parts of my body clench.

Our feet scuffed up endless steps. From time to time we passed a window.

"Are we almost there?" Lexi groaned.

"Yes." Gregorio stomped along above me. Although I never would have pegged him as an athlete, the stairs didn't seem to bother him. How often did he come up here?

"You won't believe what you can see from up here." Gregorio sounded excited.

Conversation became impossible. I was too busy panting. At the top of the stairs, a carved bench sat on a landing below a medieval painting. The whole mood changed. Snatching a key from a hidden cranny, Gregorio opened the door with the ornate, old-fashioned key. Lexi and I crowded in behind him.

Lexi's eyes swept the room. "Look at all this stuff."

In the center of the spacious room sat a four-poster bed draped with drop cloths. Furniture was also shrouded. Lexi pulled the cloth off a mirrored dressing table and another from the bench in front of it. "Mom, look at this." She was elated by her discovery.

Dust sprayed into the air, causing a major coughing fit. "Lexi, stop."

"But, Mom, this is so great." Lexi plopped down on the padded bench. "Do you think I could move this downstairs? You know, just for now?"

I snapped my attention from the paintings on the walls. "Of course not."

"I would have to ask." Gregorio ran his fingers over the inlaid wood on the dressing table. "This was my mother's."

Feeling light-headed, I grabbed the bedpost. "Do you mean this was your mother's room?" A bedroom was personal territory. Now I felt like an intruder, but I was more than curious. What in heaven's name would the poor woman be doing up here? My eyes went to the heavy drapes and huge fireplace. A woven blue and rose-colored rug covered most of the stone floor. Yes, someone could have stayed here.

"Yes, I remember playing on this rug." He glanced down at the floral pattern. "Wish I could remember her more."

The boy's sigh went straight to my heart.

"Gosh, how old were you when she, you know, died?" Lexi's forthright manner could irritate me. But not today. I wanted to know too.

"About four." His voice thickened.

The poor boy had only had a mother for four years. How difficult for Marco and hard for the little boy who ended up with a stern-faced grandmother.

The room definitely had a feminine feel to it. But it also held a lot of hurt and isolation. Why had Marco stuck his wife up here?

"Look at this." Lexi motioned me to the window. "You can see everything from here."

"Just about." Gregorio came up behind us. "There's the stable."

When I glanced down, my breath caught in my throat. Heights had always terrified me, and I grabbed the window ledge with both hands. "The scenery is spectacular. Are those vineyards off in the distance?"

"Yes, we are known for our wine. Well, and our olives. Maybe someday we can visit the vineyard."

"I would like that." When I'd done my research, the vineyards and wine had been mentioned. Turning away from the rolling hills that stretched forever, I took a breath. "Have you ever used the fireplace?" The huge stone opening was stained dark from smoke.

"I haven't used it. But it's been used." Gregorio carried a strange sadness in his voice. "It gets cold up here."

Anger simmered behind my eyes. How dare Marco isolate that young mother up here. "Why didn't your mother live downstairs?"

Outside, a brisk wind kicked up, rattling the mullioned windowpanes. I could only imagine how frightening that would sound at night. "She wanted to be alone." Then Gregorio's face brightened. "Want to see the dungeon?"

"Yes, yes." Clapping her hands together, Lexi turned from the window. "What fun!"

Fun? "Where is it?" My head was reeling.

Mouth gaping, Gregorio looked at me as if I'd just fallen off a turnip truck. "In a castle the dungeon is always in the basement."

Lexi and I exchanged a look. Trepidation slowed my steps as we followed Gregorio out of the room. He locked up and tucked the key away. Gregorio seemed so sad as we followed him down those forbidding stone steps. Why had he brought us up here? The room seemed so personal and he hardly knew us.

Maybe Marco would answer my questions. But I would have to phrase them very carefully.

When we exited at the foot of the steps, there stood his grandmother. I nearly jumped out of my shoes. Her forbidding look was enough to give me nightmares.

"Gregorio, what are you doing?" Although her question was pointed, her voice was soft. Ama obviously cared very much for her grandson.

Hands fumbling in his pockets, Gregorio shifted in his boots. My heart went out to him.

"He was just giving us a tour," Lexi offered breezily, eyes circling between Gregorio and his grandmother. "Great view from up there."

That was my girl. Always ready with an answer, even though the question wasn't intended for her.

"I see." But Ama continued to focus on her grandson. "Have you had lunch?"

"We've been in class, Nonna." Suddenly, Gregorio became very interested in the portraits that stretched along the wall on the first floor. "This was a typical fourteenth century study of the countryside."

To my astonishment, he rambled on, spewing some pretty impressive information. The boy definitely had a leg up on art history. To my relief, Ama drifted away. As soon as she'd disappeared down the corridor, he cut the monologue and crooked a finger. "Come."

We followed tight on his heels. This boy knew every secret corridor in the place. "Was all that fourteenth century stuff true...about the painting?" I had to ask.

"Most of it. Reginaldo, one of the tutors, was really into art." Shuffling along, he led us to another elevator in the back. By that time, I had no idea where we were.

"But he wasn't American," Gregorio continued, lifting a shoulder. "You know. No connections at Harvard. No friends in high place, my father says."

"Oh, but I…" No way did I want Marco to think I had influence at the university.

"Isn't this amazing?" Lexi squeezed my arm.

"I know." Gregorio opened the cleverly hidden elevator door. After making sure no one was looking, he ushered us inside. "For a long time, no one else had an elevator to their dungeon."

Oh, really? "And now?"

"A few have them. How do you say it?"

"Copy cats," Lexi provided with a pleased grin.

"Yes. I think so." He closed the metal door and pushed a button. Lexi giggled.

"What?" Gregorio gave her a patient smile, and for the first time I saw the age difference. He seemed more sophisticated than Lexi. "My father's very progressive in that way."

I snorted and then broke into a cough. Progressive? A man who kept his wife in a tower?

He shrugged. "Of course we don't use the dungeon anymore."

Okay, I wondered how recently it had been used.

"My father had a huge wine cellar built down here. That was really why he added the elevator."

Cold seeped into my bones as the elevator slowly descended. Lexi seemed too excited to notice. This experience might run pretty close to one of the fairy tales she used to love. In *Hansel and*

Gretel, the children wound up imprisoned.

Finally, we reached the bottom. The elevator stopped with a jolt, and Gregorio pushed the door open. We stepped out into dank darkness. Lexi fell against me, quivering. I squeezed her arm. But I wasn't feeling that brave myself. A cold chill iced my spine. With a crisp click, Gregorio flipped a switch on the wall.

Overhead neon lights flickered to life. Lexi released a breath and pulled away. "This is really creepy."

"Yeah. Creepy," Gregorio said, a smile lifting his voice. "All the dungeons are like this." His tone implied this was the best thing since sliced bread.

I erupted into laughter and Gregorio gave me an injured glance.

"Oh, I'm not laughing at you. It's just that we don't have dungeons in our country." I tried to explain. "In our basements we just do the laundry."

Gregorio shook his head as if that were equally puzzling. We moved ahead, our feet scuffing on the earthen floor. You didn't have to walk far to find the dungeon. A hallway on the left led to two cells with iron bars, facing each other. "There are separate cells." I felt as if we were on a movie set.

Although I knew nothing about dungeons these looked long, narrow and dark. "Maybe we'll read *The Count of Monte Cristo* sometime," I murmured.

"Oh, Mom, stop." Lexi turned to Gregorio. "The Count lived in prison for years and years."

His expression never changed. "Sometimes that happens."

I crossed my arms tight to keep from shivering. The elevator looked pretty tempting right then. Another hallway led in the opposite direction. "What's down here?"

"Only the torture chamber." His tone was matter of fact.

"Yuk!" Lexi squealed. "Your family tortured people down here?"

"Of course. Those times were very difficult. People always wanted to take your land and kill your family. Some of your own people might turn into spies."

Okay, with that I did an about-face. No way was I headed down that dark hallway. "That's terrible."

Back at the elevator, I waited for them. All I wanted was to be carried back up to the light and sanity. I never would have made it in medieval times.

"So you don't want to see the wine cellar?" Gregorio asked, an injured look on his face.

"Um, not today."

"Yeah, some other time." Huddling next to me, Lexi nodded.

Gregorio held the door open. Lexi and I barreled into the elevator, shivering when he clicked off the light in the lower chambers. Joining us, he pressed the button for the first floor. By that time, I was starting to feel a serious disconnect between my life and the life that Gregorio lived. How could I prepare him for the world of Harvard and Boston when he was surrounded by this past?

Feeling damp and gritty, I wanted to clean up before lunch. My hope was I could scoot into the kitchen and grab some sandwiches for Lexi and myself, avoiding the dining room.

While these plans pulled together in my mind, the elevator stopped. Gregorio opened the door and we stepped out.

Marco stood at the door to the dining room with a young, dark-haired beauty. They were having an animated conversation. She wore crisp white slacks and a white top accented by a trailing blue and green scarf that moved with her slender body. Her laughter sounded like a breeze teasing crystal wind chimes.

"I forgot Gabriella was coming." Gregorio rammed a hand through his long curls before running it down his wrinkled breeches.

Who the heck was Gabriella?

Chapter 7

Staring down the corridor at the most feminine woman I'd ever
seen, I wanted the floor to swallow me. Cobwebs clung to my hair
from our foray into the dungeon. My beige slacks and blue top
were wrinkled from the heat. Hair that would not stay in the
barrette tickled the base of my neck. I was a brown pigeon while
Gabriella was an exotic tropical bird. Lexi seemed entranced by the
newcomer. But Gregorio? Not so much.

All smiles, Marco gestured to us. "Come and meet Gabriella."

Oh, how I wanted to be back in that elevator, pushing the
button for the second floor. But no, I was an employee. As I
inched forward, my smile felt stiff. This was how I'd felt meeting
the parent of a troubled student on Parents Night. Only Gregorio
wasn't the troubled student. No, I was thinking of Marco. The man
was full of surprises.

"How wonderful!" Gabriella whirled toward us. Her scarf
floated on the air while her long dark curls tumbled in distracting
abundance. "So happy to meet you. I'm Gabriella di la Fontagna."

"Christina Newhart." I extended one hand. Gabriella looked
very young. "And this is my daughter Lexi."

Before I knew it, Lexi was doing a light bob, as if she were greeting the Queen of England. I choked on a laugh. We both needed a class in royal courtesies. "Pleased to meet you, I'm sure," Lexi said. Face reddening, she darted her eyes to me and I smiled.

"Yes, of course. How sweet." The tropical bird seemed fascinated by Lexi's purple hair. Maybe vivid colors were Gabriella's thing. But a nod was apparently all Lexi merited. With another swirl of that fanciful, floating scarf, she held both hands out to Gregorio. "Gregorio, my darling. How nice to have a school mate!"

Face brick red, Gregorio kept his hands jammed in his pockets. "Gabriella." One word was all he could handle? Her graceful hands flitted to her scarf.

"Oh, my. Guess I don't even get a hug." She regarded Marco through thick, lowered lashes.

Marco gave a suppressed sigh, as if Gregorio needed more training. Was that going to become my job too? The more time I spent with Gregorio, the more I realized he was a sweet boy going through a difficult time. The isolation of the castle and his tragic past sure weren't helping things.

Day by day, I was being fed pieces of life at the castle. Right now, it seemed to be very complicated. Did Gabriella know Marco's background? Did she realize his last wife had been imprisoned in the tower?

"Gabriella's come for lunch." Marco turned to me, dark eyes flashing. "You'll join us?"

But I was already edging down the hall toward the elevator. "Oh, sorry but we have plans." The words came out sounding stilted and ridiculous.

Marco and Lexi both turned to me with astonishment. But the satisfied look on Gabriella's face kept me from hustling off. She didn't want me to stay. So I was staying. "Well, if you insist."

"But of course. Excellent. We will have a nice lunch, no?" Marco waved a hand to the dining room. Trailing behind Marco and Gabriella, I studied her. The girl didn't shop in Macy's or Nordstrom. Oh no, I pictured this young woman sitting next to Beyoncé at the spring shows in Milan. My beige pants tightened around my waist and my flats felt scuffed and boring.

"The doors are open." Lexi came to a stop.

"What?" Yes, indeed, the french doors of the dining room had been opened to an outdoor patio. Sheer drapes billowed invitingly from either side of the doors. We stepped out into mild summer sunshine. A long plank table with eight chairs spanned the stone patio. The fountain featuring some god, maybe Neptune, filled the air with sparkling moisture. The sun's rays were splintered by the leafy trees that towered above us with historic majesty. Marco gestured. I slid onto a chair with Lexi on one side and Marco on the other.

Across from us, Gabriella cozied up to Marco. With a long-suffering sigh, Gregorio took a seat next to her. Of course, it was way past a decent lunch time in the States. The boy was probably starving. Marco's mother arrived, looking regal in one of her long, flowing ensembles the color of the sky. Gold earrings hung from her ears, and another astonishing jewel hung from her neck, this time an opal. A servant stepped forward to seat her at the other end of the table.

"Mother, you've met Gabriella."

"Of course." Ama snapped open a napkin. "I knew both your father and your grandfather."

Was the comment meant to accent her youth? Gabriella's smile wavered.

"Yes, of course. So nice that our families know each other." Marco continued with the conversation. "Gabriella was driving past."

The Queen Mother's delicate brows lifted. I had to agree. How does one simply happen to be in the neighborhood of a castle? I thought back to the boat and the dock—the whole process used to arrive at the gates.

Marco seemed totally unaware. Maybe women stopped by every day. While waiters filled water goblets and served wine, he chatted with Gabriella about Gregorio's studies—as if he really understood what we were doing. I refused to get upset. When I felt Gregorio's eyes on me, I gave him what I hoped was a reassuring smile. This gorgeous, airy day with a gentle breeze wafting all sorts of wonderful scents from the garden called for carefree conversation. The boy seemed to relax under my encouragement.

Ama began giving Gabriella a history lesson and I sat back. Listening to a long list of when various renovations had been made to the castle, I squeezed Lexi's hand. She seemed totally engaged. This was better than reading about history in some textbook. After serving the beverages, staff brought baskets of bread to the table. The scent of the fresh bread, no doubt baked this morning, made my stomach growl. I ducked my head. The butter that accompanied the bread was formed into little designs that sure looked like Marco's coat of arms.

Although I'd never been much for wine during the day, it might be time I started. Looking over the land that spilled before us in undulating waves, I was amazed by the beauty. What was I doing sitting here with Lexi, lapping up history under the trees on this delightful day with a colorful group of people I didn't know? Taking a chance had paid off. My friends Reena and Maddie would agree.

The pasta was the most wonderful I'd ever eaten, served with a sauce that did not overwhelm it. The delicate coat of the fish was easily broken by my fork. While I savored the meal, Gabriella played with her fork and made eyes at Marco, who responded in kind. Ama whispered in Gregorio's ear and I wondered what she was saying. Although the older woman wasn't at the top of my hit parade, she cared for her grandson. That counted with me.

"What is this stuff?" Lexi's voice shredded the still air.

I looked down. "Pasta." *Please don't ruin this, Lexi.* Checking my wine glass, I realized that I hadn't emptied it. Had she? My heart sank.

Face reddening, Gregorio leaned forward. "Gnocchi."

"What the heck is Know She?"

To my embarrassment, Marco had stopped talking. He looked away from Gabriella's beauty and turned a sharper gaze to my daughter. The fragrant moist bread lodged in my throat. I grabbed my water glass.

"Gnocchi is made with fresh eggs," Ama said in her gravelly voice. "You break the eggs into the center of the shredded potatoes and carefully circle with your fingers."

Lexi drew back. "That sounds complicated."

"It sounds wonderful. And tastes even better." What was I saying? I scooped up a forkful.

"This is Gregorio's favorite." Ama's eyes pierced Gabriella, as if she should have known this. "The dish is made especially for the Crown Prince."

Gabriella's laugh tinkled on the air like a precious silver bell. The kind that can drive you out of your mind. She gave a baleful look to the spoonful on her plate. "So sorry. Way too many calories for me."

Yes, in those pencil slim pants under her draped shirt, was the slim body of a model. Of that I was sure. "But it's delicious." I took another forkful. Feeling Ama's approving eyes on me, I said, "Maybe the staff could teach me sometime."

Wouldn't that be great? I pictured myself wowing Reena and Maddie with my culinary skills. Maybe I'd even give lessons at the Rec Center.

Lexi snorted but Gregorio smiled. "I can teach you," he said softly but with the rich timbre of his father's voice. Promises of things to come. "It's kind of fun. And tastes so good." Bringing his fingers to his lips, he kissed them, maybe like some chefs he'd seen on TV. Then his face turned as red as the radicchio.

"The student instructing the teacher." Gabriella raised her glass.

Marco studied his son with visible disapproval. Was cooking

not considered manly enough for a Crown Prince? The king jerked his attention back to me. "And calculus? That is going well?"

"Yes, indeed." Not the time to delicately tell him that we were busy with trigonometry, that I was trying to bring Gregorio up to speed. When I looked up, Lexi was giving me a curious look. She knew we weren't working with calculus since she'd been sitting in the class. I'd have to talk to my daughter so she didn't blow my cover.

"Signora Newhart will get my son into Harvard," Marco confided to Gabriella.

Her lips formed an O, round and luscious. Did she even realize the importance of this past bit of news? Did she care? Marco seemed captivated by those lips. And for some reason I was becoming increasingly irritated.

To my relief, everyone went back to the meal. I tried not to eavesdrop on the others' conversations, but I was not to be spared. Because she wasn't eating. Gabriella had time to talk. "Gregorio, tell us what you have been learning."

Maybe she'd already asked Marco about the lessons but he didn't have a clue.

Brandishing one of the heavy silver forks, Marco said, "Yes, Gregorio. Tell us."

My heart sank as I watched Gregorio struggle. He'd been chewing, and I hoped he didn't choke.

Averting her eyes, Ama tensed. Gabriella was definitely not her favorite person. My guess was, Ama didn't want this young woman to have any knowledge of what went on in this castle. The

Queen Mother was a secretive woman.

"We've been reading *The Great Gatsby*," I offered. Gregorio threw me a grateful look. Hand shaking, he lifted his water goblet. The poor boy managed to spill water on what was left of his gnocchi.

Gabriella tipped up her beautifully sloped nose. "What is this Gatsby thing?"

"A classic," I said. "In America, that is."

One slender shoulder lifted dismissively. "Well, America."

Lacing his hands together, Marco abandoned his meal, his attention drawn to his struggling teenager. "Tell us, my son, about this book."

Gregorio's eyes lifted to mine. I nodded. He liked the book and he seemed to get it.

"It's about a bootlegger named Gatsby."

"Bootlegger." More distaste on Gabriella's side. "What is this bootlegger thing? So he makes shoes?"

"Smuggler." Marco supplied the word as if every well-bred Royal should know what that meant. Ama's eyes sparkled, as if she wanted to hear more.

Eating had slowed, the food forgotten. "Well, Gatsby loves a girl named Daisy."

Gabriella sent a simpering smile in Marco's direction. "So Gregorio is reading a love story, eh?"

The teacher in me roared to life. "Of sorts," I said in my best academic voice. "The book is about class differences and how they affect relationships—the fabric of society."

To my delight, Gabriella slouched back and reached for her wine. She'd been chastened. And she didn't like it.

"Daisy falls in love with Gatsby, but he has to go off to war, so she marries someone else." Lexi joined the discussion.

Marco shrugged his broad shoulders as if he understood perfectly.

"But when he comes back, he decides to make a lot of money so Daisy will love him again." Gregorio jumped back into the fray.

"He makes money," Marco said the words as if he were trying to understand. "So he has no estate. No trust?"

"No, Father. He is a poor man," Gregorio said softly.

"But she is married now, no?" Gabriella had picked up that key point. I was beginning to enjoy this lively discussion. In class, my students often pointed out the similar conflicts. But now I had the royal point of view.

"Daisy loves Jay Gatsby," Gregorio says with wonder. "Her husband hasn't treated her well."

"Yes. Poor Gatsby. He doesn't get it." Lexi says. "And he gets killed."

"Does the husband take his vengeance?" Marco asked, eyes sparking. "Does he challenge Gatsby to a duel?"

My mind went to the assortment of swords, knives and daggers displayed on the walls. Well, I couldn't help it. My laughter spilled over the table. Marco was applying his own life, his own set of social standards to this classic tale. One look at the group and I swallowed my laughter. They were taking this very seriously.

Gabriella had fallen silent. All this talk of strange marriages might have caught her by surprise. And she might not like it.

Wearing a sly smile, Ama regarded Marco and her grandson. Gregorio had gone back to his gnocchi.

"So much for these fairy tales. What about the mathematics?" Marco waved a knife in the air.

Did men always go back to numbers?

"He's doing very well." But I was getting ahead of myself.

Gregorio understood the concepts. I could see that. But I sensed that his heart wasn't in trigonometry, so calculus might be a slog. This passion I'd seen today during our discussions? No, he didn't hold this keen interest in math.

Sitting back, I thought that over as the servants deftly exchanged empty plates with a fresh salad.

"Salad now?" Lexi said, giving her plate a nudge. "Why isn't it served at the beginning?"

This had been a long morning, beginning with my lessons with Rudolfo and ending with a tour of the lower chambers. As I devoted myself to the salad, I looked forward to stretching out on my bed, drawing up the soft comforter. I could sink into a food coma while the breeze wafted through the open doors of the balcony.

"Lexi and I are going to town this afternoon," Gregorio announced.

My head snapped up. "What?"

Lips tight, Marco looked from Gregorio to me. Ama looked equally alarmed. When had the two of them cooked this up?

My employer's eyes drilled into me. "You will accompany them, of course."

"Of course." The nap would have to wait.

"Milo will take you. It is done." Marco turned back to Gabriella, who threw him a kittenish smile. How would they be spending their afternoon? When the profiteroles were served, I didn't think I'd be able to finish three of the dainty puffs filled with some sort of cream filling. Somehow I managed.

Chapter 8

On the ride into town, Lexi and Gregorio were curiously quiet. Had they hoped they'd escape without me? That wasn't going to happen. Life on an island was unrolling a lot faster than I'd imagined. Still, I was glad Lexi and Gregorio were getting along. If she had nothing to do but drag herself off to class, it would have been a very long summer.

Vitas drove the limo again, with Milo riding shotgun. His profile was set in stern lines. Getting into the limo, I'd reached for the door handle but Milo beat me to it. "My job."

Okay. Well then. He opened the door.

Lexi had taken a suspiciously long amount of time getting ready. In fact, I'd been spread out on the bed nodding off after that huge lunch when she finally tapped on my door. I'd barely had time to sweep my hair up into a ponytail and apply some mascara and lip gloss. My beige pants would have to do. I'd slipped into the peasant top with the purple embroidery and grabbed an old straw hat from the armoire.

My spirits lifted as the limo cruised toward town. This time I could enjoy the scenery. When I cracked my window open, the smell of lavender filled the air. The lush purple plants brightened the countryside. In the distance, expansive rows of grape vines made me curious. Was this all Marco's vineyard? I closed the window. Wasn't everything on the island his?

Excitement banished my earlier fatigue. We were going into the village. I would get to see more of Napolitano. Okay, I didn't know the language, but wasn't this summer all about adventure? A chance to see a new country?

Looking over at Lexi and Gregorio, I wondered how this friendship had developed. Their phones may have played a role. Guilt washed over me. I'd told Marco we needed access to the wi-fi so Gregorio could order books or do some research online. For all I knew, Gregorio and Lexi were zinging emails and texts back and forth.

But that wasn't a bad thing, and I wouldn't worry about their budding friendship now. As far as I could tell, there was no reason for concern. Not yet. Gregorio seemed like a polite, intellectually curious young man. I liked him, and the two of them were just friends. Maybe kids in their teens could do that. Friendship with a man? I wouldn't know what that was.

"What will we do when we get to town?" I asked Gregorio. For some reason Milo had not put up the glass this time. Maybe he was interested in this little group. Or maybe Marco had told Milo to keep tabs on us.

Gregorio consulted his watch. "The markets will still be open. During the summer, the people bring their vegetables and fruits to the town market."

"I hope they bring more than fruits and vegetables." Lexi threw her head back onto the leather seat. She was looking way too comfortable in this limousine.

Eyes sparkling, Gregorio pivoted toward her. "Lexi, you have never seen such beauty. Everything is fresh. The lettuce is crisp and alive. Some of the vegetables even have bits of dirt still on them." His enthusiasm made me smile.

"Dirt?" Lexi wrinkled her nose. When I pinched her, she winced and threw me a wicked look.

"Sounds great. Can't wait to see it." I was not about to let Lexi's mood get me down, and I thought I caught the edge of a grin on Milo's profile. Did he have a wife and children? The driver Vitas was like a sphinx. And today those two did not talk. Maybe Gregorio was our secret weapon. He would understand their conversation and could translate for us. Perhaps that's what kept them quiet today.

The drive that had seemed so long when we arrived now passed quickly. The small cottages with turf rooftops looked homey and charming. A woman was hanging clothes out on a line. To her frustration, the breeze sent them flapping. When she caught sight of the car, she smoothed the curls that had escaped from her pink head scarf and bobbed into a curtsy. So they knew the royal limousine.

What a terrible invasion of privacy this would be to have people recognize you wherever you went. Shrinking back, I was happy to be an unknown visitor on this excursion.

Before too long the colorful village appeared, and Vitas took a turn. The cobblestone road vibrated under our tires. Lexi sat up to peer through windows that I now realized were shaded. We were encased in privacy. At home I would plod through the mall, anonymous except for occasionally encountering a student. Here we were people of interest, and I didn't know how I felt about that.

The streets continued to narrow until I felt I could reach out and touch the ochre walls as we rolled past. Finally, we came to a square where older people sat on benches under fig trees. Men gestured with their pipes as they talked. Children clung to their mother's hands or pulled carts filled with bags. The bright sun glittered off water spraying from a fountain. The square felt invigorating and I couldn't wait to walk around. Perched on the edge of her seat, Lexi also looked eager. All thoughts of Marco, Gabriella and that stilted lunch faded. We were here and I was sharing a new experience with my daughter, along with an excellent guide.

When Milo opened the door, I jumped out with Lexi right behind me.

"Wow, will you look at this?" Lexi twirled around to take it all in. I hoped that the sudden silence of the crowd was caused by the royal limo, not Lexi's bare midriff or shorts. Her gladiator sandals made her legs look longer than ever. But I wasn't going to worry about my daughter on such a gorgeous day.

Coming around the back of the limo, Gregorio glanced at his watch with that distinctive Rolex styling. "Come back in two hours, Milo."

Milo nodded. "Yes, Your Highness. As you wish."

Astonishment left Lexi and me mute. With those few words,

Gregorio had changed from student to royal heir, with people at his command. Watching the black limousine glide away and disappear, I wondered at the power of this young man. And I was curious. "Your father doesn't leave you with security?" I was thinking of the monarchy of Great Britain and how their security people were so important.

"No one would harm us," Gregorio said with uncharacteristic nonchalance. "My father would draw and quarter them."

A chuckle dried on my lips. My student seemed completely serious. But then he gave me a playful grin. He could be a tease, and I liked that side of my new pupil. Near the square sat an enclosure with something that sure looked like a guillotine but without the blade. The wood was weathered and suspiciously stained. A brass plate marked the spot and I wondered if this was historical. "Do you ever use that?" I pointed.

"Not lately." His set expression told me nothing.

"Mom, I think he's kidding you," Lexi said in an undertone as we followed Gregorio down the lane.

"First, they would have to spend time in the dungeon." Turning, Gregorio gave a little wiggle of his brows.

I waved a warning finger. "I could flunk you on your first test for that."

His face drained. The boy was so sensitive. "Kidding, just kidding."

We were still new to each other. And our differences involved more than personalities. Here, cultures were involved.

We followed him down a row of shiny windows. The smell of

baking blanketed the street beneath the lighter scent of flowers. Petunias and foreign blooms I didn't recognize spilled from earthen pots. Up above, flowers draped from balconies and what looked like rooftop patios. While Lexi and I tried to take it all in, the townspeople smiled.

"Gregorio, I have a question."

He turned and dipped his head as if he were listening.

"What country do you belong to? Italy, Greece or perhaps Spain?" Those all seemed like possibilities from the sound of the language.

He gave me a solemn headshake. "Oh, no, Profesora. We are an independent principality. Think of Monaco. Everyone would want us for our tax revenue, but my family would never agree."

Thinking of the history of this area, I could understand that and turned my attention back to the shops.

Wherever we walked, people dipped and curtsied to "Your Royal Highness." I fell behind him to watch the interplay between Gregorio and the people who would one day call him King. The whole scene was fascinating.

At one point, Lexi turned to Gregorio. "Should I also be curtsying to you?"

"If you like," Gregorio responded. But at the end his smile cracked and so did his voice. "Just kidding. No. Please."

To my horror, she elbowed him in the ribs, as if they were cruising the halls between classes. "I wasn't going to do it anyway."

I heard the market before I actually saw it. Voices tunneled down the narrow street, while laundry flapped overhead. We broke out into the open. At the end of the street stretched lines of stalls covered by colorful canopies. The royal red and green seemed to be the colors here, but what I now recognized as the official logo marking the tables was dwarfed by the abundant produce. Eggplant, beans and tomatoes were heaped on the tables, along with figs and citrus fruit. Their scent tingled in the air.

As he strolled along the stalls, Gregorio chose avocados, tomatoes, dark green spinach and thick heads of broccoli. The shopkeepers seemed to know him, and Gregorio called them by name. "Lorenzo, how is your mother doing?"

"Better, Your Royal Highness," the man said, looking pleased. "I will tell her you asked about her."

"Please do."

Where had this comfort level come from?

"Rosa Maria, where is your baby today, eh?" Gregorio playfully peeked around one stall.

The woman put a finger to her lips and lifted a terry cloth covering to reveal a sleeping baby in a carrying seat.

Lexi looked as amazed as I felt by Gregorio's transformation. The teenager held a natural comfort with the people, and he remembered all their names. Perhaps they appreciated the respect he had for their merchandise.

"How do you know when those are ripe?" Lexi asked, pointing to the avocados. Taking one in his hand, Gregorio squeezed it ever so slightly with his thumb, returning the first two to the pile. On the third avocado, he nodded. "Perfect. Feel." And he handed her the avocado. "It gives a little bit."

I loved seeing the pleased smile lighten Lexi's features. At home, the only thing she cooked was frozen pizza. Maybe this market visit would inspire her.

"You like food, Gregorio," I said as we continued down the aisle.

"Yes, I do." And he patted his stomach. Although he tried to laugh it off, I felt terrible. Boys were so sensitive at this age.

"No, I meant you know a lot about produce. You're growing," I told him, trying to offer hope. "You'll see. Why, Lexi grew like a weed last year."

"Mother, please." My daughter tossed back her purple hair, which had been attracting quite a bit of attention.

"I spend some time in the kitchen," Gregorio said, as if he were admitting that he'd gone out carousing at night. "My grandmother likes to cook."

Now, that was a surprise and hard to picture. "Your grandmother is very fond of you."

Smiling, he snatched up a bundle of fresh lettuce and handed it to the woman behind the counter. "Nonna is very strict but she is special too." A warm smile softened his features.

"She loves you very much." If Ama had to choose between her own son and Gregorio, Marco might lose out.

"I wish I had a grandmother," Lexi murmured with such a longing that my throat swelled.

Gregorio wheeled around. "You have no grandmother? No nonna?" The words held such shock and compassion.

I cleared my throat. "We're short in that area. My mother died two years ago. It was very hard for both of us. And Lexi's grandparents on her father's side are gone."

His round face lengthened. "I know how that is. Nonna is the only grandmother I have left."

"What about your mother's mother?" I wanted to know more about Bianca.

"Oh, no." And his face closed. "She was gone before my mother had me."

The air had turned serious and we moved on to the next table.

Wearing broad smiles, shopkeepers waited patiently while Gregorio made his selections. They quickly snapped up whatever he chose and bundled it into bags. Eventually, Lexi and I each ended up with a burlap tote over one shoulder.

And as we passed the stalls, the men continued to dip their heads while the women curtsied. "Your Royal Highness" greeted him wherever he turned. The first time she heard it, Lexi giggled, but by the time we reached the last of the stalls she was not laughing. I hoped today wouldn't ruin their budding friendship. But maybe a little distance wouldn't be a bad thing.

His subjects liked him. That much was evident, but I wondered how they felt about Marco.

Turning, Gregorio lifted his sunglasses. "So, what do you think?"

"Fabulous. Almost makes me want to cook."

His smile widened. "I know."

Eyes searching, Lexi twirled around. "No chocolate? Any pastries?"

Gregorio jerked his head toward the end of the stalls. "Up ahead. Maybe I've saved the best for last, eh?"

The scent of fresh bakery grew denser. I gave up any hope of losing weight this summer. Why not indulge myself? Entering a tiny shop, we chose amaretto cookies doused in powdered sugar and chocolate croissants still warm from the oven, along with almond biscotti and three boxes of assorted truffles. Outside, he handed one box to Lexi and another to me. The third box was probably for Ama.

As we strolled along, the sun grew warmer. Up ahead a woman was selling fresh juice. My throat felt parched. "I'd like to buy one of those. Gregorio, what kind of money will they accept here?" Reena and Maddie had both tucked some leftover euros from their last trip into my purse before I left. "Or maybe they'll take American dollars?"

Before I could reach into my purse, Gregorio stopped me. "Your money will not be good here." Handing his bag of groceries to Lexi, he approached the smiling woman and returned with three tall, frosty cups.

The fruit juice tasted heavenly. We moved on, and I felt very pleased, almost as if this were an exotic vacation. But by that time, the sun was at its hottest peak. "Is there a place where I can buy sunblock?" I could feel a burn start on my cheeks.

"Of course. Just one moment." And with that, he dashed into a store front that certainly didn't look like a pharmacy. The bottle he handed to me upon his return was the same brand we used in the States. But he wouldn't accept anything for it and that had to stop.

On our way back to meet Milo and Vitas, we crossed a street where teenage boys were kicking a soccer ball. Probably about Gregorio's age, they laughed and shouted. For a second he stood watching them. But when they stopped playing and stared, he twisted away and kept going. I caught a certain sadness in his expression and my heart squeezed. Was he lonely at times in that huge castle? "Where do they go to school?" I asked.

"Oh, we have a school here on the island."

"But you would not go to that school?"

"Never." Shaking his head, he looked so much like his father. "Impossible, Profesora."

I didn't question him, but he'd given me a lot to think about. Our path had led us back to the fountain. The three of us collapsed onto a bench where I dabbed lotion on my burning cheeks. The splash of the water and final sips of the citrusy drink relaxed me. I wanted to remember this day for a long time.

Jumping up, I grabbed my phone from my bag. "Gregorio, you and Lexi smile." I backed away.

I'd never seen Gregorio move so fast. On his feet in a flash, he snatched the phone from my hand. "Profesora, no."

I was crushed. "You don't understand. I want a memento of today."

His curls bobbed when he shook his head. "My father does not allow pictures. The villagers know that. They have been warned." He still held the phone. And he was dangerously close to the fountain.

The villagers had all disappeared. What was this? "All right. No need to get dramatic. I won't take a picture." I held out my hand. Slowly, he handed my phone back and stood waiting until I shoved it into my bag.

"Please understand," Gregorio said slowly. "My father likes to remain 'below the radar.' That's how he looks at it. I am so glad you have come here, Signora. But we have rules. My father was very worried about my future. Especially after Reginaldo." He sat down next to us. Once again, we were a threesome.

"What about Reginaldo?" I had to ask.

"My father thinks his time with me was useless."

I cringed. Would I have to weigh every academic choice I made? No way did I want to be judged "useless."

"This is the best day I've had in a long time," he said so seriously that my heart went out to him. "Do not make a mistake. Please."

Now, that sounded ominous. The sun slid behind a cloud and the landscape dimmed.

After ten minutes or so, the limo arrived. If Milo thought it strange to see Gregorio's haul of fruit and vegetables, he said nothing. The bags were stowed in the trunk. All the way back to the castle the car was filled with their earthy, fresh smell.

By the time we reached the castle, my excitement had mellowed into exhaustion. The day had been full—from class and the dungeons to meeting Marco's girlfriend and the trip to town. With a huge yawn, Lexi disappeared. Making my way through the cool, quiet halls, I eventually found the kitchen.

"May I please have a tray tonight in my room?" I asked

Constanza, the cook. This called for a lot of hand gestures. Thank goodness a tray was sitting on a side table. She was shelling peas at the kitchen sink, her arms and hands brown from the sun.

"Si, si." With a wave of her hand, she nodded.

"And one for my daughter?" I added.

"But of course."

"Thank you." On my way to the room, it hit me that the staff probably watched our every move. Anyone from outside might be viewed as a possible threat.

The elevator seemed to move so slowly. Falling back against the rich wooden paneling, I inhaled Marco's cologne, a heady mix of man and a rich spicy scent no doubt brought from far away.

The Orient. Or the moon.

Maybe I'd gotten sunstroke today.

Later, stretched out on my bed after a quick dinner tray, I relived my day. Maybe I should have been intimidated by everything I'd seen. The tower, the dungeon and nearly having my phone taken away…again. But nervous excitement kept me sleepless. I wandered to my balcony more than once to stare at the moon and eat truffles.

Chapter 9

The soft summer air held a hint of moisture as I made my way to
the stables. Had it rained during the night? The grass looked dewy
and the bushes drooped with moisture. To have so much greenery
around me felt like a gift. Reaching out a hand, I swept the leaves
of what looked like a camellia bush. Yes, definitely damp. I pressed
my wet palm to my dry jeans.

This place was pretty darned amazing. If I were home right
now, I'd be walking briskly around my neighborhood for exercise
before heading off to teach summer school classes. But my
neighborhood never looked like this—naturally wild and beautiful.
No cheery little brick homes were set along the pathway. No black
mailbox sat waiting for the mail carrier who always came promptly
at two thirty. No, this was another world.

And I had no place in it. Not really.

Staring down at my boots, I was glad I'd tossed them into the
suitcase. My instincts had been right, even though they almost took
me over the weight limit. Horseback riding certainly hadn't been on
my mind when I left home.

"Good morning Rudolfo." I greeted my elderly teacher as I
entered the stable.

His face creased into a sunburst of wrinkles, his faded blue eyes twinkling. "Good morn-ing." I smiled at the effort he made to speak English.

Inhaling, I savored the rich smell of hay, horses and everything that went with them. Strange how I was coming to enjoy the stables.

When I first suggested the riding lessons to Lexi, she would have no part of it. She was in eighth grade, the age when other girls can be cruel. Baring her arms during the summer had about killed her. Although we'd worked for months with a therapist after the accident, Lexi still didn't accept them. Could I blame her? How would I feel to have the purplish burns running up my arm? And I did not want to subject her to more surgery. Acceptance was the only route and maybe some more grafts when Lexi was ready.

Rudolfo disappeared into Tesoro's stall. I could hear her nicker softly. On my way out, I'd stopped in the kitchen to grab some carrots. Now I pulled them out of my shirt pocket.

"You are stealing from the kitchen?" Marco's teasing voice made me turn.

My boots skidded in the hay. "I brought these for Tesoro."

Elbows on the edge of Diablo's stall, Marco threw me a crooked smile. For a minute I couldn't help comparing him to the stallion he usually rode. Both were powerful and proud.

Feeling defensive, I waved the carrots in my hand. "Constanza told me it was all right." Okay, that was a stretch. Maybe I'd interpreted her sweet smile as approval.

The stall door creaked as Marco slowly pushed it open and

came toward me, dipping his head. Men in America would kill for that thick hair. Hands on his narrow hips, he swung up those eyes that could feel like warm chocolate. "So. How is it going with you?"

I froze. The carrot almost dropped from my hand. "What do you mean? Gregorio's lessons?"

Leaning against Tesoro's stall way too close to me, he nodded. "Of course, the lessons. But everything else too."

Wow, it was warm in this stable. His question made me uncomfortable. I had my hands full trying to suit the trig lessons to where Gregorio was. Reginaldo had spent way too much time on art and not enough on math. But I wasn't going to say that.

"Gregorio is a ...good student"

"Good?" Throwing back his head, Marco laughed, the confident sound of a man who knew his world would always be in order. The muscles worked in his throat. But I shouldn't be staring. "The ones before you did not think so."

The ones before me? Pay attention, Christina. "You mean the other teachers?"

"Yes, yes, of course." His dark eyes swept up to the rafters where doves cooed in the soft light filtering through the cracks. "Un-mo-tivated. I think that it was how they described my son. The future king of Napolitano." Was that disgust or despair in his voice?

No way would I let Gregorio be kicked to the curb like that. "Gregorio is intellectually curious."

I could see that the terminology had caught and held with His

Majesty.

"Intellectually curious." He turned the words over as if he were tasting a new type of pasta sauce. Was it to his liking? Marco's eyes sparkled. "I agree. This is a good thing, no?"

"Yes and no." What was I saying? I'd become distracted. Swept off track by a wave of scent rolling off this man. A combination of sweat and cologne, laced nicely with his roguish smile.

Then Marco drew even closer, as if to share some secret. As if he did not want Rudolfo to hear. But Rudolfo had quietly disappeared into his office. "Tell me…"

My mind blanked. Oh lordy, if he asked me to explain some calculus concept right now, I'd be lost. No way did I want to lose this gig that could fund Lexi's college.

"Have you ever met this Leonardo…"

Who was he talking about? "Leonardo…" My mind spun. "…you mean DaVinci?"

He erupted in laughter. The doves scattered. Behind me, I felt Tesoro give her head a shake, as if trying to clear it. Maybe every female had this response to the King of Napolitano. Stunned, I lifted another carrot over my shoulder. Tesoro snared it, munching with contentment.

"No, not Da Vinci," Marco sputtered. "DaVinci is dead. DiCaprio."

"Oh, my. No." So we were back to movie stars. The ones who he thought lived in Pittsburg. Or Capri.

"Oh, well." He hitched a shoulder and I could see that I was losing credibility. Did he know how large my country was?

"So, this Jay Gatsby person Gregorio talked about at lunch…is he mourned in your country?"

Now, I had to take this seriously. Although we'd had a limited interaction, I knew that Marco did not like to be laughed at. After all, he was king, but perhaps a very isolated monarch.

"He only exists in a book." Then it hit me. "Or in the movie. Would you like to see it?"

"There is a Jay Gatsby movie?" His face brightened.

"Of course. It's old but very…colorful." Since he seemed familiar with Leonardo DiCaprio, I'd show that version instead of the Robert Redford one.

Rubbing his hands together, Marco seemed elated. "I will have Milo order this Jay Gatsby film for movie night."

"Movie night?" That sounded interesting.

"Yes, we have a theater. It is small but adequate. My mother likes to watch films."

So that was how he knew the movie stars. Well, movie night would be more interesting than reading in my room or streaming movies onto my phone.

"What kind of movie do you usually watch?" Did they watch Italian films? French? Or perhaps the British comedies. Now that made me smile.

"*The Godfather.* I like those very much. Much machismo no?" Arms out, he bulked up his biceps.

"No. Yes, I mean. Very macho." I couldn't laugh. I just could not. Marco could put Al Pacino to shame with his soulful eyes. Rudolfo had poked his head out of the tack room once or twice. "I

114

should get riding if I'm going to be ready for class today."

"Yes, yes. I will not keep you." But Marco still had something on his mind.

The man was so close that I could smell coffee on his breath. I was already pressed against the wood, with Tesoro nuzzling my hair. "What did you think of Gabriella?"

Okay, I was not expecting that. The breath whooshed from my chest, leaving me a bit dizzy, "Gabriella?"

"Yes, yes." His voice roughened with impatience. "The girl who came for lunch."

Girl? Well, if that didn't say it all. "Yes, I remember. Well...she is very pretty." More like ground-shaking gorgeous.

He hitched up a shoulder. "This I know. But do you think she and Gregorio....do you think she would make a good mother for my son? This is very important, no?"

"No." The words blurted out, sharp and decisive.

Marco jerked back. "No, that is not important?"

Pushing away from Tesoro's tickling, I shook my head to clear it. "Yes, it's very important that the woman you choose will be someone ...motherly."

"Ah, yes. Motherly." The firm set of his lips told me what he thought of that.

Oh, man. Deep frown lines appeared between his eyes. I was so in over my head.

"You may have already discussed this with Gabriella but if not, you might ask her how she feels about children, especially Gregorio." Marco's relationships were none of my business, but

Gregorio was.

"Yes, of course. Very good idea." Oh, my word. This had just dawned on him?

When Marco's hand rasped along his chin, I could feel it in my bones. They were melting. I hadn't felt a man's stubble against my skin for such a long time. Too long.

His hearty clap on my shoulder took me off guard, though. In fact, it nearly sent me to the ground. Did he think I was Milo?

"Very good, Profesora. Very good." One finger came up. "But now I must go order the film, no?" And he strode off, probably to find Milo or Gregorio.

I watched him leave. How could I help it? Shoulders straight and head high, Marco walked like a king. Confident. Imperious. And totally hot.

But I wasn't going to go there. As Rudolfo led Tesoro from her stall, I rubbed my sore shoulder. The king may have left a bruise. Then I chuckled. Who would believe this? I could almost picture the shocked look on Reena's face. Standing at our open doorways between classes, we often compared notes. I'd love to hear what she thought of Marco. Maybe I'd send a text message and a picture.

But pictures weren't allowed. Thank goodness Gregorio had clued me in about that.

"Signora?" Rudolfo stood at my elbow. Tesoro was waiting.

After leading my sweet mount outside, murmuring pleasantries all the way, I climbed into the saddle. Mounting came easy to me now. What a thrill it was to hoist myself up. The ground looked far away as I patted Tesoro's neck. Weren't we in this together?

Rudolfo came alongside me on his quarter horse. He was a man of few words but those eyes spoke volumes. I think he liked me. Maybe he felt sorry for me.

"What do we practice today? Trotting around the paddock? Cantering?" The latter had become my favorite. I loved the easy lope that Tesoro slipped into so gracefully.

We were one. Females together.

When Rudolfo gestured toward the open field, I saw that he'd opened the gate of the paddock. What was this?

"We're going outside?" Excitement spiraled through me. This was different. This was new. Was I ready? My thighs tightened while anxiety played tic tat toe on my chest. Restless, Tesoro shifted beneath me.

Rudolfo waved us through. I sucked in a deep breath as my horse pushed ahead as if anticipating a good stretch of the legs. Well, me too. I was up for this and Rudolfo must think I was ready. Tesoro would take care of me. That much I knew. Hadn't she always been meek and responsive in the corral?

Sliding off his mount, Rudolfo closed the gate behind us. The sun had burned away the dew. Wild grasses released their scent on the morning breeze, along with the lavender.

Once Rudolfo was back on his horse, we were off. Tesoro took up the relaxed canter I loved. My body moved to the rhythm. Soon we were in the woods, taking the trails that Gregorio and Lexi no doubt took. I needed this and sat up straighter in the saddle.

Oh my. Didn't see that branch coming. I ducked, but not before the willowy branch had whipped across my cheek. Boy, that smarted. I wanted to check to see if I was bleeding but Tesoro was picking up speed. I didn't want to lose my grip on the reins.

Turning around, Rudolfo made a squatting motion. What was he saying? His lips moved but the words came to me in unintelligible chunks.

"Duck?" I called out. "Are you telling me to bend over?"

Whap. This time the branch came from the side.

Good heavens. Crouching over the horse, I tried to murmur sweet nothings to my partner. "Now, Tesoro, let's take it easy."

His lips pursed into a tight knot, Rudolfo turned back to me again. What the heck was he saying? Tesoro was straining at the tight reins, shaking her head the way I did to loosen my ponytail. This girl wanted to run. Our outing was getting scary. "Not now. Slow down, Tesoro."

She shook her head again, that golden mane ending up in my teeth. So much for comradery.

Just when I thought I might die on this horse, the path emptied into a clearing. Those pesky bushes and saplings were left behind. "Good girl, good girl." I patted Tesoro's neck but she seemed to shake me off.

Holding up his reins, Rudolfo showed me how he'd tightened his. Why of course. But when I tightened the reins, Tesoro—my buddy, my friend—came to a halt. We stood there in the clearing, perfectly still. Crickets chirped around us. Birds sang from the trees. But we weren't going anywhere. Her tail swished behind me. Nonchalant as all get out, Tesoro lowered her head and munched the grasses. I sneezed. Maybe all this outside beauty was getting to me. For one exhausted moment, I wanted to slide off the darned mare and limp back to the stables. How far could that be?

Thighs burning, hands stinging and behind aching, I was feeling pretty old. Beyond my "sell date," as the kids would say. Not at all like that Gabriella who had flitted into the castle like some exotic bird.

Rudolfo nudged his mount next to mine and peered at me from beneath those shaggy brows. "O-kay?"

I expelled a sigh. "Sure. I'm fine. O-kay." No way was I going down like this. I brought my head up.

Nodding, Rudolfo again took the lead. I must have imagined that grin tilting his lips. After all, he was a kind man. Loosening the reins, I clucked to Tesoro.

Nothing. No motion. None whatsoever. She wanted to eat the grass.

Up ahead, Rudolfo swiveled around in his seat. "Tesoro, *tu vieni.*"

The darn horse bolted forward like she'd been touched with a prod.

All the rest of the ride from hell, I was painfully alert. Every twitch of Tesoro's ears, I was ready to collapse over her neck like the darned pasta we ate almost every night. Somewhere along the way, Rudolfo must have circled back. When the stable came into view, I wanted to weep.

My entire body felt tense and achy from holding my body erect. Rudolfo dismounted, came over and grabbed Tesoro's reins.

"Thank you. Oh, thank you." I slid to the ground, my boots

hitting the ground with a painful lurch.

"Si, si." He threw that out casually. Not very encouraging. Clucking to Tesoro, Rudolfo led her back to the stall. No way would I take off her saddle and stroke her down today. She'd turned on me. As I limped from the stable, I thought I heard Rudolfo crooning a tune to Tesoro.

Really? This felt all around traitorous.

Or had they both been making fun of me?

With a sniff, I kept walking. The uneven ground made it difficult. Every part of my body ached. In trying to avoid injury, it seemed that I'd irritated every tendon in my body, from my shoulders to my calves. That big inviting bathtub adjoining my room? No time for that now. But tonight I would spend quality time in that tub.

***

In the classroom later that morning, we finished *Great Gatsby*. "Told you the guy dies in the end," I heard Lexi whisper to Gregorio.

"That is life." His face was set in acceptance. What other sadness had Gregorio accepted in his lifetime? The loss of his mother was probably at the top of the list. My heart went out to him. How had she died? Bianca must have been very young.

The lesson ended. I assigned the first three chapters of *To Kill A Mockingbird*.

"Your father, I mean, His Majesty, mentioned that we might have movie night tonight," I told Gregorio.

"Which movie?" Lexi threw out the name of the latest

Dystopian thriller.

"He'd like to stream *The Great Gatsby*."

"Awesome." Gregorio's eyes lit up. He'd picked that phrase up from Lexi. "He will understand what I am studying."

"Apparently you have your own movie theater?"

"You do?" Lexi looked at her classmate with amazement. "I can't believe that."

Stacking his books together, Gregorio stood. How was it possible that he seemed taller than when we'd arrived? "It's a small one."

"Are you kidding me? At least you have a theater. We have to watch movies in our living room."

"Oh, isn't that too bad," I teased, turning off the overhead lights. "You poor, deprived girl. At least we're able to watch movies. When I was your age…"

"Here we go again." Lexi rolled her eyes at Gregorio. A hot flush of embarrassment flowed through me. When would Lexi learn to appreciate what she had? Maybe this summer brush with privilege would only make her more critical of her life back home.

"Would you like to see the theater?" Gregorio asked as we filed from the room.

"Can we?" Lexi's eyes lit up.

"How far is it?" Every muscle in my body was screaming *no*.

"Not far. After all, it's in the castle." And Gregorio was off.

This castle was huge. The theater could be three blocks away. Limping along behind him, I wondered if in time he would assume the carriage his father wore so well. My mother had actually made me walk with a book on my head. Today, that seemed ridiculous. But Gregorio might benefit from it.

The route seemed to take us into the other part of the castle, a section I hadn't explored yet. Body protesting, I tried to keep up. As long as I kept them in sight, I was good. But I sure didn't want to get lost. I might run into Ama.

"Will there be popcorn?" Lexi was asking with a giggle when I caught up to them at a juncture of hallways.

"No. Why do you ask?" Gregorio didn't bother to disguise the horror in his eyes. "Is that necessary?"

"Popcorn is an important part of movies at home," I explained, digging a fist into my aching back. "Usually as expensive as the movie itself."

Gregorio seemed to be turning that over in his mind as we passed into the western section of the castle. Here the walls were more crowded. Were these paintings of former monarchs? Ecclesiastics? Even in the low light, the golden frames glittered. Reaching the end of one hall, Gregorio went through a door and motioned to us to follow.

"These staircases are so darn cold." I shivered. From now on, I would have to carry a sweater or hoodie.

"You get used to it," Gregorio said.

But as we passed a doorway that looked familiar, I paused. No way was I going to wimp out and ask how far it was. The bathtub was on my mind. "Maybe I'll wait until tonight to see the theater." Although I hated to send the two of them off on their own, my aching body was telling me I needed a long, hot soak in that tub.

Chapter 10

The knock on the door echoed through my room. Had I nodded off? The bath water was still warm. The room smelled of the jasmine soap. Reaching around the stool next to the tub, I found the thick white robe.

"Mom. Where are you?" Lexi had come to get me. What time was it?

"Hold on." Quickly, I got out, toweled off and fastened the robe securely around me. "I'm coming!"

But when I opened the door, Lexi wasn't alone. Seeing me in my robe, Gregorio dropped his eyes.

"The movie will start without us." Lexi's eyes swept over me. "Were you taking a bath?"

"Yes, did I sleep through dinner?" What time was it? Afternoon light still fell through the balcony windows.

"They changed the time for the movie." Lexi bristled with impatience.

"Sorry, but Nonna wants to come," Gregorio explained. "She doesn't like to stay up late so the movie will be in the afternoon."

"I'll pull on some clothes." I hid a yawn behind one hand.

"His Majesty is looking forward to seeing the Gatsby movie."

Gregorio smiled. Was he pleased that his father was taking an interest?

"His Majesty? You call your own father that?" Lexi's voice held more than a little sarcasm. Maybe the horrified expression on my face tipped her off. We played by the rules of the house. Well, in this case, the castle.

"Sorry, sorry," Lexi said quickly.

Gregorio's shoulders eased. At least she was smart enough to know that she shouldn't bite the hand that fed her. Of everyone here, Gregorio had been the most welcoming.

"Give me a minute." I started to close the door.

"We can wait in my room." Lexi turned.

I pointed to a bench in the hallway. "How about over there."

Gregorio got the message and sat down with a little smile. Giving me The Look, Lexi followed.

"I'll be right back." I closed the door, irritated because I hated to be late. As a teacher, I worked on a schedule and I expected the same from my students.

My hair was damp, so I twined it into a loose braid in the back. Pulling on my beige slacks, I topped them with a soft pink shell and grabbed a navy sweater on my way out the door.

Minutes later and after a trek down semi-dark halls, I sank into one of the blue leather recliners. Back home we had stadium seating in the movie theaters, and it wasn't unusual to feel popcorn beneath your feet. This theater had blue and gray oriental runners in front of the three short rows of seats. An enormous screen had been lowered from the ceiling. I could feel a neck ache coming on.

Now, how could I recline this seat?

"Let me help you, Profesora." In a second, Gregorio was at my side. I nodded to Ama across the narrow aisle. Lexi figured it out by herself. Soon she was draped over the recliner as if she were sunbathing in our yard back home.

Gregorio flipped a lever and my chair slid back. "Thank you." This felt great.

With a sweet nod he went back to his grandmother. Looking around, I tried to count the seats. Maybe Marco brought groups of friends here. I hadn't noticed any movie theaters in the small village.

The door opened and Marco arrived, bringing a breath of fresh air with him. He must have been riding. With his hair tousled and his linen shirt creased, the man gave disheveled a whole new vibe. His clapping hands echoed in the theater as he met my eyes. "So, we will watch this *Great Gatsby* movie. And then over dinner, we could discuss, no?"

No! I want to shout to the vaulted ceiling. But I couldn't. And was this so bad, being forced to watch Leonardo DiCaprio on the broad screen? After Marco had taken his seat next to his mother, the room darkened and the movie began.

"Oh, man, this theater is so cool," Lexi murmured. "My friends would be so jealous."

"Absolutely no pictures," I reminded her.

With a sigh, she settled back.

Although I'd loved Leonardo DiCaprio in the role of Gatsby, Robert Redford played Gatsby as more vulnerable. Wasn't that the charm of the tycoon who'd worked hard to win the hand of an upper-class woman beyond his reach?

A covert glance or two told me that the royal family was entranced by the movie, although Ama's lips curled during some of the scenes. All of the giddy splendor of the roaring twenties played out on the screen. But I'd seen this movie before. My mind wandered. Although I never thought I'd miss cooking my own meals, I did. Or maybe what I really missed was the freedom to cook or order a pizza, if I liked.

But who was I to complain because someone else was doing all the cooking? This blue leather was oh, so comfortable. I settled back.

The next thing I knew, Lexi was shaking me. "Mom, wake up. The movie's over."

When I struggled to sit up, the recliner came upright with a snap. Had I been dreaming? Marco had been in my dreams but I couldn't recall how. I darted my eyes across the aisle where he was having an animated conversation with his mother.

"I'm starving," Lexi said, hopping to her feet.

Getting up, I combed my fingers through my hair and wiped off my cheek, flushing when the skin felt damp. Had my mouth been open?

"And now, dinner." Marco was already heading toward the door. I dragged my feet. These flats had never felt so heavy. Tonight I would have been thrilled to have a meal delivered to my room. But that wouldn't be allowed. I hoped Marco didn't expect me to lead a discussion. Eyes averted, Ama seemed to feel the same lack of enthusiasm.

While Marco, Ama and Gregorio took the elevator, Lexi and I headed for the stairs. "Hang onto that leather strap."

"Mom, I'm not a child."

No, she wasn't. If I'd hoped that this time away from bad influences would tame my daughter, the summer wasn't turning out like that. Instead, she seemed to be off on her own. Back home during the spring, Lexi had lost my trust when she'd asked to spend the night at a friend's house. When the police called late that night, I'd learned that she'd been at a party that got out of hand. The parents weren't at home and the neighbors had called. To my daughter's dismay, I became more vigilant.

When we reached the first floor, the scent of food filled the hallway. Marco waited at the door of the dining room. The faint flush in his cheeks made him even more handsome. "We must discuss this Gatsby, no?" he said as we stepped inside. A platter of sausages, olives and cheese sat on a sideboard. Carrying a small plate, Ama was picking and choosing in that delicate way she had before taking her seat. Lexi and I followed suit.

As the servers made the rounds with platters of mouthwatering pasta, Marco dove right in. "So why didn't this Jay Gatsby fellow win the hand of Daisy?" He looked perplexed, as his son had been.

"Papa, he is not the same class as Daisy." Gregorio took a stab at it. After all, he knew how his father thought.

"But in America all things are possible." Marco talked and ate. "Is that not so, Profesora?"

"Indeed, many things are possible in the States." What did I know about the upper echelons of society? "But I guess we still have some sort of class structure." How could I explain the excesses practiced by the wealthy? The world trips. The two thousand-dollar handbags. The garages filled with collector cars.

"You guess?" Marco looked bemused and disappointed.

Apparently, I had to be an expert on all things. But I sure wasn't feeling like an expert today. "You cannot buy everything with money." Now I was spouting clichés? This man apparently could purchase everything.

Gregorio did not look up. At his grandmother's urging, he'd taken another serving of the tortelloni.

Marco wasn't finished. "But America is the place where any man can have his dream. Is this not right?"

How could I explain the difficult contradictions of my own country? "Many people find that they can work very hard and, for example, open a restaurant or start their own company. Some call that the 'American Dream.' Social acceptance might be different. It cannot always be bought. We still have our problems."

Gregorio was listening to me carefully and I didn't want to discourage him. He wouldn't be leaving for the United States tomorrow, so we had time. Someday he would be a tall attractive man, like his father. Certainly, that helped.

The plates had been cleared and we were lingering. I was about to leave when Marco clapped his hands. "Bring me one of the dessert wines," he told Alfredo the server, rattling off something else in his own language.

I pushed back from the table. "It's been such a long day,

beginning with my early morning riding lesson." Which had been disastrous.

"Dessert wine?" Lexi's eyes lit up. Across from us, Gregorio chuckled.

"I'm sure that His Excellency…" On my right, Ama frowned at me. "…His Majesty is talking about wine for the adults."

Marco twirled an empty wine glass in his fingers. "In my country we teach our children to drink responsibly. And to do that they must sample the product. Especially Gregorio for he will be in charge of the vineyards one day."

Yes, one day he would be king. But tonight he wasn't looking very pleased about that. I thought back to the boys kicking the soccer ball around in the village. If Gregorio had a choice, would he choose that life? Probably not. He'd never known it.

Alfredo swept into the room bearing a silver tray with the most beautiful glasses I'd ever seen. The cut crystal gleamed under the chandelier.

"Please? Come on, Mom." Lexi had put her hands together as if she were pleading. When was the last time she'd asked me for something?

"Maybe just a taste of my wine." It wasn't as if she were going to get into a car and drive around the island.

At a nod from Marco, Alfredo began to pour. Whatever the wine was, it was a rich, dark red and smelled wonderful when I lifted it to my lips. Down at the end of the table, Marco lifted his glass, sniffed the wine and smiled. "See what you think." His eyes challenged me.

The first sip was delightful. "Oh, my." A fruity warmth traveled through my veins. Maybe I was tired. Maybe I was overheated by that intense look in Marco's eyes.

And maybe I was imagining things.

Next to me, Lexi sipped. Her lips pursed. I was happy when she set her glass down. "Not for me."

Fine with me. Many things were an acquired taste and she had plenty of time to appreciate a fine dessert wine.

Although Gregorio and Ama took measured sips, they didn't seem to have the same reaction we did.

"You like it?" Marco asked me.

"I love it. What's in this? I think I taste a little orange and maybe apricot."

"Very good, Profesora." Marco beamed. The rush in my head must have been from the dessert wine, not from his smile. "The wine is the heart of my estate," Marco told me as if he were imparting a secret. "For many ages—at least two centuries—my ancestors have tended the grapes to create this flavor. And Gregorio must know how to manage the family company."

That task seemed monumental. One glance at my student told me this was more than he could fathom right now.

"It is important that my son Gregorio know everything about the wine. From the vineyard to the wooden casks. Everything." And he gestured to the poor boy.

Meanwhile, Gregorio had become very interested in his dessert wine. Still, the red circle on each cheek did not come from the wine. No, I thought it came from being the subject of the conversation. Gregorio did not like to be noticed. If it wasn't his father, it was Ama always asking him to do more, to be more. And that wasn't what the teenage years were about. At least, not to me.

"...and so I think the ball would be a good idea," Marco was saying when I tuned back into the conversation. "An excellent way for me to see a broader variety of women. I'm not so sure about Gabriella."

A smile tickled Gregorio's lips. The rest of them were waiting. "Pardon me?" What on earth was he talking about?

"We will have a ball, in say, two weeks' time? A splendid ball." Marco looked more than pleased. "Like the Jay Gatsby ball. You know, to attract more women."

"Because..." My mind was whirling.

He tapped a finger on the table. "Time is passing. Of course I am in excellent shape, but I am not a young man anymore."

I was speechless.

Pushing back his chair, Marco stood as if to attest to his physical condition. I could hear Reena declaring him "one fine specimen of a man," the way she did when she totally approved.

Oh mercy. My chair scraped back. Ama looked at me in surprise. Now, when it came to royalty there were rules about everything, including the table. I suppose it wasn't polite to leave when His Excellency. His Majesty. Whoever—was still on his feet. But this had been a very long day. "Excuse me. Lexi?"

We escaped. That night we took the elevator upstairs.

"A ball," Lexi said. "What will I wear?"

"We'll find something in the village." What? A tablecloth? The idea made me giggle.

As I fell asleep that night, how I wished that in the morning Milo would whisk me away to the airport. This summertime gig might be safe for Lexi.

But I was beginning to wonder if it was safe for me.

Chapter 11

In the days to come, the castle hummed with preparations for the gala affair that would drum up candidates to be Marco's queen. Was this weird or what? And I felt responsible for this disgusting show.

Back in Pennsylvania, the farmers would have livestock auctions. Prize cows would be studied and discussed while auctioneers rattled off their attributes. Long ago, my father had sometimes taken me. As a child, I'd been fascinated by the speed of the process. Later, I would think back and be disgusted.

"The barn smelled like the state fair," I'd told my mother with excitement when we returned.

"Time to wash up, Christina," Dad would say, smiling at my mother. Their marriage had looked so effortless. Had I been naïve to expect the same?

My marriage to Wallace had been a disaster. I'd been blind-sided. The Newharts were friends of my parents, so my choice had been preapproved—or so I thought. What could go wrong? He was tall, handsome and charming. In the beginning Wallace had hidden his drinking very well—but so had his father.

While he studied for his doctoral degree, I went to work at the local high school and helped put him through school. Those first years weren't very romantic. Wallace had to study a lot. Later I would remember those empty beer cans I'd find in the trash the mornings after he'd been working on his thesis.

By the time he was instated as a professor at the local university, he was a closet drinker. But I thought I'd be able to change him. Limit his drinking. My pregnancy had been a surprise, but I welcomed it. Surely a baby would help Wallace get his priorities straight.

He only drank more. By the time Lexi was three, I knew I'd chosen the wrong man. How many times had I thought back, wishing I'd separated from him earlier, sooner. Maybe then the accident with Lexi never would have happened.

I tried not to think about it. Paralyzing guilt swept over me whenever I thought back.

And now I was here, as far from Pittsburgh as a woman could be. The upcoming gala affair filled me with a sense of dread. Marco had gone crazy. Everyone was supposed to dress as their favorite movie or TV character, which seemed kind of childish. And of course most of the shows were American. Our TV shows were streamed across the globe.

"I'm so glad you came here," Gregorio told me one June day when the air hung heavy in the classroom. Picking up my notebook, I fanned myself.

"That's very sweet. Do you mean so you have Lexi to ride with?" Almost every afternoon, they escaped to the woods. When I caught sight of them from an upstairs window, I marveled at her confidence, which seemed to grow every day.

"No, well, of course I like hanging out with Lexi." Stretching out an elbow, he leaned his head on one hand. "I mean, you talked my father into opening up the wi-fi."

Gregorio looked over at Lexi, lips squinched to one side. Lexi playfully socked him on the arm. "Gregorio's the brother I never had."

"That's very nice." I'd wanted more children, but not with Wallace. And now? Now I was in my early forties. Those years were behind me. Would menopause knock on my door soon? Didn't matter anyway. That part of my life was over. Thankfully, my future was laid out for me and I was content. I loved teaching and was committed to funding my IRA, although Lexi's college might take me off track.

But I pushed those worries aside. We continued to explore American lit and then went back to some trig problems that had given them both trouble. The air felt so close in here today and I'd forgotten to fill my thermos with water.

"How do you turn on the air conditioning?" I asked when we'd finished with math. As time passed, it became evident to me that math wasn't Gregorio's strong point. Constant ratios didn't intrigue him. He didn't have the same passion for math that he had for literature. The boy was an avid reader. He devoured our book list as if they were his favorite stromboli. Those discussions were such fun. Math never called for interesting interpretations.

But now in this heat, I could hardly think.

"Air conditioning?" Gregorio pointed to a large circular design on the wall. I thought it was some sort of decoration. "There is our air conditioning and then the one on the floor. Our system is centuries old and draws cool air from the basement." Was he kidding? My blouse was sticking to me like plastic wrap. Then I remembered how cold it had been on that lower level.

I began packing up my books. "Well, it's not enough. Can't we buy an air conditioner in town?"

"They don't have them. We would have to go across the water." The last was said with reverence.

Across the water? "Maybe it's time." Suddenly I'd had enough of castle life.

"Why don't you cool off in the pool in the afternoons?" Gregorio asked.

"Great idea." Lexi slammed her book closed. She was going to ace trig next year. Mary Lou Derwent would be amazed, and I would feel so proud.

"The pool?" I patted the bun that kept my hair off my neck.

"Gregorio told me all about it." Excitement brought Lexi to her feet. "We should sneak out there. Marco, er, I mean His Majesty wouldn't mind, would he, Gregorio?"

"Probably not." Getting up, Gregorio stretched. It seemed that he had grown since our arrival. "You don't have to sneak out. There are towels in the cabinets. The staff will make sure you have everything."

"I didn't bring a bathing suit." The thought had never crossed my mind. Besides, the idea of displaying myself at the pool made me feel nervous. And it might be difficult for Lexi. The scar on her arm didn't need the sun.

"Don't worry. We're about the same size. I brought a couple suits." Lexi ran a hand across her forehead.

"You are four inches taller than me." I gave her The Look as I swiped at the beading on my upper lip. It must be ninety degrees in here. How would we ever make it through the summer? We crowded into the elevator and it slowly descended to the second floor.

"Later." Gregorio nodded to Lexi before loping off. "Three o'clock?"

"Yep, see you there."

"Are you having a good time with Gregorio?" I watched him swing down the hall toward the family wing. The historical portraits and wall hangings were so familiar to him. He paid them no mind. But I still stopped and stared, my mind buzzing with questions. I wished this were like a museum, where an explanation was posted next to each painting. Lexi left for the pool. I opened my balcony doors to catch a breeze and went online to email Reena and Maddie.

***

In the next few days, the heat intensified. The sun I'd welcomed upon arrival became oppressive.

"Let's go to the pool, Mom," Lexi complained one day after class. We were both lying on my bed like two fish that had been dragged onshore by a careless fisherman and cast aside.

"I didn't bring a suit, remember?" A bathing suit had been the last thing on my mind as I'd crammed the suitcase full prior our departure. Everything had been so rushed, so hurried. In my heart, I was afraid to slow down. I might reconsider. Our departure had been more like an escape rather than a planned summer away.

"Mom, I told you. I brought three."

This was a losing contest. The air was sweltering in here. I peered over at my daughter, who always wore a rash guard with her suit to protect her arm. "I can't fit into one of your suits. The length, for one thing."

"They're all two-piece."

"Oh, goody. No way."

Flipping over onto her stomach, Lexi peered over at me. "Are you kidding? All my friends used to tell me you were hot."

What? My heart stopped. "They did not."

Lexi yawned. "Yes, they did. Jeff Sassano had you for the class right before lunch. Sometimes he'd stop at my table in the lunchroom to give me the reading. Those hot pink slacks you wore sometimes? They made you a ten, or so Jeff said." Lexi chortled while I thought back. Those slacks still fit, but I hadn't brought them.

Grabbing an extra pillow, I covered my face. The thought of the boys checking me out made me uncomfortable. Still, I'd liked Jeff. He at least spoke up in class and became part of the discussion.

Whipping the pillow from my face, Lexi tossed it to the floor. "Come on, Mom. Gregorio showed me where the pool is. No one ever uses it and he's gone off to town today on some sort of mission for his dad."

"His Majesty," I reminded her softly.

By this time, Lexi had slid off the bed, the brocade coverlet releasing her slim body with a soft sigh. "Well, if you won't come, I'm out of here."

"No, Lexi. Wait." That did it. No way was I letting her spend time in a pool without me.

I followed her to her room where she dug through a drawer and tossed out a blue bikini. "Here. This should be fine."

"Give me a minute." Heart pounding, I balled the suit into one fist and hurried back to my room. Ten minutes later we were hoofing down the hall toward the family wing. Over the blue bikini, I wore a long white t-shirt emblazoned with the Pittsburgh Steelers logo. Our flip flops flapped noisily. I'd crammed a hat on my head and wore a pair of sunglasses. Over my arm was a tote packed with books.

"We're not going to the beach, Mom," Lexi said with a smile. "You don't have to worry about the students seeing you."

That had been a constant concern back home. In our suburb there was very little I could do without bumping into a student or two who would wave and call out, "Hey, Mrs. Newhart!"

But today I wouldn't see anyone I knew, which was a great relief. I followed Lexi down a winding staircase to an undiscovered patio on the other side of the castle. The pool was hidden from sight by a tall ridge of alder trees.

"Oh, my." Before us stretched a pool with water the color of the sky. "An infinity pool." The expansive pool had a hot tub at one end and was surrounded by comfortable lounge chairs, with patio umbrellas. The slide must mark the deep end.

"No diving on the shallow side, Lexi."

She turned to give me an aggravated sigh. "Mom, I'm not a child."

"Yes, I know that." Burning, choking, drowning—didn't all mothers seek out possible dangers? I shivered in the hot sun.

Meanwhile, Lexi went to a glassed-in cabinet to one side and grabbed two towels. She seemed very familiar with everything.

We both spread the towels on our chairs. I lay back, reaching for my books. I was skimming through *Animal Farm*. The book was short but chock full of concepts that brought animated classroom discussions, some of them disturbing. Did I dare open that can of worms for my royal student? The idea of equality was central to that book. This island might be a place where some people were "more equal" than others. Leaving that book in the tote, I picked up a romance. Today I wanted to relax.

Tossing her sunglasses onto her towel, Lexi kicked off her flip flops and went to the edge of the pool. Was this tall, confident girl really my daughter? My heart clutched with pride and wonder at how she'd grown. But her growth wasn't merely physical. No, she'd matured. Twirling her hair into a long braid, she hesitated for only a second before diving. The entire time she was under water, I held my breath.

The silence stretched. Lexi didn't emerge. Leaving my book, I jumped up, my heart in my throat. When I caught my foot on the chair, I didn't even feel the pain. "Lexi? Lexi!" I was at the edge in seconds.

The water erupted. Water splashed everywhere. Bobbing in the water, she laughed up at me. "I could hardly touch the bottom. This pool is so deep."

I pressed a hand to my galloping heart. "Darn you, Lexi! Don't try to touch the bottom, okay?"

Smiling up at me, she treaded water in her aqua sun guard and bottom. "Not to worry. Come on in." Giving a wave, she began to do laps with long, assured strokes.

Oh, this heat. It took my breath away. Looking around, I saw no one. Relief released something inside me. The day was beautiful and we had access to this gorgeous pool. I was being foolish. Flinging aside my hat and sunglasses, I dove in, joining my daughter. We did laps together until my legs felt jiggly and my arms, like lead. Then I flipped into a back float while Lexi continued to perfect her dives. The privacy cocooned us.

Finding the ladder, I eventually pulled myself out. The sun that had felt so punishing earlier now felt welcome on my wet skin. Back on the lounge chair, I waited ten minutes or so until I dried off. Then I slathered myself with sunblock that I'd bought in town. Well, I hadn't actually purchased it and that was a problem. I wanted to pay my own way here but how could I manage that?

Ramon, one of the dining room staff, appeared. "May I bring you something, Signora Newhart?"

"Oh, water, I guess. Lexi!" I called out. "Do you want anything."

"Sure." And she named her favorite pop. "With lemon, please. Thank you, Ramon."

Hmm. Something she must have learned from Gregorio and very European. Here they had lemon with everything. Ramon retreated into a secret door I hadn't noticed earlier. Cramming my hat back on my head, I grabbed my sunglasses and my book. And I was being paid for this? Not bad.

Closing my eyes, I felt any tension dissipate. Once I'd taken a yoga class with Reena at the rec center. We'd learned deep breathing. Now I filled my lungs with air and slowly released it through my parted lips. Never in my life would I have imagined myself in a setting like this.

Lexi must have returned. I heard her footsteps and the chair next to me creaked. "Isn't this wonderful?"

"Yes, it is." But who was this? Opening my eyes, I gulped. Hard.

Leaning back on his elbows, Marco smiled at me. If I'd suspected that he had a great body, his swim trunks confirmed it. The man was ripped, as my daughter would say. "Your Majesty." Shocked, I struggled to get up and go for that curtsy. I should act professional. But his hand stopped me, his touch searing my arm.

"No, no, Profesora. That is not necessary." Dropping his hand, he also dropped his eyes, suddenly unsure of himself.

"Gregorio told us we could use the pool." Still, I felt like an interloper.

"But of course. I'm sorry I didn't think of it earlier. This is like a microwave out here." He glanced off into the distance with disgust. "Isn't that what you say when the day is very hot?"

Marco must have learned all his idioms from American TV

shows. I tugged at the bottom of my bikini. "I think you mean oven. Today is as hot as an oven."

I glanced over in time to see his eyes skim my body. A smile tipped one corner of his lips. I tugged at my towel, but unfortunately I was sitting on it. "My goodness, it is hot."

His chest expanded when he took a deep breath. Jerking his eyes away, Marco went back to studying the horizon. "A good day for the grapes."

My laugh came out in a very unladylike snort. "The grapes?"

"Yes, my grapes like hot, dry weather." He sounded insulted.

"Pardon me. I didn't know."

"You are…pardoned." His lips lifted into a saucy grin. "I will not put you in the dungeon. Gregorio tells me that you have had a tour."

"Unfortunately, yes." I shivered at the thought of that dark, damp prison.

Apparently that earned me another pat on the arm. When he leaned back onto his elbows again, I was glad I was wearing dark glasses. It was hard not to stare. This guy could have been on the cover of one of those magazines for men. "So, you like my pool?"

Everything was personal with him.

"Oh yes. I mean, I'm very grateful…that we can use it. You're very generous." I was stumbling. Although I could be articulate in front of a classroom, that sense of calm seemed to have evaporated on the heated summer air that was good for his grapes.

When he turned onto one side to face me, I had the advantage of another angle—and I liked it. Wallace had been scholarly but had rickets as a child. His chest was practically concave, not that there was anything he could do about it.

But Marco? Oh, this was another landscape entirely and I wasn't thinking about the grapes.

"I've been thinking," he murmured. When His Majesty leaned toward me, a whiff of man-in the-hot-sun rolled over me. I took a sip of my water. Adjusting the sunglasses that had fit fine the moment before, I inhaled.

Falling off the chaise right now would not be cool. "Yes, Your Majesty?" Maybe he couldn't see my blush. "What were you thinking about?"

To my own surprise, I hoped it would not be Gabriella.

"This party we're having. Is there anything I've forgotten?"

Now this stumped me. How would I know? I'd never planned a gala. The Homecoming dance at Providence didn't measure up to what Marco had in mind. "I'm sure you have thought of everything."

"Yes, well. I think so. But I will check." Raising a hand, he brushed it over his chin. The movement was slow, hypnotic and very sexy. But His Majesty, my employer, probably wasn't aware of that. Was he?

"We will all have a wonderful time." Here he patted his chest, fingers trailing through the dark hair that patterned his upper body. Although I'd never given it much thought, I decided that all men should have chest hair.

"And I will be Gatsby!"

"But of course. You should be Jay Gatsby if you like." What

would his guests think of that? But maybe they had never seen the movie, much less read the book.

While we talked, Lexi continued to swim laps, her careful rhythm soothing me.

"Have you heard from your friend. Your…" Here he searched for the words as I wondered who the heck he was talking about. "The woman who will know how to make sure that Gregorio is not disappointed. You know, your friend who will get him into Harvard."

"Oh, right. No, not yet." But I would follow up with her tonight. "It's been so busy."

How lame. I didn't miss the twitch of his lips. Here I was, lolling about on a chaise, sipping water with lemon floating in it. Not a bad life.

"I will check my inbox. Maybe I'll have a message from Mary." A quick flick of my eyes ensured me that my ankles were crossed. Fibbing wasn't my thing. And yet I seemed to be doing a lot of it lately. Another sip of my water and I settled back onto the cushions. A woman could get used to this. Marco's voice provided a backdrop while I closed my eyes, brain turning to mush.

"…so you would help me, yes?"

"Yes. I will check my emails tonight." Mary Carmichael. Got it.

Looking up, I caught him staring at me, his face empty.

"Gabriella is not emailing you. Is she?" He looked horrified. "Are the two of you friends now?"

What was he talking about? Gabriella and me as friends? Was he crazy? The girl who had probably never worked a day in her life and me who faced an uncertain retirement? What an unlikely friendship.

I'd lost track of the conversation. Why couldn't I think straight around him?

"No, of course we're not friends. I only met her that one time at lunch. I'm sorry. What were you saying?" I waved a hand vaguely— the way I'd seen him do himself when he'd lost his train of thought.

He gave an abrupt sigh, the way he did with Gregorio. "I was asking you if you would help me. You know, look over the women who come to the party. The single women, of course," he hastened to add.

"Yes, of course. For what?" Was he afraid they might steal from him? Take some of the scented soaps liberally supplied in the first floor powder rooms?

"You must look for the right qualities that I might miss."

Oh, I should have been flattered. But I needed to know more. "What qualities are you looking for?"

Wearing an inscrutable smile, he leaned back on the aqua and blue cushions and closed his eyes. Now it was my turn to study him again, undetected. "I think I would like someone who is…fun."

Now that was a surprise. "Do you mean someone who could ride with you?"

"Is that important?" He opened one eye, which made it seem he was winking.

What were we saying? Oh yes, common interests. "Yes, I would think so. After all, you want to spend time together. That's what a good relationship is all about. And you like to ride."

Back to fingering his chin. "Yes, probably so."

And this was news to him? Was he thinking of marrying some hapless woman, only to leave her wandering around in this huge castle? Or tucked away in the tower? A chill settled over me. I shivered.

"You are cold?" Reaching behind himself, he grabbed his towel.

"No. Of course not. It's hot out here."

"Well good." He tucked the towel under his chair. "So we would ride. Together." He looked very serious and totally joyless at the idea.

"You could show her your...vines."

This got some traction with him. A quick nod. "Yes, she will appreciate my grapes. Perhaps she will help me with the St. Michael's Day party."

"Perhaps. What is that?" Marco didn't strike me as a religious man but what did I really know about him?

Eyebrows lifting, he glanced over with horror, as if I'd just questioned the existence of Santa Claus. "St. Michael's Day is when we harvest the grapes. Very important day."

I'd never heard of it before. "Oh, I'm sorry. We don't have that in the States. Not that I know of."

"Such a disgrace. I had no idea." He shook his head in disgust. America had dropped in his estimation. "Now, back to this party business." Marco would not be distracted.

Oh, so the party was about business? Jay Gatsby might have agreed.

"So, this woman, this one right woman." He held up one finger.

Oh my. I was beginning to feel sorry for the one he ended up choosing.

"...she should ride with me."

"And enjoy your movies," I prompted.

"Oh, yes." His patted his swimming trunks, which of course had no pockets. "I should have a paper and pen. Will you send me this list?"

It was hard to swallow my exasperation. Was the man helpless? "Yes, of course."

He began to rattle off qualities. Some made sense. Some did not. I totally understood that she should enjoy motherhood, but not crying into her pillow at night? What was that about?

"And she should be funny," I said when I thought we'd run out of becoming qualities for the woman who would become Gregorio's new mother.

"Fine, yes." Marco didn't seem to see the value of a good joke shared. "And she should be beautiful."

"Oh, of course." The party no doubt would be filled with gorgeous women wearing gorgeous costumes. Well, I didn't have to stay long.

"And charming."

"Right." How would I remember all this?

Deep in concentration, he ran a fingertip over his lower lip. My stomach did a swan dive.

Lexi arrived and splattered me with cold water.

"Stop, stop." I smiled up at her. What would she think if she heard about this conversation? Should I have her ask Gregorio what he wanted in a new mother or would that be rude?

Jumping up, I gathered my things. The past hour had been totally unsettling. As I packed up, Marco strode to the diving board and executed a perfect dive that would earn a ten at the Olympics. When he surfaced, he threw back his curly hair and smiled. His teeth gleamed in the bright sunlight.

"See you later." I pulled my t-shirt on over my damp suit.

"Later, Profesora?" He laughed. "Don't forget the list."

Together Lexi and I disappeared through the door that would take us to our quarters, the area that housed guests and some of the servants, I'd come to realize. The light inside seemed so dim after the brightness of the pool area. I jumped back when Ama appeared from behind a pillar. Why was the woman always creeping about? She beckoned.

What did she want? "Lexi, you can go ahead."

Giving me a concerned look, Lexi paused until I made a shushing motion with my hands. I tugged at the t-shirt. Certainly I could handle Marco's mother.

Chapter 12

Was I supposed to curtsy to Marco's mother? I wasn't sure about that. *Well, here goes.* Holding my towel around my waist, I slid my left foot back. My flip flop caught on the tile but I managed to keep my balance.

"Do you have a costume for the party?" Ama smiled. How strange. The only time I saw her smile was when she was talking to Gregorio. I stood upright.

"No. Not yet. I was planning on going into the village to see what the shops had. Lexi will need something too."

"Come. I may have something." With a mischievous smile, she trotted off. Now, this was a totally new side of Ama and it was a welcome change.

What else could I do but follow her? Clutching my tote and hoping my towel stayed tightly around my waist, I followed Ama into the family quarters. While my flip flops sounded absurdly loud, her skirts swished softly against the marble floor. The corridor felt somehow sacred, all dimly lit and hung with priceless paintings.

Which one of these doors led to Marco's apartments? My cheeks heated with the reckless rogue thought. *Count to ten and pretend you are back in the corridors of Providence High School, Christina*

Bernadette. Taking a key from a hidden pocket, Ama approached a door. Were there keys to every door in the palace? Who had the key to my door?

By this time, I was having second thoughts and lagging behind. Ama and I hadn't had much interaction since my arrival. Had I imagined her disapproval? During our meals together, she hardly initiated any discussion. In fact, she spoke only to Marco and Gregorio. Today, she was smiling, as if we were high school friends picking out dresses for the prom. Okay, if she offered me tea or even a bite of baklava, I'd draw the line. Ama probably knew lots about poisoning. She had that look about her.

But today she was smiling. "Come, come." She waved me into her inner sanctum.

My breath caught in my throat. "Oh, my. How beautiful."

This was no ordinary bedroom. In fact, there was no bed. Ama must have a suite. Perhaps all of the family members did and that shouldn't surprise me. A decorator had definitely been at work here. In contrast to the rest of the castle, here the color scheme was a tasteful gray with purple and magenta accents. The side tables were exquisite with delicate spindly legs.

On every wall, paintings soared to the ceiling. No doubt she had her own collection of bucolic scenes and family members. But pride of place was given to the portrait of a gorgeous woman with dark hair standing behind a throne. Her hand rested on the shoulder of a handsome man whose uniform gleamed with ribbons and medals. A young boy stood beside them. At the sight of that smile, warmth cascaded through my body. Marco.

Ama followed my eyes. "My husband. And Marco, of course."
Her smile warmed as she took in the painting.

Was it all right to ask questions? "How old was Marco in this
painting?"

"Ten." Her eyes studied the painting with pride.

"Very handsome family." What else could I say? The family
resemblance was unmistakable. The dark hair and eyes, the
patrician nose and carved cheekbones, which were softened in
Gregorio's case.

Questions pulsed in my head but this was no time to ask them.
My eyes circled the room. Instead of one balcony, Ama's room had
two sets of french doors opening onto balconies. Between those
french doors sat a large armoire. Two gowns hung from an open
door.

Immediately catching my eye, the robin's egg blue gown
shimmered. With a modest scoop in the front, the bodice tucked
into a slim waist before falling to the floor with a full skirt. The
skirt glimmered, catching the light with hundreds of tiny crystals.

"What do you think?" Ama snagged the hanger of the dress
with one hand.

"It's beautiful. A Cinderella dress." Made of gossamer material,
the dress looked as if it might fit.

Wearing a pleased smile, Ama went to hold it up to me but I
stepped back. "My suit is still damp under this shirt. I don't want to
ruin it." To think of wearing this beautiful creation was impossible.
But it sure was tempting. Ama was being so kind, so thoughtful.
Her offer would save me the hassle of searching the village, where

I might find nothing appropriate.

When Ama spun the hanger from one hand, the fabric billowed out, issuing an invitation. "But of course," she said, whisking it back to the armoire. "So that's settled. I'll have it put in your room."

"Oh, are you sure?" What if I spilled red wine on this dream of a dress? I wasn't exactly the most coordinated person.

Ama glanced back at me while tucking the dress into the armoire. "Of course I'm sure." A slight touch of scorn tinged the words. Like Marco, she wasn't used to being questioned.

Then she motioned to the second dress, a simple linen with a high neck and a keyhole cutout falling to an A-line dress. "For your daughter?"

The dress was lovely but it was sleeveless. Now how would I get around this? Dressing Lexi had always been a challenge in the summer. "My daughter likes sleeves." There. I'd leave it at that.

Hmm. Fingering the huge sapphire at her neck, Ama seemed to ponder options. "Perhaps a jacket of some sort?"

"Maybe that would work." Was she kidding me? The weather continued to be hot and muggy. Despite what Gregorio had said about their pseudo air conditioning, the castle still felt uncomfortable.

"For you to decide. His Majesty is inviting guests… of his own rank, of course."

"Of course." Ah, now we were back on familiar footing. I was the hired governess, nothing more.

Her dark eyes bored into me. "My son has expectations of you and your daughter for this event."

Right. And buying little peasant dresses in town wouldn't pass muster. "I understand."

Her grim smile was back, kind of like the witch who lured Hansel and Gretel. "The dresses will be in your room tonight. What you do with them will be up to you." Then she crossed her arms at her waist, hands disappearing into the full cuffs.

Our girl-to-girl chat was over. "Thank you so much, Your Grace."

Her head tilted to one side. I probably had the wrong title. *So shoot me.*

Somehow I escaped from the room, my head whirling like the fabric of that exquisite dress. So Marco had "expectations." And I would have a hand in sorting through girls who would meet them.

Those poor young women.

Back in my room, I changed and went to find Lexi next door. "Maybe we shouldn't go."

Propped up on the satin pillows, Lexi was reading. Now the book was tossed aside. "Are you kidding? Miss this ball? Gregorio says the food is going to be fabulous and they're having fireworks. We're going."

Had I seen her this excited since we arrived? "I know, I know." Nerves did a tango in my tummy.

Sliding off the bed, Lexi came over to the balcony windows where I was standing. She gently put her hands on my arms. "Hey, are you thinking about Marco? I saw how he looked at you today."

Twisting away, I flapped one hand. "Nonsense. You have a

great imagination." What had she seen?

"No really, Mom. He was totally checking you out."

My nerves sang as if I were careening down a zipline. "That's ridiculous. I have to get a one-piece suit."

"No way. You're very…well-preserved." Then Lexi squinched her face together, knowing the term wasn't quite right.

"What? Am I an olive?" I didn't know whether to laugh or cry.

Dinner that night was quiet. Lexi and I had been blitzed by the sun, I think. Marco and Ama took the lead discussing food for the party, along with the shapes of the ice sculptures.

"But it's summer." How many times would I remind myself to think before I spoke? This wasn't my party and certainly not my money. If they wanted to decorate with ice sculptures, that was up to them.

"But of course." Marco brushed my interruption away. "We will have to enjoy ourselves very quickly then, no? Before the ice melts?"

Ama chuckled but Gregorio burst into laughter. "Oh, Papa."

His father gave him a stern look. I nearly dropped my fork. Was this the term Gregorio used for his father in their private quarters? "Papa" sounded so cozy and I wanted to believe that they had that kind of relationship.

"Your Majesty," Gregorio amended before laughter again rumbled deep in his stomach. "Sometimes you make me laugh."

"And why is this?" Marco's features were set in sharp angles.

The man didn't like to be laughed at. I thought back to my conversation with Lexi that afternoon. Parenting often meant that your children pointed things out that you didn't want to hear. But Marco didn't know that.

"Nothing, Father." Gregorio took the napkin from his lap. "May I be excused?"

Ama darted Marco a sharp look. How I wished I'd taken supper in my room. Sometimes I felt as if we were seeing a movie play out before us, Lexi and me. No family is perfect. I knew that. But the tension between the two of them had a deeper base. At least that was my guess. And what roll did Ama play in all that?

Shortly after that, Lexi and I excused ourselves too. But the night was young, and I didn't feel like going upstairs yet. "Let's go out to the patio." Although I would have loved to sit by the pool, that area was visible to the family. I wanted privacy.

So we found our way out to the fountain, where the breeze was cool and the shadows lengthened.

"Hey, let's try the maze." Lexi pointed to the high bushes that had been my downfall on that first day.

"No way. I'm not trying that in the dark." We perched on one of the stone benches that encircled the fountain.

"Man, these are hard." She fell silent. We sat together, listening to the fountain bubble and splash. "Mom, sometimes I wish we were home."

Well, so much for sharing that peaceful moment.

What she really meant was she wished she were near her friends, who had gotten her into plenty of trouble. "This is only for the summer. Make the most of it. In October you'll look back at this and wonder if these days had been real."

"Yeah. No one's having a ball back home." Her cheeks split into a grin.

"Speaking of the ball, Ama picked out two dresses for us."

Her brows went up. "Really? Are they decent?"

"Oh, very decent. Wait 'til you see." Throwing back my head, I glanced up at the moon, now a slice in the sky. "Just think, Lexi. This same moon is smiling down on our friends right now."

"You make it sound as if they're right around the corner." Her words sounded sad.

"Do you wish they were?" Now, why had I asked this question? I knew the answer.

"Yeah, yeah I do."

My little girl sounded so lost. The reckless sophomore who would try anything once was gone. In her place was this vulnerable teen. I squeezed her hand. "But I'm here."

She slipped her hand away. "I know that, Mom. Sometimes you're my mother. Other times, you're my teacher." Lexi made a face that told me what she thought of that.

"I know you didn't want this, Lexi." How I wished I hadn't even started this conversation. "But I think this summer might be good for you in the end."

"Why do parents always think they know what's best for us."

"Because we've been there. Believe it or not, I was fourteen once. The feelings are the same." But the temptations are not. Time changed everything. No way could I ever have envisioned the kind of situations Lexi now faced. "Teenage years can be very confusing."

Nothing from my daughter.

"Maybe we should go up now." I stood up and turned toward the castle. Could anyone see us down here? My eyes swept the building that extended forever, with lots of windows staring down at us.

"Think I'll stay here for a while."

Was Lexi waiting for someone? Sometimes it was so hard. She'd been penned up for a couple weeks now. Although I wanted to trust her, she'd given me reason to question her. "Thirty minutes, Lexi. I'm going to read for a while. Knock on my door when you get in."

Chapter 13

After that first disastrous day riding in the woods, things got better. Tesoro and I seem to have struck a truce. Rudolfo and I continued riding in the fields and woods. How I wished my friends could see me. Okay, I was proud of myself. I loved riding in the early morning hours when the sun was peeking over the horizon. And I was learning. How often had I told my students that school taught you how to learn? Riding was all about learning.

How pleased I was when Rudolfo finally taught me how to saddle Tesoro. How to place the blanket exactly right. I was so careful cinching the girth so it didn't pinch her but was tight enough so it wouldn't slide off, taking me with it. Slipping the bit into Tesoro's mouth had taken some courage on my part. Although she was spritely and lean, the mare had huge teeth—or so they seemed to me. But the day Rudolfo guided me through the positioning of the bit, Tesoro accepted me sweetly. What an accomplishment.

Our rides were great fun, although Rudolfo took pretty much the same route every time. When I'd asked Lexi where she went with Gregorio, she became vague—the way she acted when she didn't want me to know what she was doing. So I didn't pry.

Giving her some space became my goal. Our relationship was changing. We were developing trust. I didn't want to spoil that.

The classes were going well. Mary Carmichael had emailed me with information about how to find a testing center in Italy. She'd also sent links to sites that had preparation tips for the tests Gregorio should take.

Everything was fine, or so I told myself as preparations continued for the ball.

Summer had come stealing across the fields, the lavender so beautiful that it made my heart hurt. Staff worked in the gardens almost every day, snipping and pruning. Ama was a rose fanatic, or so Gregorio told me. The flower beds around the castle held more than twenty varieties. The scent of roses sweetened the air when I walked out in the evening. Everything here looked so vibrant, as if it were plucked from a movie. I should feel peaceful, content with all this beauty. But I didn't. For some unknown reason, I felt constantly on alert, always in a confused state.

Was all that Marco's fault?

Was he my problem?

***

Early one morning as I came out from the tack room, saddle in my arms, I ran smack into Marco. His Majesty was dressed in those form fitting breeches and boots with one of his linen shirts. No way was I curtsying. The weight of all that hand-tooled leather could land me flat on my face. Rudolfo was nowhere in sight. Marco was holding Tesoro's reins, murmuring to her as she nuzzled his pocket.

"Your Majesty." At least I was starting to get his title right.

In the early morning light, his eyes were soft as suede. And he looked a bit embarrassed. "Do you mind if I join you this morning?"

Ride with him? Heck no. With one heave, I positioned the saddle on Tesoro's blanketed back. "Why, of course, Your Majesty."

But I sounded as if he'd offered me my choice of poisons. He gave a short laugh. Had I offended him? "Profesora. If you would prefer to ride alone, or with Rudolfo, of course that is fine. I was about to go out and thought we might ride together."

"No problem. Sure." I couldn't even look at him. This was a man who would drive any woman crazy. But I could not think of him that way.

I sucked in a breath. The rich scent of hay and horse almost gagged me. Had he deliberately started syncing his riding time with my own? I didn't want to insult Marco by refusing to join him, although riding with the King and Diablo would not be a relaxed start to my morning.

He stood waiting and his uncertainty made him seem so vulnerable.

"Really. I'd love to have you join me." Somehow I injected the words with enthusiasm.

Within minutes, he'd saddled Diablo and we were off. Tesoro didn't seem to mind cantering out with the larger stallion. Of course we fell back behind them.

Because all of my slacks would have been ruined by riding, I'd fallen into wearing jeans with a long-sleeved T-shirt to protect my arms from the sun as well as the branches that could whip out from anywhere. My hair was tugged back in a barrette at the base of my neck.

Across the fields we flew. The pace was a little faster than what Rudolfo and I had been doing. But Diablo's legs were longer than those of delicate Tesoro. I felt exhilarated and free. But we were falling behind a bit. Glancing back, Marco slowed.

"Sorry, I'm not used to going so fast," I managed to pant out as we cantered up to them.

"Of course. Thoughtless of me." Easing up, he fell back until we were riding side by side.

"Are you enjoying it?" he asked, his eyes sliding over my top and jeans as if he'd never seen anything like them. What did women here wear to ride? I pictured a red jacket and black breeches, but maybe that was only for the British.

"Yes. Rudolfo has been very kind."

"Oh no. I meant, are you enjoying the lessons with Gregorio. This position."

We'd taken one of the paths into the woods and the cool air was welcome. The smell of damp earth surrounded us and the air was very still, as if every creature in the forest were watching their king.

"Gregorio is an eager student."

"This I'm glad to hear."

"Didn't his other tutors find him to be a good student?" That would surprise me. I'd expected a spoiled young man whose father could afford to hire a tutor from across the sea. Gregorio and his charming humility had been a welcome surprise.

"I'd heard that he didn't study. The tutor before you, Reginaldo, felt that Gregorio had no attitude for math. I think that was what he said." Marco was getting huffy about the former tutor.

"Do you mean aptitude?" I asked softly. Did I dare question him?

He shrugged. "Maybe. Aptitude. Attitude. All is the same."

Ah yes. So he wanted to create his own language.

I leapt to Gregoria's defense. "I would say that his geometry and trig need a little work but he is catching on quickly." No way did I want to throw another teacher under the bus, but I had to speak up for my student. "Were you good in math?"

His eyes fell. "I think I was adequate. My tutors usually told my father that I had promise. I think that's how they phrased it."

"Well, there you have it. Like father, like son. And you carried that into your college years?"

"No." He lifted troubled eyes. "Profesora, I did not go to college."

His words were almost whispered, more a confession than a statement of fact. I must have jerked on the reins because Tesoro reared her head. Stunned, I patted her neck and loosened the reins. She settled while my thoughts churned.

"But why?" As soon as the words were out, I wanted to reel them back. Marco's academic career was none of my business. But his admission explained so much.

Our pace had slowed and I was glad. I wanted to hear every word.

163

"My father died when I was seventeen. He had taught me so much by that time. I'd worked in the vineyards since I was a child. Knew the grapes as if they were siblings. But I was not ready, of course, for the responsibilities. For four years, my mother acted as Regent. After that, I ascended to the throne."

It wasn't hard to picture Ama directing the castle and the kingdom. Now I understood her authoritarian mannerisms. Had it been hard for her to step back? So Marco hadn't enjoyed any carefree years as a student prince. Sure, college could be a grind, but it also fostered independence and deep friendships. As I sat there in the sunlight flickering through the trees, I wanted that for Gregorio. And I felt bad that Marco hadn't had that opportunity.

"Gregorio will go to the university." The words were a pronouncement, not a wish. "He will have all that I did not have."

"Of course. I would have been thrilled to have a boy like Gregorio in my class." At least then he would have had companionship. "Does he have friends?"

"Why, of course." We'd reached an overhanging branch and I started to duck. Moving ahead, Marco held it back with one sweep of his arm.

"Profesora, please." With a nod of his head, he motioned for me to pass. Now, if Rudolfo had done that for me when we first ventured out of the paddock, I would have been saved from those scratches that took a few days to heal.

To either side of the path, the land fell away, forested with saplings that jostled for light under the taller trees. "You will meet some of Gregorio's friends at the party. The ball." He seemed to be testing the words, trying to find the right words.

"I look forward to that. It's nice for teenagers to have friends, as long as they don't get him into any trouble."

My words slowed. By that time the trail had narrowed. Marco broke away and took the lead. He cut quite a figure on the black stallion. How could I ever have mistaken him for a stable boy? Turning around, he said, "Trouble?" He had a way of analyzing things.

"Bad habits." Here I had to be careful. He might have second thoughts about letting Gregorio hang out with my daughter if he knew about Lexi's situation. She'd be crushed.

"High school is an interesting time," I said slowly. "Kids do a lot of experimenting, you know, to find out what suits them. Their parents might not agree."

Marco seemed to let that settle, a frown bringing those brows together in concentration. "I see. But then they should not do these things."

"Or you will put them in the dungeon?"

Grinning, he drew back. "Oh, no. I would not do that."

Maybe Gregorio would never do anything to upset his father. But that seemed almost unnatural. How did a teenager learn if he or she did not test the boundaries? He turned back to face the trail. Up ahead the trees thinned. We came out into the soft morning sunlight. A mist teased the rolling field that was a rich green. This was the point where Rudolfo usually turned around. We would circle back, using a path that led to the stables.

Diablo was straining at the bit, as if he knew what lay ahead.

But I tightened my hold on Tesoro's reins, uncertain of this new route. "Aren't we going back?"

The grin on Marco's face sent a shiver of apprehension through me. Or was that excitement? "I'd like to show you something. Up ahead." And he nodded his head with that wild mane of hair.

"Sure." This sounded like a challenge and I completely lost my head. "No problem." No way was I backing down.

"Magnifico." At a signal from Marco, Diablo surged ahead, muscles working in his dark shiny coat. When I loosened the reins, Tesoro didn't need to feel the pressure of my thighs urging her forward. We were off. Keeping my head low, I tried to post as Rudolfo had taught me, but this rhythm was different. My hair clip tumbled out. Before long I was gasping for air, my hair flying into my mouth. But boy, this was fun. Was this what Lexi and Gregorio did after they'd disappeared into the woods? The only difference was that Lexi had been given lessons. But Rudolfo had taught me well.

Up ahead, Marco rode the stallion as if they were one, his head lowering over the horse's neck. Diablo's gait looked wild and free, but always under the hand of Marco. At the pool, I'd been given more than a glimpse of my employer's muscular chest. No red riding coat and top hat for this man. The cuffs were rolled up on strong forearms. Those buff-colored breeches fit him like a second skin.

Maybe that's when it happened. Maybe I was thinking too much about the breeches and not enough about the ground and Tesoro's pace. My heart lurched when I felt the horse stumble. She went down and I went flying. Oh my heavens. The ground came up to meet me and I braced myself. When I landed, I could feel the impact clear through to my teeth.

Mercy me, had I killed his favorite horse?

Rolling over, I stared up. Clouds moved across the sky. Or was my head spinning? Marco was there in an instant. "Are you all right? Christina, talk to me."

Had I ever heard my name from his lips? Usually it was *Signora Newhart* or *Profesora*. I struggled to sit up but felt so dizzy.

Marco stopped me. "Do you have any injuries?" His hands ran down my arms, gentle but thorough. The same treatment was given to my legs. *Oh mercy.*

"And inside? How do you feel? Do you have pain anywhere?" Hands poised above me, he looked ready to continue his careful inspection.

"No, I'm fine." I felt a little bruised but no need to go any further.

Suddenly I was pressed to his chest, while he smoothed the hair from my forehead. His heart pulsed under my hand and my own had gone crazy.

"Is Tesoro all right?" I looked up at him, "I'm so sorry, Marco...Your Majesty."

"She is fine." His breath felt warm on my face as he turned to look. "She is eating grass, as usual."

"Well, fine. I mean, good."

Marco had the longest lashes I'd ever seen on a man. Dark and sooty, they framed his intense eyes. Didn't look as if he'd shaved yet that morning. The dark stubble added to his rugged look. His etched lips opened. "Profesora?" More blinking of those lashes.

"Yes, Your Majesty?" The words felt tight in my throat.

"You...you are very beautiful." The words were said in wonder. Almost as a question. I should have felt insulted. But if Marco was having trouble with his eyesight, so be it. Had anyone ever told me I was beautiful? I think my husband had told me I was pretty.

When Marco gave a shake of his head and loosened his hold, I came to my senses. "Can you get up? I will help."

All righty. End of that magic moment. Clutching his arms for balance, I stood, my jeans and shirt damp and grass-stained from the tumble. "I'm all right. Really."

Oh, my word. I won't be able to sit for a week.

Looking down, he dropped his arms. I watched his chest rise and fall. Somehow I maintained my balance while he slammed the heel of one hand against his forehead. "*Stupido.* I thought you had crossed the fields before. Show-off."

I drew myself up. "Are you calling me a show-off?"

Knifing a hand though those wild curls, he shook his head, much the same way Diablo shook his mane. "No, no. *I* am the show-off."

Then he chuckled. "My mother, she tells me that all the time."

With the mention of his mother, my sanity returned. "I should have been more careful with Tesoro. Are you sure she's all right?"

Pulling away, he grabbed Tesoro's reins and knelt. Marco ran his hands down the horse's legs, pausing at times to check something out. Knowing how those hands felt, I shivered as I watched.

"She is fine," he pronounced, jumping to his feet. "And you are fine also?"

The crisp inquiry brought us back to the employer-employee relationship. "Yes, yes, nothing broken." I shook out a leg as if to prove it. Talk about being stupid. I must have looked crazy.

Looking away, Marco studied the horizon. "Do you wish to go back or can we continue? It's only a little way."

So there was a destination? This wasn't a wild joy ride? "Of course. Let's continue."

Capturing Tesoro's reins, he helped get me back into the saddle by lacing both hands below me. Stepping into that pocket, I vaulted up and somehow made it with one try. My backside complained but what could I do about that? A hot bath was all I wanted right now. But no way would I complain.

This was all part of the job. I held the worn leather reins in my hands.

What did he want to show me? At a much slower pace, we found another path that led to a road. The mist had cleared and eventually we came to row after row of vines that stretched forever. "Oh my goodness. Is this your vineyard?"

Looking very pleased, he pulled up next to me. "Some of it, yes. Come." Sliding from his saddle, he led Diablo to one of the rows, where the grapes were dark purple. Dismounting, I followed. We left the horses to graze and I followed him down one of the rows. The rich smell of grapes was almost intoxicating.

His long fingers skimmed the vines until he stopped and gently tugged off a few grapes. "A taste?" Marco held them up to me.

I hesitated. These grapes might be coated with insecticides. As if he read my mind, Marco said, "Don't worry. The sprinkler system traveled over this field very early this morning."

Good enough for me. He seemed so eager to have me taste them. I popped one into my mouth. His eyes on me, I bit down. Flavor exploded in my mouth. Now, I was a woman who bought whatever wine was on sale that week. The taste of Marco's grapes made all my taste buds stand up and plead for more. I'd never tasted anything like this grape.

The sounds of appreciation coming from my mouth brought a smile from Marco. He was as delighted as a little boy on Christmas morning. "So you like my grapes?" He waited.

"They taste amazing."

His eyes swept the vineyard with pride. "This is only one of my vineyards. But this vine?" His eyes traveled along the gnarled row with affection. "This is one of the wines I will serve at the party."

"But these grapes won't be wine by next weekend, right?" I tried to get my mind around what he was saying.

"Oh, no, Profesora. No." And he grinned as if I'd said the most ridiculous thing. "These grapes won't be harvested until late August or September. Fine wines have to be aged. That is what my guests will taste. Wine perfected by age in my casks."

Okay then. The sun was rising higher. One glance at my watch told me that I'd stayed too long. "This has been delightful but I have to get back for class, Your Majesty."

"Call me Marco," he said in a husky tone I'd never heard

before. "When we are in private. Marco, please."

The words sent heat blazing through me. I pushed back my tangled hair. "What will your mother say?" The words were out before I thought. Not unusual for me.

"Christina…" He paused, his eyes flicked over me while I savored the sound of my name on his lips, much as I've savored his grapes. "May I call you Christina, Profesora?"

My name on this man's tongue turned my legs to pasta. The cooked kind. "Okay. I guess so." My voice came out as foggy as the field we'd traveled this morning.

"Christina," he said again, as if he were enjoying my name, "my mother knows well that I am the king of the castle."

Well, it didn't even occur to me to remind him that the phrase was a time-worn cliché and how I did hate clichés. "I'm such a mess." Ducking my head, I ran my fingers through my hair to untangle the knots.

Marco's hand lifted as if he wanted to help. Our eyes met. The sun beat down. His hand dropped. Turning, I stumbled toward Tesoro.

Both quiet, we rode home through the fields that had almost been my undoing. I wouldn't trust myself to be alone with Marco again.

Chapter 14

What a commotion. And to think that reading about Jay Gatsby in class had set this gala in motion. I'd have to be more careful. About a lot of things. Over the last few days, that morning ride with Marco had replayed in my mind a million times. I felt so confused.

But first, I had to deal with this party. Outside, the staff had been busy setting up tables on either side of the fountain and arranging chairs. I couldn't help checking on them from the balcony. A crew had put down a portable wooden dance floor hours ago. The trees and bushes were strung with lights. The orchestra was tuning their instruments as I struggled to get into my dress without tearing it. Why would any seamstress put covered buttons up the back where a woman couldn't reach?

Just then the door shot open, banging against the wall and sending me through the ceiling. "Lexi, be careful. You'll damage the walls." That's all I'd need—a bill for damages when we left to go home.

"What's wrong?" Lexi's old *Frozen* bathrobe billowed around her as she crossed the floor with her long legs. "I thought you'd be ready by now."

"These buttons are impossible." Turning, I motioned to my

back.

"That's the problem? Mom, I thought you were dying in here." Mumbling she turned me around. Maybe someday she'd be patient with me. But this wasn't that day.

"Why did I agree to this? What a foolish idea. We won't know anyone." I tried to turn, but Lexi wouldn't let me. "Maybe I'll have a tray sent up. Stay in my room."

"What? Absolutely not." The buttons that hadn't behaved were fastening nicely under my daughter's fingers. "Since when does a Newhart chicken out? There. Finished." She stepped back, looking pleased.

I slowly turned. "I'm being practical. What's with the robe? Why aren't you dressed?"

Lexi gave me the once-over with her eyes. "You're definitely going. That dress looks fabulous on you. Look." And she gestured to the long mirror.

I stepped closer. A breeze wafted through the open french doors, and the wide skirt of the gown fluttered around me in soft waves, the tiny gems winking up at me. "Oh, my word." I fingered the neckline, modest but revealing. "I can't wear this. Why I look like…"

"Cinderella." Lexi circled me, tugging here and there.

"Exactly." I studied the mirror. "How can I go looking like a fairy tale? Maybe I should have chosen another movie—something that isn't childish. Sleek. Sophisticated." At least, that's what I pictured.

"Why? Everyone knows the story of Cinderella." Lexi wore a

secret smile. "Mom, you look amazing. Wait 'til M–everyone sees you."

"Don't you think it's a bit much?" The skirt was so full. But I did like the dainty cap sleeves. Any toning in my arms was strictly hereditary. I never had the time or money to work out at one of those places where the girls wore spandex and worried about stomach rolls that weren't even there. My mother had looked physically fit well into her mature years. Scrubbing her own floors had helped those arms.

"Did you bring Grandma's pearls?"

"Yes, I didn't have time to take them to the safety deposit box." Our neighborhood had experienced some break-ins during the last couple of months before we left. Pulling out the lower drawer of the elegant dresser, I dug under my lingerie until I felt the frayed silk bag. "Here you go. You can do the honors."

Taking the pearls out, Lexi placed them around my throat and fastened the safety clasp. Fingering my mother's precious pearls, I could almost hear her in my ear. "Things are what they are, Christina. If you can't change it, roll with it." Mom had been a roll-with-it sort of person, although she could dig her heels in when it counted, like buying me my first two-wheel bike. Mom and Dad had always come through for me when it counted.

While I stood there dreaming, Lexi started pulling at my hair. "What are you doing?" I'd spent an hour pinning my hair into this tight knot.

"Mom, you have beautiful hair. You have to wear it down. What the heck is this? A french twist?" Closing my eyes, I felt her tug at my hair.

"I wore it this way to my senior prom." Thank goodness my high school had invited students to come without dates or I never would have gone. That night I'd worn a french twist with the pink tea-length dress that my mother had sewn for me. Giggling nervously with my girlfriends at our table, I'd tried not to pay attention to the couples swirling across the floor.

Plugging in a curling iron and grabbing a brush from the dressing table, Lexi went to work.

Seeing that intent look on her face made me nervous. "Lexi, don't go crazy now. This is me, your mother."

"Exactly. And it's about time you lived up to your potential."

"You are t-telling *me* that?" I tried not to smile. How many times had I said that to Lexi?

"Keep your eyes shut." She stopped working until I did just that. What was I doing? I felt foolish, as if I were playing dress-ups. "That's enough, honey," I finally said. "We should get down there. The orchestra has started to play."

Lexi steered me to the mirror. "Like it?"

"Oh my." I hardly recognized myself. Long curls tumbled to my shoulders. In the fading light, my dark blonde hair caught a few highlights. Lexi swept my long bangs to one side and stepped back. I looked so different. My friend Reena's voice sounded in my ear. *Maybe this is the night for different.*

"I'll be right back." Lexi bustled from the room.

While she was gone, I peered down at the courtyard that had been transformed with the magic that only gobs of money could bring about. Marco would be pleased.

In two minutes, Lexi was back with her makeup bag.

"Not for me." I held up a hand as if warding off Ebola. I hated all that stuff and never knew what to do with it, although every Christmas I found an eye shadow palette in my stocking. But I closed my eyes while Lexi swiped my lids with her brush and worked with pencils. And she didn't stop there. Apparently, my lips weren't prominent enough. Another set of brushes came out.

"So this is where your allowance goes every week?"

"Not really. Why do you think I babysit so much?"

"I thought you enjoyed children. And I'm proud of you for being so independent."

"Right." Finally, she stepped back. I went back to the mirror, the gown rustling around my ankles. "Oh, I don't think…"

The knock at the door was sharp. "Come in!" Would it be Ama, coming to see how I looked in the dress she'd so generously loaned me?

But it was Enrico, one of Marco's footmen. "They are waiting for you, Profesora."

They were? Who was "they"? "All right. We're coming. Thank you, Enrico."

He disappeared. I went to smooth my hair, but Lexi stopped me.

"Mom, don't ruin it. Please."

Grabbing my small beaded handbag, the same bag I'd carried to the prom, I sucked in a breath. "Go and get dressed. I'll meet you outside."

She gave me a soft push with her hands. "Can't wait to see what they think of you."

My stomach clenched at the thought. We stepped into the quiet corridor. Closing the door behind me, I pressed a hand to my stomach and reminded myself to breathe. With so many guests attending, I could hide in the crowd. At least, that was my intention.

The long gown pulled at me with each step so I couldn't hurry toward the elevator. The ride down to the first-floor level seemed to take forever. Maybe it would malfunction, and I could hide in here all night. But the thought brought on a terrible attack of claustrophobia. In any case, Lexi would come searching for me. How I wished she were with me now. When the elevator finally stopped with a lurch, I hurried out into the hallway.

Laughter bubbled into the first floor on a breeze flowing from the french doors that had been left open in almost every room I passed. Marco might be taking this opportunity to show off his castle. Beneath the chatter of people talking, the orchestra provided a stringed backdrop with a bit of brass. As I slowed my steps, I thought I recognized the James Bond theme from *Goldfinger*.

If I was asked what movie I was from, I would say *Cinderella*.

Eyes down, I hurried past guests in the foyer and escaped into the fresh air. What a beautiful night for a party. Was I really living this dream? Back on Willard Street, they'd be getting ready for the summer block party. My special bacon and brown sugar beans would be ready in my pyrex dish. Lexi would help me haul our lawn chairs over to the Walkers' house because they had the biggest back yard.

Glancing past the fountain into the falling dusk, I took in the mystical scene. Tiny white lights were suspended above the guests and wrapped the palm trees set about the terrace in enormous blue pots. To either side rose an ice sculpture of a dolphin. Around each sculpture, shrimp and crab legs were heaped alongside crystal dishes with sauces. Grilles sat on the side patio and the smells coming from that area were enough to make my mouth water. But the snug fit of this bodice reminded me that I couldn't eat much.

Standing to one side, I took it all in, knowing that I wasn't really a part of all this. No problem. I'd stay in the background. Waiters circulated with flutes of champagne. Although I wasn't much of a drinker, the waiters didn't have any pop. I whisked a flute from the tray and the waiter smiled.

Clutching my glass of bubbly wonderfulness, I looked around. Not one familiar face. I upended the glass, feeling a flush sear my cheeks. "Profesora!" I turned as Gregorio broke through the crowd.

"Don't you look dashing." He wore a tuxedo and tonight he looked like a young man who might go to Harvard. "What movie are you from?"

"Movie?" For a second he looked confused.

"Your costume. Are you James Bond?"

"Oh, that. No. Didn't Nonna tell you?"

"Tell me what?" Another waiter appeared, taking the empty flute from my numb fingers and handing me a replacement.

"I guess people complained that they didn't have movie

costumes. So, my father changed it to formal wear."

Embarrassment rolled through me in hot waves. "I didn't get the message."

Gregorio gave me an encouraging smile. "Don't worry. You look beautiful. Did you bring that dress with you?"

"No. Your grandmother loaned this to me." And I gestured toward the full skirt, a contrast to the clinging gowns other women were wearing tonight. I felt frumpy, not that I would ever wear a dress like that. No way could I afford it.

"Nonna gave that to you?" Gregorio's smooth brow, so like his father's, creased and his eyes clouded.

Dumping my champagne into the nearest planter, I straightened. So, this is how it was. How naïve I'd been to think Ama felt concerned for me. "But Lexi...I think she..."

But Gregorio's eyes had slid past me. "Lexi?" His mouth had fallen open.

Turning, I choked. Lexi was wearing green tights and a filmy top that encompassed her arms with mere wisps of fabric. Wings sprouted from her back and that's what tipped me off. "Let me guess...."

"Tinkerbell!" Her arms flew out as if she really might fly. And oh, how I wanted to fly away with her at that moment.

"It's that Peter Pan show," she told Gregorio, who still wore a quizzical smile.

"But where did you get this costume?" I asked.

She gave me a sly look. "Amazon."

"Oh, my word. Here?"

"Yep, Gregorio helped me."

My student was trying to look innocent. In halting speech that flushed his cheeks, Gregorio quickly explained. His words were barely coherent and I held up a hand. "Not to worry. You look lovely." Although I wasn't sure about those tights, no way would I make her as uncomfortable as I felt. This night would be special for her, a party to tell her friends about at home.

"Gregorio was just telling me that they'd scrapped the movie idea."

"How many days ago was the theme changed?" Lexi wasn't taking this well.

"A few." Gregorio stuffed his hands into his pockets. "I don't know. Does it matter?"

He was right, of course. "No, it doesn't." Why ruin the evening? Ama wanted us to feel out of place but I would deal with her later.

While we talked, night had fallen, making the party even more magical. And providing more cover. It would be easy to slip away now, which was exactly what I planned to do.

"Christina." Only one person said my name like that. Fighting a bad case of the shivers, I turned.

Marco was the epitome of privileged cool tonight. He must have decided to tame those curls with pomade. Brushed back, his hair glistened under the lights. In the crisp black and white tuxedo, he looked elegant, more handsome than a man had a right to be.

He studied my dress, eyes traveling over me as if they had GPS targeting. Were the crystals on the skirt a little much. I had no right to them, and my cheeks burned. I had to explain. "I didn't know."

His brows rose in question. "Know what?"

"I thought we were still being movie characters."

"Oh, I see." His eyes twinkled. "And you are?"

"Cinderella." Lexi came to my defense. "Doesn't she look great?"

My hand went to my hair, which seemed to be the center of his attention. Why had I let Lexi do this to me?

"Cinderella." He gave the name a knowing twist that sent a chill down my back.

The night air rustled my skirt and did crazy things with the curls Lexi had created. My hair was going to be a problem, but I didn't plan to stay long.

As if she really were sassy Tinkerbell, Lexi set her hands on her hips. "We thought we..."

But I stopped Lexi right there. Marco had gone to a great deal of trouble. No way did I want him to know about Ama and whatever trick she had pulled on us. Or had she? Had a notice been slipped under the wrong door? That was probably it. When I got back to the room, I might find an envelope under the Oriental rug in front of the door.

Rubbing his hands together, Marco looked as if he had to move along. "You both look very nice. Now, Profesora, we must talk about tonight, no? Our plans."

Gregorio and Lexi took off, quickly swallowed up by the guests.

"I think I should go up and change." Even my pearls felt pathetic. All around us, women sparkled with what were surely real rubies, sapphires and diamonds.

"What?" His square jaw moved with impatience. "Nonsense. Now I will introduce them to you, one by one. My sister-in-law Sofia has come up with a list."

"What list?" My head was whirling. The lights above me seemed to swim. "You have a sister-in-law?"

"Yes, Bianca's older sister." When Marco drew closer, I thought I might faint. He was wearing that cologne again. The kind that could turn a woman's bones to cooked pasta. I was becoming noodleized. When he leaned toward me, I could see each bristle on his rugged chin, although he was more clean-shaven than usual.

"The prospects," he whispered, as if this were an undercover operation.

As his warm breath bathed my neck, I tried to bring order to my thoughts. "Right. Of course." *Buck up, Christina. He needs some help. You have a mission to accomplish.*

"Ah, here you are." And with that, a lovely looking woman dressed in a fashionable moss green dress appeared at his side. Compared to many of the pencil slim women tonight, this woman looked comfortable—as if she enjoyed dinner and didn't give a fig what anyone thought. She gave me a broad, accepting smile. I liked her immediately.

"Sofia, I want you to meet Gregorio's tutor, Christina."

I began a quick attempt at a curtesy, but her hand squeezed my elbow. "None of that for me. I'm just a peasant." Her sparkling eyes swung to Marco and a brow lifted. "Has she been spending too much time with your mother?"

Either Marco did not catch the comment about Ama or he decided to ignore it. He produced a slip of paper from an inner pocket. "Christina, this is the list Sofia has prepared. Elena, Chiara and Izabella. Do you think we have time for more?" His eyes flitted between Sofia and me.

Sofia's laughter bubbled into the warm night air. "The evening is young, Marco. We'll do what we can." Thank goodness one of us understood what this was about.

Oh my. I followed the direction of Marco's eyes. Gabriella was making her way toward us. Her silver lame gown shimmered on her skeletal frame like liquid foil. At her neck was a collar of pearls. Had Elizabeth Taylor worn that in *Cleopatra*? This group looked like the type that could afford it.

Gabriella didn't look happy. "Marco. Marco?" Her peeved voice raked across my nerves. I tried not to stare at that necklace that made my mother's pearls look paltry. "I've been looking everywhere for you."

Marco's face froze but not before I noted the twitch in his right temple. Had she been hounding him? "Gabriella, so glad you could come. Nice to see you again." The words were polite and distancing, as if she were an old friend he hadn't seen in years. He did a quick European air kiss.

"But, but Marco…"

Taking Gabriella's elbow, Sofia steered her away from Marco. "Has your mother come with you tonight, dear?"

"Well yes, she's here somewhere." Gabriella's smoky lavender eyes did a sweep of the crowd before circling back to Marco.

"She probably needs some food," Sofia said. I had to hand it to her. She sounded really concerned. "Your Majesty, are the food stations open?"

"Oh, yes, of course." He swept a hand toward the long tables where waiters had arranged colorful platters of tenderloin, lobster and enough roasted vegetables to make Julia Child happy. "Have a wonderful time, Gabriella."

Feeling sorry for the girl, I was stunned into silence. She hadn't even made the list.

Gabriella slinked off to find her parents. And the games began. Teaming up, Sofia and Marco made their way through the guests, with me trailing behind. I felt very much like the caboose behind the royal train but I didn't mind. Sofia had a teasing way with Marco. I liked watching the two of them play off each other. She was fun.

Sofia waved to another dark-haired beauty who wasn't a day over twenty-five, if that.

"Ah, Chiara!" The woman with dark wavy hair and brown eyes turned. Of course she was delighted to find the host next to her. Although I tried to tuck myself behind Sofia, she drew aside. "I'd like you to meet Signora Newhart. She is Gregorio's tutor."

"How nice." Chiara fingered her champagne flute nervously.

"With her help, Gregorio will go to Harvard," Marco announced.

Oh no, oh no. Not that again. Alarm jolted me forward. I narrowly missed stepping on Chiara's silver sandal. "Oh, Your Majesty, we are preparing him for the tests that could make him eligible for

Harvard. The admission process is very competitive."

"Yes," Sofia broke in, her eyes dancing. "Many things in life are competitive." Did she throw a coquettish look my way?

I was still reeling from Marco's announcement. His expectations were high and they made me uncomfortable.

As Chiara spoke with Marco, the conversation was polite but lackluster. The girl actually talked about the weather. Young and uncertain, she waited for him to take the lead, with Sofia prodding the poor young woman.

I was relieved when Marco excused himself and led us away. "Maybe we will come back to her later," he murmured.

"Not if you are smart," Sofia threw out, which almost made me laugh. Then she added, "But you are all wise, of course."

"No need to flatter me." Marco leveled a playful look at Sofia. "Next?"

Sofia's eyes scanned the crowd. "Elena? Yes, there she is."

Waiters wove their way through the crowd with trays of appetizers that smelled yummy. I was starving and by that time I didn't care if I gained five pounds tonight. I was going to eat. My mouth was full of tenderloin and french bread when we reached Elena. I could only wave when Marco introduced her. Another young woman who bordered on anorexia, she held up a hand when a waiter did another pass with the tenderloin. "Nothing for me, please." And she leaned closer to Sofia. "Bread is so fattening."

Was she looking at me? No way would I be kicked to the curb by a girl who needed to eat more if she knew what was good for her. Snaring another small bite of beef and bread, I kept nibbling.

"Do you like my gown, Your Majesty?" Elena smoothed one hand over a hip. That bone had an edge that rivaled the rocks surrounding the fountain. "Mama took me to Milan the day after we received your invitation."

"Oh, she shouldn't have gone to all that trouble." Sofia's disapproval was obvious. At a startled look from Marco, Sofia must have realized what she'd said. "I mean, that was a lot of trouble."

"Mama says a girl has to look her best." Her blonde hair shimmered when she tilted her head to give Marco a coy smile. "We are hoping I will be married soon."

"Who is the lucky man?" Marco asked without batting an eye.

I choked on the bread. While Sofia patted me on the back, I grabbed a glass of water from a waiter.

"Well, well…" Elena faltered before recovering herself. "My father will decide."

Sofia and I exchanged a look. A darkness flickered over Marco's features.

Sofia jumped in. "Just be sure that your father's choice is also your choice."

"Yes, well." Tears welling in her eyes, Elena gave some excuse and drifted away.

"Next time show more mercy, Marco," Sofia whispered.

Animated conversation flowed around us while the orchestra played. Everyone seemed to be having a good time. Tiny bites of tiramisu were making the rounds and of course I grabbed one.

"Come, come." Marco urged me, as if I were Tesoro or Diablo, here to perform at his will. Had "Will attend social functions" been a part of our contract? I probably should have read that more carefully. "People will want to meet my profesora. And, of course, you must help me choose my queen."

Now, I doubted very much that anyone wanted to meet me. And helping Marco vette his next wife was making me uncomfortable. True, many beautiful women were here tonight. But were they kind? Could they mother Gregorio and give him good advice? I hated this process, and yet I wanted Gregorio to be happy.

But if my employer, who was paying me an outlandish amount of money, wanted me to screen prospective wives, well then, I'd do my best. Handing a waiter my empty glass, I prepared myself to meet the next young woman.

Izabella appeared with a swirl of color and motion. Bracelets sparkled on her arms and huge green emeralds quivered from her ears. The earrings matched her eyes, her gown and an enormous emerald suspended from her neck. I couldn't imagine wearing anything that heavy and I rubbed the back of my neck in commiseration. She was what my mother would have called "well put together."

"Lovely party, Your Majesty." Not hesitating for a moment, she leaned forward for the customary double cheek greeting. Sofia caught Marco's eyes over Izabella's well-coiffed head and smiled, as if she were tolerating a child. "The food is ever so delicious."

"So nice to see you, Izabella. Thank you for coming."

"But of course." She turned to me expectantly. "I don't believe we've met."

Marco leapt into action, his hand gentle on the small of my back. "May I introduce. Christina Newhart...from America."

"An American? So, you must be the teacher they are talking about."

My smile wobbled. Who was talking about me?

Marco didn't bat an eye. "Signora Newhart is, how you say, bringing Gregorio up to speed. For Harvard."

Her glossed lips formed an oval. How I wished Marco would stop with the Harvard intro. Thank goodness Gregorio wasn't around. He winced every time he heard those words. My goal, as I now saw it, was preparing the poor boy to be emotionally ready to enter the world of Harvard if his test scores worked in his favor.

The orchestra had struck up "When I Fall in Love." My heart twisted. The song sang about forever. Did that really happen for anyone?

"Oh, I love this song." Izabella's hands came to her chest in an almost childish gesture. She slid a not-so-subtle glance in Marco's direction. Staring off into the distance, he appeared to be humming. Sofia wore a small smile.

Time for me to exit. "Guess I should check with Lexi," I murmured.

"Oh no. We must dance." With that, Marco swung me into his arms.

My breath caught in my throat. I clung to his arm for support. Chuckling, Sofia led Izabella away. The poor girl looked as if she'd just been in a hit-and-run accident.

"What are we doing?" I stared at him in all his blazing lordship.

That playful grin? Marco clearly thought he had license to do anything. Maybe he was right. Holding my right arm out as if we were going to waltz, he grinned. "Why, we are dancing, of course."

This was crazy. But very exciting. I pushed back a bit and we were off. I couldn't remember the last time I'd waltzed. Wallace hadn't been much for dancing.

"Are you feeling like Jay Gatsby tonight? Does this gala meet with your approval?" I had to smile up at him. He looked so pleased.

Marco's square chin went up and his arm tightened around my waist. "Do I look like him? The Jay Gatsby character?"

The truth was, he looked better. "Oh, yes. You could have been in the movie...along with this castle."

That went over well. He chuckled under his breath. "I'm glad you are here, Christina Newhart from America. You have made my home more...lively."

"Lively? Well, um, good." I'd been called many things. But not lively. Little mousy me? No way.

A breeze had kicked up and my hair would not behave. Marco surprised me by capturing one of my curls in his fingers. Now, I know we can't feel our hair. Not really. Not unless it's torn out at the root. But I felt his fingers, felt the stroke. Saw his eyes turn to velvet when he murmured, "So soft."

I swallowed the biggest lump ever in my throat and somehow sucked in a breath. "Back to dancing, Jay Gatsby, er, Your Majesty."

His raucous laughter made others turn. And I so did not want to be the center of attention. I was really messing this up. "Sorry, Your Majesty. I'm just not used to all this."

"But you like to tease me, yes?" Marco's eyes glittered.

"Yes, I do." And I laughed. "It's fun to tease you, but not too often."

"I love that." With that he threw back his head and roared. Out of the corner of my eye, I caught a glimpse of Ama talking to someone. Hearing her son's antics, she shook her head in disapproval. I couldn't blame her.

"I won't tease you anymore."

His smile collapsed. "Oh, but I want you to. Please. Tease me."

"You are incorrigible."

His Majesty tossed my observation off with a shrug. "I don't know what that means. So I will have to look it up."

"Oh, don't bother. Let me save you the trouble." Almost magnetically our bodies moved closer. My left arm rested on his shoulder and oh my, his shoulders were broad. Where was I? "Incorrigible means naughty."

Marco's arm tightened around me. "I think I like that." He was getting the wrong impression.

"B-bad naughty. You know."

But he didn't know. I could see that in his laughing eyes. Or if he knew, he didn't care. Kings have that license, I supposed. He nipped his lower lip as if he were thinking. Then his eyes moved over me, leaving chills in their wake. "You look lovely tonight, Profesora. So…"

I waited. Time seemed suspended while he searched for words.

But I had heard "lovely." First he called me beautiful. Now he called me lovely.

"I haven't seen that dress in a long time."

"What?" *Stay with the program, Christina.* Marco was swirling me about, and my head was whirling right with us. I felt so disoriented. We'd just passed the fountain. Were we creating a scene? Of course, he was the host and that tuxedo emphasized his broad shoulders and trim hips. But Marco's charming smile would catch attention wherever he went, especially among eligible young ladies and their scheming mothers, or so I supposed.

But back to my gown, which was swirling nicely at that point, as if it were made for waltzing. "So you've seen the dress." I wondered what else Ama had in her magical closet?

"Ah, yes." His words were a sigh.

My excitement deflated. "You don't like it? I'm sorry I thought we were dressing as movie characters."

"And you are Cinderella, yes, I know." But that light in his eyes had dimmed. A sudden weight pressed on my chest. I tripped. Our steps slowed. "You see, that was Bianca's dress. And it was very expensive, as I recall. I suppose my mother did not want to part with it." Here he clucked and shook his head. "My mother can be something else, as you Americans say."

The fabric of the dress burned my skin, or so I thought just then.

"Really, I hadn't noticed." His mother was something else all right, but I'd deal with that later. Back to the dress. "So the dress belonged to Bianca, Gregorio's mother."

"Yes, but Gregorio would not remember. He was too little."
The night had lost its sparkle, and the music receded. Marco gave
me a small shake. "Do not feel sad, Profesora. Please. What
happened was sad, but not for you. You bring your own charm to
the dress."

What had happened to Bianca? But I didn't dare ask. Most
Europeans thought Americans were too bold, too brash and I was
determined that I would not be that way.

"Why do you squeeze your eyes shut."

My eyes flew open. This was just a natural reflex with me. when
I didn't want to face something. Thank goodness I never did it
while driving. But Lexi kidded me about it all the time.

"I'm so sorry for bringing up painful memories. I wouldn't have
worn the dress, had I known."

His featured darkened with concern. "But you didn't know. My
mother made a mistake."

Well, he had that one right. An intentional mistake.

"She means well. You are a big help to me and to Gregorio."
The song had ended. As if she'd overheard our conversation, Ama
appeared at my elbow.

"Mama, are you having a good time?" Marco was such a good
son.

Ama wore her usual stern expression, a lady waiting for the
worst to happen. "Where have Gregorio and your daughter gone?"
She addressed her comments to me.

Glancing around, I bristled at the accusation in her voice. "Are
they missing?"

When was the last time I'd seen Lexi?

Chapter 15

"They are here somewhere." Marco's eyes swept the crowd. The orchestra was playing "Somewhere my Love," another one of my favorite songs. My mind spun. Had I been so busy dancing that I couldn't keep track of my own child?

I'd brought Lexi here to save her from her wild friends and their experimentation. Yes, Gregorio was my student, but had I been ignoring my daughter? After all, Lexi was still Lexi.

"Come. We will look." As he took my hand, Marco spoke into his lapel. What was this? "Milo, we are looking for Gregorio. Please track him."

Track him? Did Marco have some sort of device on his son? At first that appalled me. Then I felt grateful. Wherever Gregorio was, Lexi was probably with him. I tried to keep up as he rushed me from the fountain up to the patio.

"We'll get a good view from here."

Scanning the crowd below, I slid my hand from Marco's. How hard could it be to find Lexi's purple hair? But I didn't see her anywhere.

Marco kept looking until finally he said, "No, I do not see them. Where would they be?" He turned to me.

My mind leapt ahead, as always, just like the time Lexi was supposed to be at a slumber party at Merrilee's. That night something just didn't feel right. And yes, I'd gone snooping, sweeping one hand under Lexi's pillow to see if she'd taken her pajamas. They were gone and for a while, I'd relaxed. Even watched *Mrs. Maisel* episodes on TV.

But the police call later that night shattered my calm. I drove to the station to pick up my daughter. She was shame-faced, her eyes ringed with makeup smeared by tears. There had been a wild party at another girl's house. So wild that a neighbor had called the police. She had lied to me.

That had just been the beginning. But I wouldn't think about all that now.

"Does Gregorio have a special place?" I asked, turning from the party and a carefree life that certainly wasn't mine. "A private place."

"Well, yes. His room. But what would they be doing there?" Marco's voice slowed. I could tell he wasn't used to thinking about stuff like this. After all, the castle was isolated. When he turned, our eyes locked—two parents having the same thought. Just then a slight ping sounded. Marco bent to his lapel, clicked something and listened. "Right. Yes, that makes sense. Thank you, Milo."

He turned. "Follow me. Gregorio is in his quarters."

Scrambling after him, I followed him to the royal family's private rooms. The halls were quiet and the lighting, subdued. All the action was happening outside. At least I hoped it was.

Our footsteps were cushioned by the long runner. Tonight, I

was barely aware of the elegance surrounding me. Where was my daughter? The two of them had been getting along but I'd been busy with lesson plans and horseback riding...with Marco.

Please, please, Lexi. Don't disappoint me. Not when we'd been making progress mending our relationship. I didn't want to be thrust back into the role of warden.

Marco stopped and knocked on one of the recessed doors. "Gregorio? May we come in?" His powerful frame vibrated with impatience. He knocked again. Nothing. We waited.

With a shrug, Marco tested the knob. It turned in his hands. I released a ragged breath. Whatever they were doing, it couldn't be too private.

Like Ama's quarters, Gregorio had a suite. The décor and the lavish furnishings were a contrast to the pieces of clothing draped haphazardly on the priceless chairs. A pair of pants here, a sweater there. A magnificent desk rose along the wall, the laptop a modern anachronism on its leather surface.

Music blared from behind a closed door, but I would have recognized Lexi's giggle anywhere. Frowning, Marco advanced. "Gregorio? We are looking for you," he bellowed.

Gone was the calm and collected parent. Marco's obvious concern almost made me feel better.

Checking back with me, he raised one brow. I must have looked terrified because he softly said, "Profesora, we have found them. What could be wrong?"

Was this man born yesterday? Plenty could be wrong. Although it wasn't easy, I had to downplay my concern. I'd brought Lexi here under false pretenses. Marco had expected a boy, a possible companion for Gregorio. Instead, I'd had Lexi in tow. No way did I want to explain that she was here because she needed watching. Marco opened the door and I followed, my heart beating wildly, almost in time to the music the kids were blasting.

A cool breeze blew through Gregorio's room from the open balcony doors. Marco nodded to me. "They are outside."

My relief came quick but still left questions. Although I felt really uncomfortable going into Gregorio's bedroom, I edged along behind Marco. Gregorio poked his head inside. "Father? What are you doing here?" He stepped toward a stack of electronics and the music stopped.

"Looking for you." Hands on hips, Marco sniffed, as if embarrassed that he'd been brought so low. What royal father had to search for his own child?

From the balcony, a thin trail of smoke curled inside.

In the distance I could hear the party, still going on. At least Marco's departure hadn't caused any alarm. Well, not for anyone but his mother.

By this time, I was on the balcony, studying Lexi, who had coiled her legs into a knot in a wrought iron chair. Her spangled wings lay on the concrete floor next to an ash tray that Gregorio tried to kick aside.

With a mellow look on her face, she peered up at me through a wreath of smoke. Unlike Gregorio, she still held the cigarette.

No way did I want to make a scene. I sniffed the air. Although I'd never smoked, this didn't smell like any cigarette I'd ever smelled at parties. My silence seemed to have an effect. Dropping the cigarette, she ground it into the stones with her Tinkerbell boot.

"So, this is about cigarettes, Gregorio? Nothing more?" Thank goodness Marco had jumped into the fray.

"The party got boring and we wanted a cigarette," Gregorio said. His face flushed.

"Boring?" Marco roared. "You are calling our party...our gala...boring?" Marco's dark brows disappeared under that mass of dark curls.

"For us," Lexi said softly, with a quick glance at Gregorio. "It's a grown-up party."

Marco made a dismissive sound with his lips. Obviously, he expected everyone to be entranced with the party he'd planned so carefully. I felt bad for him. "You two—" he jabbed an imperial finger at them, "—are almost adults."

"But you aren't," I jumped in, just to clarify. "Not yet. You are definitely not adults. So you don't have the privileges of adults. The r-right to decide to do...whatever it is you are doing." I was still uncomfortable with them being in Gregorio's bedroom.

"Exactly." Marco gave a curt nod.

My patience fraying, I wanted to get my daughter alone. Had we ended up right back in the same situation we'd left far behind? "We'll talk about this later, Your Majesty."

He stepped back. I waved her through the room while Marco and Gregorio stared stonily at each other.

Stomping like a five-year-old child, Lexi followed me to the door. Anger rolled off her in waves. The whole situation exhausted me. This was what Wallace had never seen or handled by being the missing father. From what I understood, despite the accident that had changed Lexi's life, she was very good when she was with Wallace. Maybe she was wishing that he would ask her to live with him—the more permissive parent. This attitude? He never got to see it. "It's just a cigarette, Mom."

As she brushed past, Marco turned to me. "Christina, it is just a cigarette."

What? Was he familiar with the other kind of cigarette and could he distinguish one from the other? I was so upset, I couldn't speak. Words failed me. How could I explain this without making Lexi look like teen-age trouble?

At the door, Marco turned. "Gregorio, we will talk later."

"Can I go back to the party?" His son stood there looking repentant and helpless.

Chuckling, Marco turned to me. "The party that was so boring," he murmured to me under his breath.

But he lost the grin when he faced his son again. "Yes, but don't tell Ama about this. She will ask. Just tell her you were…showing Lexi the dungeons."

"No!" Lexi and I said at once.

"Really, Marco." I shook my head at him. "What would two people be doing down there?"

He seemed to turn that over. Such an innocent. This man was going to have a hard time with Gregorio's teenage years if he didn't wise up.

"Mom, what about me?" By this time, we were in the hallway. Lexi turned with a questioning look.

Was she kidding? "Keep walking, Missy. The party's over for you."

The look Lexi speared my way could have taken down an elephant. Sure, it hurt but I pretended not to notice. The two of them took off down the hall. Gregorio followed her partway and then turned off at the first stairway.

Sometimes parenting could be exhausting. A hand on my shoulder, Marco brought me to a halt. "It was just a cigarette, Christina. The European cigarettes can smell different."

Oh, well. "But I don't want her smoking. Where will that lead?"

"What would be so bad? Hmm?" The back of his hand brushed my cheek when he tucked a curl behind my ear.

Just when I was trying to keep myself in check, he had to go and do that. My whole body quivered. What had we been talking about? "At least they weren't…" My words and thoughts drifted off. I was mesmerized by those eyes again.

"Oh, no." With a decisive shake of his head, Marco's features set into forbidding lines. "That cannot happen. Would not happen. After all, Gregorio will be king one day."

My back straightened. What was he saying? What did being king have to do with anything? Marco might be my employer but I wasn't letting this pass. Pivoting, I faced off with His Royal and oh, so irritating Majesty. Over his shoulder hung a portrait of one of his ancestors. The guy in the painting might be from two centuries earlier but he sure looked as if he were sneering at me.

You're not good enough. I felt the force of that dismissive look. But this time I wasn't taking that —not from anyone. "I'm not sure I understand what you're saying."

Marco bit his lip, the way he did when he realized he should choose his words more carefully. "It's just that there are expectations for my son, Christina. And he would not want to ruin them by any...indiscretion with Lexi." Too late, he realized what he'd just said. His face flushed.

My own skin felt burning hot. The man fried my mind. And he'd hurt my feelings terribly. "Really." Well, that just about tore it. My hands went to my hips and I was ready to do battle. The silly romantic dancing out on the back patio was long forgotten. In unguarded moments people could be seen for what they really are.

And Marco was sure looking like a stuck-up, pompous idiot.

But I needed a little clarification first. When my mother was alive, she often warned me about jumping to conclusions. So I sucked in a breath, but the air felt stale and dry in my throat. "Do I understand you to say that my daughter might be a bad influence? Do you think that coming back to his room was her idea?"

Marco directed a level look my way, as if we were standing in his office and this was our first meeting. "Of course not, Profesora."

Oh. Well. So we were back to keeping our roles separate. He was the king and I was the governess. My satisfaction was short-lived. A little piece of my heart wanted to hear my name spoken softly, just one more time.

That wasn't going to happen. He darted a look toward the end of the hall. "Could we talk about this another time? I have guests…"

"But of course, Your Majesty." My tone hit its mark. "When heads are cooler."

Giving me a startled look, Marco ran his fingers through his hair, as if to check the temperature. "My head…is not hot."

This was getting worse by the minute. Marco looked adorable when he was out of his depth.

"This is not about your head or your hair. Please don't take me literally. But we're both upset…"

Dropping his eyes, he tugged at the sleeve of his tuxedo. "I am not upset. But you are being unreasonable."

Opening my mouth, I snapped it shut again. Time to back away so I wouldn't say things I might regret later. I had to keep this position. Gather my wits about me—another one of my mother's favorite phrases. "Good night, then."

Before he could answer, I whirled around and dashed for the stairs. Grabbing the handrail, I lifted my skirt with my left hand so I wouldn't tumble down the steps.

"Good night, Cinderella," Marco called down the stairwell, his voice echoing.

My footsteps faltered on the stone steps. Fingers tight on the leather strap, I kept going. And I made sure both my shoes stayed on my feet.

Chapter 16

A nightmare clung to me as I pulled myself from sleep the next day. I was lost at sea. Not a good thought. I was in some kind of boat—maybe like the one that brought us here—but it was bucking the waves, threatening to capsize. Clutching Lexi, I was desperate not to lose her.

What was that about? Sheet tucked around my chin, I studied the morning light filtering through a slit between the drapes. Dust motes danced on the air.

Dancing. I sucked in a shivery breath, remembering how I'd felt in Marco's arms.

But I would not think about that disastrous party where I'd been forced to judge other women under the laughing eyes of Marco Napolitano. Thank goodness last night I'd put a note on the door that the staff didn't have to make my bed. At first that gesture had seemed thoughtful and charming—like a quality hotel. But now I found it intrusive, as if they were tracking my whereabouts with every move or pawing through my things. And perhaps they were. Marco's words to Milo about finding Gregorio the night before stayed with me.

My thoughts raced as I pulled on my jeans, a white t-shirt and my boots. When I stuck my head out onto the balcony, the morning felt cool. I welcomed it. The low mist creeping over the landscape gave it a ghostly appearance. After I quietly shut the balcony doors, I slipped into a green hoodie. Yanking my hair up into a ponytail, I didn't bother with makeup.

Last night had been a parade of women wearing all kinds of makeup enhancements I'd never seen before. Rhinestones spiraled above their smoky eyes, often outlined in kohl with other subtle colors. Lipstick shades ranged from a garish turquoise to bright orange. Too much—the whole affair had been too much.

Marco's friends and family were definitely a different world and I was an unwelcome visitor. The trick Ama had played on me with the dress still rankled. She wanted me to look out of place, to *feel* as if I didn't belong here. I couldn't decide whether I should get even in some equally petty way or if I should rise above it. My mother's voice whispered in my ears. "Move on, sweetheart," she would say. With a sigh, I zipped up my hoodie.

Not wanting to awaken Lexi, I crept out the door and gently closed it. The castle felt so quiet. Class began at nine, so I had plenty of time to grab something in the kitchen and take a quick ride on Tesoro to clear my head.

Because the elevator had a certain low-key clatter that might be magnified in this silence, I scurried down the stairs. When I reached the kitchen, staff were cleaning up after last night. Huge pots stood on counters along with trays and buffet serving pans. Crystal and silver serving pieces were grouped on another with cleaning cloths ready.

Constanza had been hard at work. The scent of fresh baking tempted me. Giving her a quick smile, I grabbed a cornetto, a couple of carrots and headed out. On my way to the stables, I bit into the flaky pastry. The talented cook never disappointed. The treat of warm chocolate melted on my tongue.

Outside, a beautiful morning awaited. The staff was sweeping and raking the ground. Marco did like to keep everything tidy. On two side tables, the ice sculptures had melted, leaving only sodden tablecloths. You would almost never know that last night two hundred people had laughed, sipped champagne and danced. I shook my head, thinking about the elaborate party here where he'd graded women on their queenly attributes. Maybe I should have given him a score sheet. Really, Marco was such a trip.

But he was a prize. The party had awakened me to this fact. Even without his crown, he might be a man worth wanting. Attractive. Funny. A good father.

Well. Seemed that I'd done a one-eighty with King Marco. *There will be none of that, Missy.* Popping the last bite into my mouth, I strolled over the dew-tipped grass and down the gravel path to the stable.

The quiet sound of horses munching their feed and the sweet smell of hay filled me with contentment. A tiny kitten tumbled onto the path—a fluffy ball of gray and white. "Now, who do you belong to?" Scooping up the furry mass, I peeked into an empty stall nearby. A mother cat was stretched out, nursing a passel of kittens. She barely lifted her head when I settled the kitten back at her side.

My boots echoed on the pavers as I ambled over to Tesoro's stall. Had she recognized my footsteps? The beauty hung her head out and nickered. I stroked her neck, my own head against hers while I fed her the carrots. "We're in this together, Tesoro."

Footsteps behind me made me turn.

"Ah, Signora." Rudolfo glanced at the clock on the wall. "So early today, even after the party?"

"Yes, I like early." And today I also wanted to be alone. I had to sort out my feelings about Lexi and Gregorio. Had I overreacted?

Entering the tack room, I grabbed the striped blanket I used with Tesoro and took it to her stall. "Maybe someday you'll be a mother," I muttered to her while I settled the blanket over her back. "Sure, babies might be wonderful, so soft and cuddly. But as they grow up, they can give you nothing but trouble."

The mare bobbed her head as if she understood. Or maybe she was just lowering her head to eat more hay. Seconds later, I led her from the stable.

"Alone?" Rudolfo came up behind me, giving me a worried glance.

"Yes, I'm fine alone."

But he didn't look convinced. "Tesoro knows the way home," I reminded him.

That seemed to placate Rudolfo, although he still lingered. I should be grateful. Putting one foot in the stirrup I launched myself over Tesoro's back, hoping I looked more confident than I felt.

The early morning air bathed my face, damp and clean. I drank it in as we set off at a relaxed pace. I gave Tesoro the lead and she took me into the same woods I'd traveled with Marco not too long ago. I smiled recalling the pace Marco had set. Patting Tesoro's neck, I murmured encouraging words to her. If only children were like horses and would do your bidding.

Glancing around, I took in every tree, every wildflower and even the squirrels chattering in the trees. If I'd stayed home this summer, what would I have been doing? Maybe I'd call Reena or Maddie and we'd go to the beach to loll about at the shore's edge, legs stretched out from our beach chairs. But Reena was off on her own adventure this summer. Not too long later, I checked my watch. Time to return and I circled back, giving Tesoro her head again.

And of course, she got us back to the stable, where Rudolfo waited. "I told you I'd be fine." I slipped from Tesoro's back.

The man's eyes widened and crooked his head. Marco pushed himself off from Diablo's stall, his face thunderous.

"What? Is something wrong?" Unhitching the girth, I slid the saddle off.

Stepping up with a sigh of impatience, Marco reached for it.

Although the saddle was heavy, I managed to twist away. "So independent," I heard him mutter behind my back, following me into the tack room.

"Are you over your...tantrum?" he asked, standing in my way when I went out to whisk the blanket from Tesoro's back.

"Tantrum." I pivoted to face him. "I was concerned for my daughter's safety."

He blew out a breath. "You are safe here. Your daughter is safe here. Gregorio would never do anything to harm her or compromise her."

"Right. I know. Because your son will be king one day." His words would burn in my memory a long time. But I hadn't meant to blurt that out.

"Exactly. So you understand." He didn't catch the sarcasm in my voice.

Why did I even bother? Marco was thick-headed when it came to women and so condescending. Maybe all royalty was like that.

But Marco didn't leave. As I took a brush to Tesoro, he said. "You went out alone?"

"Yes, of course." His eyes burned into my back.

"Do you think that is...safe?"

I spun around. "Yes, I was perfectly safe with Tesoro."

Marco pursed his lips. Was he laughing at me? One of his shiny boots brushed at the hay on the floor. "After class today, please come to my office. We must talk about things."

"Things." Now, that sounded ominous.

"Yes, you know, as we discussed."

What in heaven's name was he talking about? The bright morning faded. Suddenly I felt very tired. "Sure. Yes, of course." Handing the reins to Rudolfo, who hovered, I took off for the castle, trying to pull my thoughts together for class.

When I walked into the classroom that day, Gregorio and Lexi both seemed subdued. The day had become cloudy. No sunshine fell through the long, narrow windows. So we made our way through a lackluster discussion of *To Kill a Mockingbird*. I would have to come back to this later. I was thinking that the day was lost.

Then Gregorio asked, "Can this really happen in America?"

His innocence and incredulity touched me. "Yes, sadly, this kind of thing can happen in America. We have this racism in our history." I thought back to what he shared about his own country. "But if you come to America for an education, you'll hear more about this." Since I didn't want to discourage him, I left it there.

Both Gregorio and Lexi seem relieved when our minds turned to math. The wonderful thing about mathematics was that things were so clean. There were no interpretations to be discussed. I liked that about numbers.

Not long after that, I ended the class. Both of them seemed eager to scamper away. I was left alone in a room that was colder than any classroom I'd ever had. And I wasn't thinking about the temperature. The heat continued. That hadn't changed. But this room had no character. I could hardly begin decorating it with a bulletin board or anything like that. We were here to study—nothing more.

Yes, Gregorio was coming along nicely. I couldn't deny that. Soon, I would begin giving him the prep tests for the SAT. I wanted him to be fully prepared and comfortable as he sat for his exam, wherever that might be. But today the life had gone out of what I was teaching. Was I letting my personal life interfere?

Today I couldn't have lunch in the dining room. Instead, I circled through the kitchen. Giving a smile to Constanza, I grabbed some ham and cheese from the refrigerator. With a knowing smile, she cut off a slab of fresh bread. After a quick "thank you," I took my picnic outside to the fountain. As I sat there on this cloudy day, my mind went back to the party.

The evening had truly been a successful night for Marco. The gathering had given me a chance to see him with his peers. He hadn't been the only king there, that much I knew. As my eyes followed Ama through the crowd, I could tell by the way people reacted to her who was royalty. They formed their own community, secure in their entitled worlds. Royalty was a closed society. Oh, we may be invited in to serve them but it was not wise to confuse their friendliness with acceptance. Maybe I should explain that to Lexi.

Marco had made that clear. Lexi was not good enough for Gregorio. She could be a study partner but that was all. If they emailed each other after this summer, those contacts would no doubt fall off after a while. That thought brought a hollowness to my chest.

Chapter 17

My shoes slid on the pavers where we'd danced last night. The memory slowed my steps. When I squeezed my eyes shut tight, Marco's arms were around me, his laugh reverberating in my chest. That evening had been magical.

Magical nonsense.

Getting back to reality, I entered the castle and stomped toward Marco's office. Shoulders straight, I shook off my nervousness. This wasn't my first day on the job. We had business to discuss— or so he'd said. I knocked at the solid door so hard that I skinned my knuckles.

"Come in!" He sounded irritated.

My hand stinging, I pushed the door open.

"Milo– " Seated at his desk, Marco peered at me over the tops of his glasses. His face flushed as he whisked them off. They disappeared into a desk drawer.

"Profesora. Come in. I was expecting Milo."

"But you told me to come."

"Yes, yes. Forgive me." Waving a fistful of papers, he motioned toward one of the chairs in front of his enormous desk. "Please sit down."

Stay cool, Christina. With a sigh, I sank into the chair and tried to still my mind.

"So what did you think of the party last night?" he asked as soon as I'd settled myself.

"My opinion doesn't really matter, does it? More importantly what did you think of it?" Okay, I wasn't keeping cool.

Marco laughed—one of those explosions of delight. "You surprise me all the time, Profesora. Sophia was very pleased to meet you."

That coaxed a smile from me. I'd liked his sister-in-law. "She seemed very nice. Very easy to talk to." But I'd felt a little guarded with her since she had a direct line to Marco, as well as Gregorio. After all, she was his godmother.

"Now, what did you want to talk about?" I'd stick with business no matter how distracted I became. No musing about his tousled hair or the hands that had toyed with my hair only last night.

He drew back, as if surprised. "I wanted your opinion on the prospects, of course. You know, the ladies you met last night."

This was getting old fast. "Then I would only be judging them on their looks. And that is hardly the measure of a woman."

My words had been sharp and one brow lifted. I hated that look on Marco. But only because I liked it too much. A tingling began in my chest. Maybe I was having a stroke or something.

"The measure of a woman?" His brow settled. Marco seemed to be struggling to get his mind around that concept.

"I'm not talking about how much she weighs or how tall she is." I began to explain but the expression on his face told me I was only confusing him. "What are you looking for in your next wife?"

Next wife. How insensitive. The words might remind him of Bianca and his terrible loss. But wasn't he the guy who put her in the tower? Watching him slump in his gilded high-back chair, I felt ashamed of myself. "The women all seem very nice."

"Nice?" He looked perplexed.

I searched my mind. "Gabriella certainly hasn't given up on you."

"But you said she does not like Gregorio."

The fact that he remembered my words touched me. "When she came for lunch that day, she didn't seem to make a genuine effort with him. Gregorio is going into his teenage years and needs attention." This felt so hypocritical. Hadn't Lexi needed attention and hadn't I failed to provide it?

"I see. Yes, of course." He played with a pen on his desk.

My mind spun ahead. I did not want to even think about Gregorio getting lost in the shuffle if Marco had a second family. And that was sure to happen. It wasn't difficult to imagine Marco marrying one of the many young women eager to sign on for that job. *Fertile Turtles.* That what they used to call young women ready to bear children. Together they'd create another royal family. What effect will that have on Gregorio? He might be crushed. On the other hand, if he were living and studying in America by that time, Marco's new wife might not matter much to him.

My concern for a boy I didn't even know existed two months ago stunned me.

Running a finger over his full lips, Marco seemed to be thinking this over. "Those are all good points. Besides, she seems to be a little silly…no?" He looked to me for agreement.

I opened my hands palms up as if to suggest *up to you*. No way did I want to get deeper into this. Rocking his head back onto his chair, he peered up at the chandelier.

My goodness, Marco had a strong neck. A neck that could cuddle a woman. A neck that had been very close to my cheek last night.

Oh mercy. I brought a hand to my cheek. What had we been saying?

"And what about Chiara?" Jerking his head back to the task, he tapped the pen against the papers in front of him. Almost like a drummer. A hot drummer.

"She is very pretty. I mean, if pretty is what you want."

So here we were again, discussing physical attributes. Was this the way it was going to go with him? Probably so. "I suppose you want your children to be attractive."

"My children?" The pencil fell. He almost levitated from the chair.

Had I been wrong? Certainly he'd considered this.

"Of course. Your children with any of the women we talked to last night would be beautiful…or very handsome. Those women were all gorgeous. But there has to be more to a marriage than looks."

Thinking back to Wallace, I couldn't control a backward glance at the marriage that had nearly destroyed me. I had been so taken by him. Tall and attractive, he was well spoken. His students loved him. Had he ever had an affair? Sometimes I wondered. But by that time the marriage was ending.

I tried to organize my thoughts. Back to Chiara. *Think of this as one of your final exams, Christina. A test on character development.* Unlike the targeted Gabriella, who had very definite opinions, Chiara had seemed somewhat shy. Ama would eat her for lunch. I had to bring that up. "Chiara is somewhat shy, isn't she?" I posed the question, glancing over at Marco and feeling my way.

Feeling my way with Marco. Nope, don't go there.

"Yes. You have a good point. She considers what she says before speaking. But that is good, no?"

His dark eyes questioned mine. Keeping my face neutral was not easy. "That is a very good quality, if you want a woman who would guard her every word with you. Who would not tell you what she was thinking."

Eyes now impenetrable, Marco retreated into some dark place. "What is it? Have I been too honest?"

He began flicking his lips with a forefinger. A slow swirling began in my stomach as I watched. "No, honesty is good. I'm just thinking back. Bianca was like that. She was a scared little kitten."

Thinking of that tiny kitten in the stable, my heart went out to the girl who had been Marco's young bride. Who'd ended up in that isolated tower room. "How young was she?"

"Eighteen when we married. We had Gregorio a year later." His eyes grew bleak as he thought back. "Now I realize she was too young. I was in my late twenties."

This was absolutely none of my business so I would not ask. I pressed my lips together but the words in my head blasted them apart anyway. "What happened to Bianca—if y-you don't mind my asking?" The last words came stuttering out. This was a minefield.

"Yes, you may ask. Because I really don't understand it, even now." He gave his head a shake. "She became so unhappy. Maybe she had always been that way. Later I thought maybe she married me to get away from her parents, who were very strict with her.

"She argued with my mother about everything, especially after having Gregorio. That room in the tower? She insisted on it after the baby. Although I loved her very much, she would not let me touch her." Marco looked so sad. "I think she took her own life, Christina."

I felt gutted. "Does Gregorio know that?"

Marco shook his head. "No. Bianca was not herself, even though I took her to the best psychologist…" He glanced at me. "Is that the right word."

"Yes. Yes it is."

"Well, he was the best in Milan. He gave her those pills. But her unhappiness grew."

"Oh dear." Now that tower room seemed even more sad. "Gregorio took us there."

"He did?" Marco looked amazed.

"Well, yes, the day that we toured the dungeon…"

Marco rolled his eyes. "Why?"

Time to recover or Gregorio might be put on the spot. "The tour was very educational. I wanted Lexi to see it. You know, kind of a glance into medieval Napolitano." What total nonsense.

He gave a dismissive guffaw. "Medieval?"

I swallowed hard. Better go back to Chiara. "Do you want a wife who would be on eggshells around you?"

Frowning, Marco gave a serious shake of his head. "That sounds very uncomfortable. Is that something they do in America? Maybe for fertility?"

I giggled. The idea of Marco crunching eggshells with his very substantial feet created quite a picture in my mind.

"You're laughing at me?" He pushed back from the desk. But not before I saw the impish tilt to his lips.

"Please forgive me." I could hardly get the words out around my giggles. "I don't want to offend Your Majesty. Walking on eggshells is a figure of speech."

His frown grew deeper. "Oh, one of those again."

"It's a phrase that Americans choose to describe how uncomfortable a person could be. You don't want your wife to feel uncomfortable around you? Afraid to say what's really on her mind?"

"No, of course not. You make me think so hard, Profesora." Resting his elbows on the arms of the chair, Marco steepled his hands in front of his lips.

"Don't you want someone who is equal to you?" The words were no sooner out of my mouth then I realized how ridiculous they were for a man who was king of all he surveyed, including his wife.

"But she would not be equal to me. Were you equal to your husband?"

"In many ways, yes."

"So it is like this in America?"

Would he reconsider sending his son over there for school? "In some ways. A husband and a wife can be unequal. I mean, perhaps one of them earns more money than the other." And didn't that sway the balance? Wallace had always controlled the checkbook.

Maybe this was a better way to put this. "Do you want a wife who would tell you only what you want to hear? For example, if your hair was all messy, should she tell you that you looked wonderful—handsome like that?"

Dear heavens, I couldn't help it. My eyes went to his dark curls. They looked fabulous to me. He raked a hand into them, improving that roguish look even more. He must have shampooed his hair this morning to wash out all that glistening gel from last night.

Keep on track.

"Don't you want a woman who can tell you when it is time to tidy up?" Had I lost my mind? I was feeling a little swoony. Maybe it was this blasted heat.

"Tidy up?" He patted his hair. The curls would not be flattened. Gregorio had those curls. They did make Marco look quite boyish. But enough of staring at his hair.

I plowed on. "When you are with your wife, do you want to have interesting conversations about world events, for example? Or do you want to only talk about the food you are eating, or, I don't know, what color to paint the hallways?"

Seeming to take this quite seriously, he ran a hand over his chin. "Now I think I see. No, I do not want to talk about paint."

"Probably not, although sometimes a couple has to deal with the everyday running of a household." My eyes flitted around the room and I nearly giggled again. This man's home was so different from anything profiled in the popular home decorating magazines.

When I glanced back, Marco was studying me. "So, what would a husband and wife talk about?"

Glancing at the newspaper on his desk, I said. "World events, for example. Things going on in the village. Or plans for your children. Every parent has great plans."

"World events?" Springing to his feet, Marco began to pace. "This does not sound very romantic. This is what a marriage is in America? And yet, people have children?"

I was making a mess of things. "At first, you might be attracted to someone by how beautiful they are or their perfume. Those things don't last. But if you don't have more enduring qualities that please you, well, then you can become lost." Something happened toward the end. The words had taken me back into the past. Tears were close and I sniffed. *Where was a tissue when you needed it?*

Coming back to his desk, Marco stared down at me, his dark brown eyes supporting my pain. "Is that what happened to you, Profesora? Did these things that you liked about your husband go away. Poof." Here he snapped his fingers.

How did we ever end up here? I did not want to talk about my ex. "What about Elena? Maybe she might be the one for you? She certainly is attractive." But skinny. Almost anorexic.

"Her mother makes me nervous," he admitted with a shrug, settling himself on the edge of the desk. "Her father died last year.

Elena's mother would probably want to live with us."

"Now that would be unusual. But some couples do it."

"That would be impossible." He raised his eyes back to the ceiling. "Who else?"

Thinking back to last night, I went over the names Sofia had so kindly provided. "Izabella. What do you think of her?" But I could not hide my smile.

"You are laughing. What is it?"

I ducked my head, "It's just that she is so noisy. All that jewelry. Do you think she wears that all the time?"

He smiled "I would always hear her coming."

We laughed together. "But what do you want in a wife?" I asked, going back to that critical point.

Marco flattened a hand on his chest, almost where his heart was. "For a wife you must have the passion, no? You should want her more than you want a good meal. You should want to take her in your arms all the time and make passionate love to her."

My breath was coming fast. His face was flushed. I pressed my back against the chair.

Shoving off from the desk, Marco went back to pacing. And this room was long. "Back to the married couples who talk about paint. I cannot believe this."

"Um, the conversation might not be about paint but maybe about the trash that needs to be taken out or why his clothing is scattered on the floor." Where was this stuff coming from? Marco's horror grew with each misspoken word tumbling from my lips.

"This does not sound very romantic." He'd come up behind me, hands gripping my chair. "I would think a man would talk about a woman's neck, how lovely it is…like a swan's."

I couldn't move. Was he looking at my neck?

"Or perhaps her eyes." He circled around and yes he was staring down on me, one hand on each of the arm rests. No way could I escape. "Maybe a husband would tell his wife that her eyes were as blue as the sea, and he wanted to swim in those eyes forever."

Good thing I was sitting down or I just might swoon. Or did women only do that in books? *Breathe, breathe.* I couldn't look up. I just couldn't.

His spicy scent enveloped me. Yes, he must have showered right before this meeting. *Oh mercy.* And now he bent closer.

"Maybe he would tell his wife that he enjoys watching her eat his grapes. Enjoys seeing her eyes grow warm with delight at the taste because he knows she would also like his wine."

Yep. Pretty soon I would faint. It was so darn hot in here.

But he wasn't finished with me. "Because no man can love a woman who does not let him know her feelings." His breath swept my cheeks and I felt my lips plump from the heat of his words.

"What woman are w-we talking about here?" My voice was a whisper.

His eyes on my lips, Marco bent his head closer. The heat banking in his eyes was too much. I closed mine and waited.

A knock sounded at the door. "Yes, come on in." Marco pushed up and away. I drew breath and heard his frustrated exhale.

Craning my apparently swanlike neck, I turned around just as Ama entered. She did not look pleased to see me. "Oh, you are busy." She slid her hands into her wide cuffs. How the woman put up with all these flowing gowns in the summer heat was beyond me.

Pushing up, I stepped aside. "I should go."

Marco gestured to his mother. "Come in, come in."

Face burning, I scurried toward the door.

"And don't forget tonight, Christina."

"Tonight?" Ama and I both said at once.

"Yes, movie night. Gregorio said he would tell you. We are watching the greasy show."

"Greasy show?" I turned that over in my mind.

Marco circled the air impatiently with one hand. "Yes, yes. Lexi told Gregorio it was very popular in your country."

Then it hit me. "Oh, *Grease*. Yes, it's about the 1950s in America."

"Good. Historical, no?" Honestly, Marco could be so cute when he tried to understand things. After his admission that he'd never been to college, I found his need to know quite charming.

"Pardon me," I said as I stepped around the woman who was a total mystery to me.

"Your face is very red," Ama said with suspicion as I edged around her.

"Yes, it is so hot. I was asking Marco to have fans sent to the nursery." And with that I left.

Chapter 18

Grease had always been one of my favorite movies and Lexi loved it too. I suspected that Gregorio had learned about the musical through my daughter. When I realized that Ama was not in Marco's little theater, I felt only relief. Maybe she wasn't here because Marco had scheduled this showing for the evening.

Marco's mother seemed pretty strait-laced. What would she think of this film that depicted the rock and roll era of America's past? Tonight the seating was different. Lexi quickly took the seat next to Gregorio on the other side of the narrow aisle. That left me next to Marco. Before I could make a switch, the movie began. I settled back to lose myself again in the story of a girl from Australia who comes to America one summer. In typical summer romance style, the innocent Sandy falls in love with a "greaser," from his slicked back hair to his boots.

And then school starts, and she discovers that he's really a hot-rodder with a reputation with the women. Reclining my seat, I looked forward to seeing the movie on this large screen. Our screen at home was tiny compared to the one in Marco's theater.

And what else was there to do at night in the castle but watch movies? Although we'd taken a couple of trips into town, the village that had felt like a leap to freedom at the beginning of the summer began to feel provincial.

Sitting beside me, Marco seemed totally engrossed in the movie. To my amazement, popcorn appeared from somewhere. "What is this?" I asked Gregorio, who was handing out the small bowls heaped with popcorn that smelled wonderful.

He shushed me with a finger to his mouth. "I hope you like the butter," he whispered. "I read there should be butter. Constanza gets ours from Ireland."

Irish butter? The very best. "Absolutely." I sank my fingers into the buttery mass. The salt made me lick my lips. Next to me, Marco followed suit.

During the classic film, I could feel him watching me, which was totally uncomfortable since I was wolfing down the popcorn. "Stop watching me," I hissed, wiping off my buttery lips.

"Why?" Marco chuckled. "I like watching you eat."

"That's very weird." My face flushed.

"Mom, be quiet." But Lexi wore a smile, as if she enjoyed scolding me.

When we came to the final rendition of "You're the One that I Want," Gregorio hunched his shoulders and moved to the music. Next to me, Marco noticed. He pointed to Gregorio and chuckled. "Did you teach him that?"

"Should I add dancing to my curriculum?" The thought made me smile.

"If he should know that to study in America, yes."

"I'll think about it. He's having fun," I whispered.

We went back to watching the movie. "Yes, this does look like fun." There was a plaintive note in Marco's voice. Was he a little boy who had lost his childhood? Had he been pushed into the role of monarch way before his time?

The movie ended. Gregorio collected the empty bowls and pop bottles. After flipping my seat into an upright position, I stood up and stretched. To my surprise, Ama was sitting right behind us. Her face was set, as if frozen by botox.

"What did you think?" I asked Gregorio as we stood at the door.

"I think they have a lot of fun in American high school." Was there a wistful note to his voice?

"Trust me, my high school is nothing like this." Lexi gave his arm a playful sock.

Marco turned to me. "Will this be the kind of students Gregorio will know at Harvard?"

"Oh, no. No." The idea of John Travolta walking down the paths at staid Harvard with slicked back hair and tight black jeans was ludicrous. "*Grease* was very popular in America because many people remembered this time, probably around the 1950s. They enjoyed the cast and the music. But that time is gone. There are no more races down the culverts, if ever there were."

"That is very good, no, Gregorio?" Reaching over, Marco ruffled Gregorio's hair as if he were four again. His son didn't look happy.

"It looked like fun," Gregorio said. "I would be happy to have such races."

"Such crazy talk." Behind me, Ama gave a disapproving huff.

Marco and I exchanged a look. "No, there will be no races at Harvard," I said with confidence. Although I'd visited the campus just outside Boston, I had no idea what happened in their classrooms. But I did hope that it wouldn't include the problems I'd run into with Lexi. If he were accepted, Gregorio would be there alone. That would concern me. Life on the island was so secluded. So protected. Even their clothing sometimes seemed like costumes, plucked from another era. Maybe that was how Marco protected himself and the family.

Once out in the corridor, Ama shuffled away. Her shoulders hunched, as if weighed down by everything she'd seen tonight.

"The movie might have been a little much for your mother." I turned to Marco, who simply smiled. "Maybe this was a bad choice for tonight."

"My mother is very conservative." His eyes followed her as she marched down the hall. "But she is also very strong."

Suddenly the corridor lined with historic mementos of Marco's past closed in on me. I choked. "I need some fresh air."

Bending his head, Marco studied me with concern. "I will come with you." He took my elbow. "Gregorio, see that Lexi gets to her room."

Gregorio turned. "Can we go to the pool for a quick dip?"

"Please, Mom?" Lexi threw in.

Marco and I exchanged a glance.

"They'll be fine," I said, not wanting to argue about this.

"They'll watch out for each other. I don't think it's safe to swim alone." Sometimes a mother gets very tired from worrying about her child. Tonight I was at that point.

The two disappeared down the hall. Marco pushed open the door leading to the patio and the fountain. The cool night air rushed to meet me, a breeze lifting my hair. "This feels so good."

Glancing over, Marco said. "Yes, wonderful." But his thoughts did not seem to be on the night air. Instead he was looking at my hair. Catching my questioning glance, he smiled and shoved his hands into his pockets.

My disappointment took me by surprise. I'd wanted him to take my hand and that was crazy.

Marco took the lead. "Come. We'll sit at the fountain." Together, we crossed the grass and settled on one of the stone benches. I didn't move away when Marco's shoulder touched mine. "Sometimes I like to sit here at night."

As we sat facing the castle, I looked up. My window was clearly visible. "I left a lamp on at the side table."

"Yes, I know." He wore a secret smile. Did he sit out here, looking at my window? No, that was wishful thinking on my part.

"It feels so good out here." Leaning back on my elbows, I drank in the night.

"What would you be doing at home right now?" Marco asked.

"Probably watching a movie or sleeping."

A soft smile teased his lips. "You must be beautiful when you sleep."

I sat up with a jerk. "What?" That comment had come out of nowhere.

Even in the darkness there was no mistaking the ruddy color working its way up Marco's cheeks. His head dropped but he zinged me with a sassy sideways glance. "You cannot blame me from wondering, Christina."

Christina? What had happened to "Profesora"?

"Wondering about what?"

When Marco smiled, lines radiated from his eyes. "Oh, many things."

"Like what?" I should have stopped there.

"Like how you look when you sleep." He turned his attention to the window. "Do you sleep on your tummy like a little girl, or on your side? Or do you lie on your back like a queen?"

"On my side." Were we going to play twenty questions? "How about you?"

"Oh, I sleep on my stomach. Have since I was a little boy."

"Wow." Now it was my turn to blush. Picturing him sleeping on his stomach brought a warm rush.

"Wow, what, Christina Newhart?"

I swallowed. Surely he could hear my dry gulp. "I'm surprised that you don't sleep on your back, like a king."

His restless groan sounded agonizing. "Sometimes I do not want to be a king."

I nearly fell back into the fountain but tightened my grip on the stone ridge. "Now, that's amazing."

"Why?" The wind kicked up. My hair blew everywhere. He captured strands in his fingers studying them as if my hair were the most interesting thing he'd ever seen. "I'm glad you do not fix your hair like those girls in the movie."

I chuckled. At the end of *Grease*, Olivia Newton John had her hair shaped into a bushy hairdo, probably plastered with hair spray. "I'm glad too."

Wearing a bemused smile, Marco let the strands slip through his fingers. "No, your hair is so soft." With that he angled his body, one shoulder slipping behind mine.

"Is it?" That was all I could say?

But I was caught by his eyes. Mesmerized by the feelings rushing though me.

"I liked dancing with you at the party." Marco closed his eyes as if he were remembering. And he hummed a line or two.

"I think you're off tune."

"What?" He pretended to be irritated. "You dare to question a king?"

Dipping his head, he was so very close. The words were whispered against my lips. They plumped. Oh, I wanted him to kiss me, but that would be very wrong. That playful glint in his eyes told me he knew that too.

Not that it stopped him.

The first kiss was soft and questioning.

"This is so…inappropriate," I murmured.

He smiled before kissing me again. "Nothing that a king does can be inappropriate. You use that word a lot."

"What word?" My vocal chords felt paralyzed. He kept kissing me, each kiss stronger, deeper.

"Inappropriate." His arms went around me. Were the stars

making me dizzy or was it Marco? "What does that mean?"

"It means something you shouldn't be doing."

This might be wrong but it felt very right—something I'd waited for all my life. The kiss went on, along with chuckles and sighs. We tried different angles, laughed when our noses bumped. But what was I doing? Pulling away, I struggled to my feet. The path was uneven and not well lit.

"Christina, no. Please." Marco reached for my hand.

"I can't. We shouldn't." And I backed away. If I stayed, another kiss could be my undoing. One kiss. That's all it took. Because I had never been kissed like that before. And these feelings? Totally new to me. New and dangerous.

***

In the days that followed I had my head in the clouds. And I smiled at how puzzled Marco would be at that expression. No way would I let myself think or feel. If I did, I would be lost. Lost in the arms of a man who'd opened my world to another life with one kiss. Other possibilities. Me. A woman of forty-two, I was in love for the first time.

Hopelessly in love with King Marco Giovanni Pietro di Napolitano.

After that night at the fountain, I avoided Marco. In the mornings, I dashed down to the kitchen to grab something to eat. Then it was off to the stable for a ride with Tesoro. To my relief and disappointment, Marco didn't show up. As Tesoro and I rode freely over the field and through the forest, I emptied my heart. The mare nickered in agreement. By the time I brushed her down,

I was exhausted physically and emotionally.

As July ground by, one breathlessly hot day after another, I pushed through the classes with Gregorio. He'd finished many of the American classics and we started on British literature, including Shakespeare. Lexi and Gregorio had a spirited discussion of *Romeo and Juliet*, which made me start to wonder.

"Nothing is going on between the two of you, right?" I asked my daughter later that evening.

Rolling her eyes, Lexi went back to stabbing at her phone. "Mom, really. He's a friend. I'm glad to have one here or I'd be alone."

"But, Lexi, you have me."

"I know. But that's different. I need friends my own age."

"Of course. He's two years older than you." And Gregorio was changing fast.

Another eyeroll. "Mom, really. He's a child. A fun guy but immature, like most boys."

I decided to leave it there.

When I located the pretests Mary Carmichael had mentioned, Gregorio seemed ready. To my relief, he did well with them. I had to play them down to Marco or he would have been packing Gregorio's suitcases or sending out announcements. We had time.

In the afternoons, Lexi and I cooled off in the pool and sometimes Gregorio joined us. But Marco did not. *Well, why would he, Christina?* My employer had made a mistake. A kiss born of a night that was oh, so romantic. I should be relieved that it hadn't gone beyond kisses. Anything more reckless was unthinkable.

One afternoon, Lexi had a summer cold and I was not brave enough to go to the pool alone with my books. That day I'd skipped lunch, so I trotted down to wheedle something from Constanza. The tantalizing smells coming from the kitchen told me the cook was working her magic. Lost in my own thoughts, I heard the voices just as I turned the corner into the kitchen. And the voices were not Constanza talking to staff. My sandals skidded on the tiles as I tried to stop before I was seen.

Gregorio and his grandmother were hunched over a pot of boiling water. He held a slotted spoon. "Take them out of the water when they have just turned," Ama told him, making a scooping motion. "They should not be brown like sausages."

What was this? The two of them chuckled together. On the long stove top in back of them, a pan simmered. Whatever was in the pan smelled heavenly.

When the two looked up, Gregorio almost dropped his spoon.

"You are cooking? How nice."

Surprise faded fast from Ama's eyes. Her long apron was a new look for the Queen Mother. "What? You have never seen two people cook?"

"Well yes. But not you!"

Gregorio's face flushed red.

Ama took the spoon from his hand. "I'll finish the gnocchi, Gregor. Don't let the chicken burn."

Gregor? I'd never heard her use that nickname with her grandson.

"I like to cook, Profesora," Gregorio told me with an apologetic look at his grandmother.

"And he's very good at it," she spoke up defensively, her delicate chin coming out.

Gregorio glowed under Ama's praise. "Nonna is an excellent cook," he told me. And he pointed to his grandmother, who could not meet my eyes.

I was speechless.

"Sit." Ama pointed to one of the stools. Grabbing a small plate, she scooped up some of the gnocchi and then spooned the chicken with mushrooms on top.

Ama handed me a fork. Under their watchful eyes, I tasted. The gnocchi and chicken yielded under my teeth and sang a love song in my mouth. Was that me groaning with delight? "How delicious. The seasoning is perfect."

"A family secret." Ama cut me off as if she were afraid I would ask for the recipe.

"Nonna often makes the main meal for us." Gregorio might be revealing more than Ama would have allowed.

My, the surprises just kept coming. Glad that I was sitting down, I couldn't stop eating. Nothing had prepared me for this revelation. Of course, I'd noticed that all three of them loved food. But this was gastronomically special—tastier than anything I'd ever had in a restaurant. "It's delicious, Gregorio."

"Tell her," Ama prodded him after I'd finished. The sampling had made me eager for dinner.

"Tell me what?" I noticed how lovingly Gregorio covered the large iron skillet.

"It is n-nothing," he finally stammered.

Ama's face fell. "It is everything. You tell her."

Gregorio's sigh reached the low arched ceiling. He gave his grandmother an exasperated glance and then turned to me. "I do not want to go to Harvard, Profesora. I do not want to run the winery."

"What?" What was he saying? But as I sat there, tasting his food, suddenly everything made sense. "The cooking?"

Ama's hands were folded into her wide sleeves, the way they were when she was about to make a pronouncement. "Gregorio wants to be a chef. And he will be one of the greatest chefs in the world."

"But I don't understand. Then why are we studying for the admission exams?"

She tilted her head at me as if to say, *how can you be such a stupid woman?*

"My father doesn't know." Misery weighed Gregorio's words.

I waved my hand across the kitchen. "He doesn't know you cook?"

"Shh." Ama quickly shushed me. "Do you want the whole world to hear you?" Her eyes skittered down the long room, checking every hallway, every door.

"He would hate it. And he will hate me for wanting it." Gregorio looked miserable. It broke my heart to see his pain. "Harvard means so much to him."

And I knew why. But I wondered if Gregorio knew the reason why Marco insisted on Harvard. "But who would run the family business if you don't?" I was thinking out loud.

"My son is still young," Ama said, as if she'd considered every angle of this question.

Yes, Marco was young. He could father many more children. Emptiness filled me. I was a silly, lovesick fool. A woman who was beyond her sell-by date. That kiss? No need to kid myself about that.

A bony hand clutched mine, bringing me to my senses. Ama's eye pierced me with the same intensity her son had turned on me so many times. "Will you help us?"

Chapter 19

It took me one week to find the courage to broach the topic of Gregorio's education with Marco. What should I do? How could I phrase this? Yes, there was no doubt in my mind, that culinary arts was what Gregorio wanted to do with his life, what he *should* do.

The kitchen scene replayed in my mind like one of those haunting tunes you cannot forget. The joy on Gregorio's face. The love in Ama's eyes, teamed with the hope for her grandchild. She wanted him to be happy. In some ways, I'd seriously misjudged her. How could I persuade Marco to want the same for his only son?

August arrived, pressing a heavy hand over the island. When we made a trip into town, even the vegetables seemed limp, drained by the blazing sun. Days stretched longer and hotter. "We are going out on the boat today," Gregorio told me one morning after class.

"A boat?" Lexi's face lit up with delight.

"Where do you have a boat?" But then I remembered arriving at the boathouse on that first day. How trepidatious I'd felt back then.

"That boathouse, Mom. When we came here." Lexi had not forgotten.

"Of course. Sure, I remember." But I was in a daze. Since discovering Gregorio and his grandmother in the kitchen that day, we had distanced ourselves from each other. That hurt. Gregorio and I had become close. But he was Marco's son. If I were going to approach Marco about Gregorio's career aspirations, I had to choose my timing perfectly. Meanwhile I'd been doing research and had discovered some top culinary arts schools.

Lexi and Gregorio disappeared to change for a day on the water. I went upstairs but not to get into a bathing suit. No way would I do that in case Marco might be coming along. When we climbed into the limo that morning, Marco was nowhere in sight. I exhaled.

The day began to look brighter. I could relax. Settling back into the plush leather, I listened as Gregorio told Lexi all about what she might see. "We will take the boat all around the island."

Excellent. That might give me more of a view of their holdings. Although I'd explored some of the land near the castle on horseback, I had no idea what else the island had to offer. In the library I'd found a map that indicated the island was much larger than what I'd seen riding Tesoro.

When we reached the wharf, a red sportscar sat outside the boathouse. Milo stood next to it, obviously standing guard.

"Oh good. My father's here already." Smiling, Gregorio nodded at the car.

My heart was in my mouth. "So he's coming?"

Gregorio cut me a sharp look. I'd disappointed him. His face fell. But I hadn't had any opportunities to talk to Marco alone. *You could have made that opportunity, Christina.*

Taking a deep breath, I got out of the car and followed Lexi and Gregorio into the cool, woody darkness. Our footsteps echoed on the moist planks. The last time I was in this boathouse, I'd been filled with misgivings. Today didn't feel much different. Yep, here sat the boat that had brought us from Milan. Avoiding Marco on a boat this size would be difficult, if not impossible.

The boat was idling and we scrambled onboard. Marco sat there, so handsome in khaki shorts and a white shirt, left unbuttoned. He looked fit and tan. My own white shorts and green top seemed conservative but I didn't care. Today wasn't about me.

After a few directions from Milo, I ended up sitting next to Marco up front. Gregorio and Lexi sat behind us. Vitas took the helm. Men untied the ropes, tossing them into the back of the boat with a heavy thud. Very slowly, Vitas eased the boat out into the sunshine. Once outside, he let it rip. Taking a scarf from my tote, I tied it around my hair.

Marco shot me a bemused look. "What?" I asked, patting my scarf.

He shrugged and I felt dismissed.

The boat slapped over the waves, sending a welcome spray. I held on to the side, not wanting to fall against Marco.

"Relax, Profesora," he murmured as the boat picked up speed. He stretched one arm behind me along the seat. "I will not bite you."

"How ridiculous. Of course not." My sunglasses were speckled with water.

Off in the distance sat a yacht at anchor. As we advanced, Vitas did not change course.

"Really? We're headed there?" I practically had to shout.

"Don't sound so surprised," Marco murmured.

But I hadn't expected a boat this size. The yacht anchored off the coastline looked huge. We approached until it loomed above us. Our boat nudged up to a ladder. Gregorio and Lexi were the first ones off the boat, climbing briskly up the ladder, like it was no big deal. Marco helped me up as the boat rocked.

"This is yours?" One hand on the ladder that made my stomach do a flip, I glanced down at him.

"Yes. This once belonged to Onassis. I think you'll like it. His estate sold off some of his yachts." Right. Said so casually. Hand on my back, Marco gave me a nudge. "Up, Profesora."

"You mean Aristotle Onassis?" Feeling weak-kneed and disoriented, I made myself climb up the ladder. *Just one foot after the other, Christina.*

"Yes, of course." Warm and steadying, Marco's hand stayed on my back.

Although I'd gotten used to the grandiosity of the castle, Marco was still full of surprises. Maybe it was always like this with him. He no doubt had lunch with presidents or prime ministers all the time.

The end of August could not come soon enough. When I got to the top, a strong arm reached out and grabbed mine. "Stefano, take her."

We'd been asked to wear shoes with rubber soles. Now my tennis shoes squeaked on the immaculate wooden deck when

Stefano helped land me on my feet.

"Mom, hurry" Lexi called from up front. "You've got to see this. They have a pool."

I glanced at Marco, who shrugged. "How do you Americans say it? No big deal."

Glancing up, I took it in. Everywhere I looked, men dressed in sparkling white stood waiting. "Trust me, Marco. Where I come from, this is a very big deal."

We'd come to a stairway. "Let's go up," Marco said, his skin glowing in the sun. "We can relax."

"Relax?" My nerves were on overdrive. Unknotting my scarf, I tucked it back in my tote. Marco led me to a seating area done in aqua and a deeper blue, similar to the chairs at his pool. Seating for a large number of people was accommodated in four or five clusters. When I sat down, the cushion of the loveseat was solid but comfortable.

A waiter arrived. "Could I get you something, Madam?"

"Orange juice?" I managed to squeak out.

"Make that two, Ignacio," Marco held up two fingers. With a subtle nod, Ignacio disappeared.

"I thought you and Lexi would like to get away from the heat," Marco said, sitting next to me.

"Yes, this is a wonderful idea. Thank you." What did it cost to take a boat like this out for the day? I didn't want him to think I was ungrateful. "It's lovely." Beyond the boat, the water stretched forever, its turquoise color deepening when clouds drifted across the sky.

"We can sit at the pool if you prefer," Marco nodded his head to a lower level, where Lexi sat laughing with Gregorio.

"I didn't bring a suit."

"Not a problem. I always keep some in the guest staterooms."

"Do you have guests often?" I pictured Gabriella stretched out on one of the deck chairs.

He lounged back, swinging his muscled calves up to a plump hassock. "But of course. Why else have a yacht? My mother didn't want to come today but sometimes Sofia comes. Her husband used to love the boat. I think he wished it were his but then of course, his illness."

The orange juice arrived in pilsner glasses beaded with moisture. My mouth was as parched as an undipped biscotti and I quickly downed a mouthful.

"I've wanted to talk to you, Christina."

Oh boy. Here it comes. Was this where I got the sack? Was this when he'd send me packing? After all, Gregorio was set up to take his test in Milan. Did the family feel they didn't need me anymore? I would be ready to leave.

Easy for my rational side to point out, but my heart didn't agree.

Marco set his drink on a glass-topped table. "I should apologize."

I shot a glance below to where the kids were cavorting on the pool deck. They hadn't heard a word. Thank goodness he was keeping his voice low. "About what?"

His brown eyes deepened. "That night. I didn't want you to

think I took advantage of you."

Every cell in my body leaned toward this man. Keeping my body upright, I exhaled a tight breath. "No need for that." My fingers traced the wavy design on the seat cushion.

"Yes, I think there is very much a need for an apology. And I will make one."

The man was really fired up about it. Made me wonder how often he apologized. "Okay, shoot."

Marco's head jerked up, and he glanced around. "Shoot?"

"It's just a..."

His wrinkled forehead smoothed again. "Ah, yes of course. One of your figures?"

"Yes, one of those figures of speech that I keep forgetting about." Sometimes his confusion could be so endearing.

Right now he was being very serious. "I don't want you to think that I would take advantage of you. You are a guest in my home. Yes, I am employing you, but I have no right to make you kiss me."

Make me? Oh, if he only knew. This apology had not been without effort. I could see that. Perspiration beaded his upper lip. Normally that would turn me off. But not with him. "You did not make me kiss you," I whispered, my voice hoarse.

"No? So you felt it too." His hand swirled between us, as if he were casting a magical circle.

My mouth was sandpaper. I took a sip of juice and the citrus hit me in the back of the throat. "Yes, I felt something."

"Well then. I do not know what to do." He sounded like a

student in one of my classes. What was the next assignment? How often did I look up after class to find a student standing at my desk with questions about the assignment because he hadn't been listening?

But Marco wasn't a young man of sixteen or seventeen. No, he was a man. A man who apparently needed reassurance.

Just then Lexi appeared, out of breath and followed by Gregorio. "Mom, can I go swimming? I can, can't I?"

"Yes, did you bring everything?" Would she want to swim without the rash guard that hid her arm from view? Had her friendship developed to that point?

"Yep, got it all and good to go."

I didn't know where that confidence had come from, but if Gregorio was the reason, I was very grateful. They disappeared.

Marco's eyes followed them. "They get on well, don't they?"

"Yes, they are friends."

"You know, at first my mother was surprised by Lexi." He grinned, remembering.

"Surprised by what?" I had to know.

"Well, she was a girl."

I blushed at that—my necessary deception.

"And then the hair." He circled his own head with a hand.

"In America, that color is not unusual."

"Oh, in Europe too," he conceded. "Anyway, now Ama thinks Gregorio has come out of his shell because of Lexi. 'Lexi takes chances.' That's what Ama said."

While I sat there, feeling pretty proud of my daughter, Marco seemed to be turning this over. Did he like a woman who took chances?

When he turned, I felt pulled into the depths of his brown eyes. "Of course, she is like you. A strong woman."

Then his eyes clouded. Did he have concerns about them? "Don't worry about them, Marco. Your Majesty. Lexi assures me that they are just friends. And I think that is the case. They will never do anything inappropriate."

Was he sunburned or was that a flush? "Please, I was out of line there too."

Now, this was getting interesting. "In what way?"

Slinging one ankle on his other knee, he played with the leather tie on his deck shoe. Admitting he'd been wrong must not come easy. "Gregorio will choose his companions himself. And your daughter is very sweet, very lively. As I said, my mother likes her. Still, I am glad that for now, they are just friends."

As I sat there wondering what that meant, Marco jumped up and stretched. The muscles of his washboard abs rippled. "Would you like a tour?"

"Sure." Eager to break the tension, I pushed myself off the cushion. "I'd love it."

Following him into a corridor, I grasped the discreet wooden railing along the wall. The yacht was like a series of hotel rooms put together. "How many staff people do you have?"

He pursed his lips "I think only fifteen."

"Only?" I snorted, not sounding very ladylike.

He opened a door for me. "Aristotle had thirty-eight. He went overboard." Marco paused, mischievous eyes finding mine. "I know he didn't actually go over the side of one of his yachts, Profesora."

"I realize that, Your Majesty."

The hallway was so narrow. His shoulder brushed mine. The scent of his recent coffee teased me as we walked. He pointed out a dining room and the hallway leading to the kitchen. "A wonderful chef, of course."

"Of course." Now, this could have been my opportunity to bring up Gregorio. Instead, I almost stumbled, thinking of all the famous people who'd walked this very corridor while they smelled the sea air.

After the fifth stateroom, I lost count. "How many are there?"

"Seventeen. And then the master suite, which is here." He threw open a door. When I poked my head inside, there was no bed. Only a sitting area with a TV and a small bar. The closed door at the end of the room must lead to the bedroom. Unlike the modernized deck above, this decor seemed charmingly dated. All rust brown and deep ochre, much like the castle. I did not sit down. This was far too removed and private. I couldn't trust myself. Marco seemed to sense my unease.

"Let's go up to the entertainment area. You will like the movie screen."

On the floor above was a large gathering room set up with multiple pits. I collapsed in one, trying to pull my wits together. Gregorio was counting on me and so was his grandmother.

Marco joined me. "Comfortable, right? Arms out to each side, he gazed around, looking pretty pleased with himself. I couldn't blame him. Obviously, this yacht hadn't been passed down for generations. Purchasing the yacht had been his achievement. Although sometimes Marco could frustrate me, he also filled me with admiration. Although his father passed away when he was relatively young, he'd worked hard to take on this responsibility and then he'd lost his wife. Yet, he'd pulled himself from grief to raise Gregorio and he'd done a pretty good job of it.

No one else was in the area. No servers lurked. Lexi and Gregorio were laughing and shouting to each other at the front of the ship. This was my chance to talk to him or I would never do it.

I cleared my throat. A breeze had kicked up, whisking across the water and under the sun drapes. I felt encouraged by the perfect setting. This was the moment. It was now or never.

"Marco, I've been wanting to talk to you…"

Marco turned. Ah, I had his full attention now. "…about Gregorio."

He nodded. "About Gregorio and Harvard. Good."

Well, he kind of had that right. "Sort of, yes."

Why had I sat on this curving sofa where he could be this close to me? Biting my lip with nervousness, I pushed back my hair.

His eyes followed my gesture. "Oh, Christina…"

My name said that way turned me to jello.

Leaning forward, he whispered, "May I? Please?"

Maybe the setting was to blame. How more romantic could life be? Later I would wonder. But so help me, I leaned into his waiting arms. Marco's lips found mine. The kiss was wonderfully familiar and more urgent than before. When he pulled away, I felt only loss, not guilt. "You will not make me apologize for kissing you this time?" he murmured, cuddling my head to his neck.

"No." How could I? His pulse beat against my forehead and my own heart synced to his rhythm.

Running a hand down my arm, he sighed. "I have missed you so much, Christina. And I don't know how this could be."

"Yes, I know." How could this be happening?

His lips took over from there. And I knew with each kiss that I would never have enough of this man. That as long as he wanted me here in his arms, so it would be.

Yep, there I was again. I even used his stilted English in my thoughts.

But Gregorio's laughter down at the pool reminded me of my mission. I pushed away. Marco sighed. His hand tender, he traced the angle of my chin as if he could not touch me enough.

I tried, oh how I tried, to collect my thoughts.

"Marco, we have to talk about Gregorio." Sitting up straight, I tried to pull together the argument I'd thought through in my room. How many times had I jotted points on my note pad and studied them? "Are you doing what you want to do with your life?"

The question surprised him. Marco's eyes flicked to the distance. "Yes, a good question, Christina. I think I am. Well, for the most part. In some ways, my life has not been what I planned."

"Well, yes. Me too."

"What happened?" His hand stroked my arm again. "How did you end up single, hm? A wonderful woman like you. I want to know. But I hope I am not being too bold."

"No. You're not." This was a person I could trust, or so I thought. "My husband was very sweet when I married him. He drank, but so did everyone else. But then it became a problem. I couldn't trust him anymore." I'd leave it there.

"And Lexi?"

"She was only four at the time of our divorce. The decree stipulated that he could not drink when he had her for the weekend. After a couple of years, he grew lax. One night, he tried to make potato pancakes with her for dinner. There was too much oil in the pan. Of course he felt terrible." My voice trembled.

"Ay." Marco hissed. In that moment he could see it. And I loved him for that.

Waiting, he looked at me. Where was I? "She's had many surgeries on that arm and it could have been worse. But I blame myself."

"Oh, Christina." Enfolding me in his arms, Marco rocked me. Of course by then I was crying. How I wished I hadn't started down this path.

I couldn't think when he kissed the top of my head. After a few moments, I gently pushed away. He held my hand while I got back on track. "But enough of that sadness. It's important that we all do what we want in this life. I love teaching or I wouldn't be in the classroom."

"You are a very good teacher," Marco muttered, playing with my fingers. "Gregorio tells me this. He never liked any of his tutors as much as he likes you."

Aw, that turned me to mush again. "I'm happy to hear that. Marco, I want only what is best for Gregorio. That's my job as a teacher. I know you feel that way too."

"Yes, of course. My son. My only child."

"Do you think Gregorio would be happy at Harvard? Is this what he wants to do? Work on a business major so that he can run the vineyard one day?" I put the question out there.

Dropping my hand, Marco frowned. "Well, I think so, yes. It is his heritage." The words were as firm and certain as the stonework in his castle.

"Have you asked him?"

His eyes narrowed. "Christina, this is not about wanting something. This is about duty. Gregorio's duty as my son."

Was there any point in going on? But I had to lay everything out for him. Oh, he may not want to hear these words but I would not stop now. "He wants to be a chef, Marco. Your Majesty. Did you know that he and Ama often cook the meals served in the dining room?"

His lips had fallen open. Marco was regarding me as if I had gone mad before his eyes. "But this, this is nonsense. Gibberish."

I don't know where he'd heard that word—probably some movie—but there it was, hurled at me. What had I expected?

My breath was coming in short gasps. I'd failed Gregorio and that thought brought such misery. Chest tight, I could hardly breathe.

But I was not giving up. Surely Marco could see the sense of this. He loved his son. "There are schools that specialize in culinary arts. Their curriculums train chefs for the best restaurants in the world."

"Enough." Stomping his feet on the floor, he jumped to his feet.

Alarmed, one of the men looked into the salon. Marco waved a hand and the man disappeared. I shrank under his fury. "I will not hear anymore. You must be mad, Christina, to ever think I would encourage Gregorio to walk away from his heritage and go off to…cook." He spat out the last word.

Doing an abrupt about-face, Marco turned on his heel and left. Crushed, I sank back in defeat. What had I done?

Chapter 20

The heat dragged on. Classes became intolerable, and I became short tempered. Even in my sleep, my argument with Marco troubled me.

I'd failed, plain and simple. Ama was no doubt waiting to hear from me. But I couldn't face her with the bad news.

"Mom, when can we go home?" Lexi moaned one day when we were trying to catch a breeze out at the pool. "I want my air conditioning back."

"Soon, Lexi. I have to fulfill my contract." Then we would be out of here. I should feel relieved. But my heart splintered at the thought of packing my bag and leaving Marco forever. Snagging the sunblock from my tote, I squirted more on my legs and smoothed it over my skin. "Won't you miss Gregorio?"

"I guess so." Lexi stared out at the pool. This summer would be one she'd remember for the rest of her life. But she may not have realized that as we sat there.

Gregorio often joined us at the pool.

"How about dinner trays in our room tonight?" I asked. "We can sit out on my balcony." If our stay at the pool stretched toward dinner, I'd often send Lexi in with a note asking for trays to be sent to our rooms. That kept me away from Marco.

"I guess so. I'll go tell Constanza." After gathering her things, Lexi left and I soon followed.

But I wasn't expecting to find Ama waiting for me in the heated shadows of the castle corridor. "Profesora." She crooked one finger, more of a command than an invitation.

I wrapped my towel tight around me. Lexi had disappeared.

Ama pulled me into a nook behind a pillar. "Any luck, my dear?"

So now I was "my dear"? How I wanted to say yes. How I wished I could say that her only grandson would have his wish. But I couldn't. "I'm afraid I failed."

Her smile wavered. "I see." So much disappointment in those two words. I felt terrible.

"Marco and I had a talk about it." My skin broke out in goosebumps as I recalled that close encounter on his yacht. "But he wouldn't hear of it. He still holds that Harvard dream for Marco."

A ragged sigh was her only answer.

"I've let you down and I'm very sorry."

To my amazement, she squeezed my arm as if we were friends, collaborators. "Let's think. Who else might have influence with him?"

"Not me. That's for sure."

"Oh, Christina." Her soulful eyes peered into mine. "You have great influence with my son. Do not discount your own worth so casually."

Clutching my towel, I shivered in the heat. "Oh, I don't think so." She had this dead wrong.

"My son has been miserable these last few days. Never have I seen him this way." Her voice was filled with wonder.

"He isn't sick, is he? Maybe some bad fish…something that he ate."

She waved my words away. "He is love sick, child. And he will not admit it."

I felt crushed. "Has Gabriella been here? I didn't see her."

Only the Queen Mother could snort in that regal way. "This has nothing to do with one of those girls." And she gave the "g" a guttural dismissal. A faint smile teased her lips. "He is in love with a woman he cannot have. Nothing makes a man crazy like that, no?"

Her words broke over me like a cold wave, chilling and thrilling at the same time. What was she talking about?

Ama moved on. "Who else can help us?"

"Sofia." The name came easily. "They are friends, right?"

She looked at me with surprise. "I never gave her much thought. After all, she is Bianca's older sister, and Bianca, poor child, was very weak. Not at all a match for my son. You say they are friends?"

"Oh, yes, I think that Sofia is very much a friend. They share confidences." I thought back to the party. "They even joke together."

"Really. Joking?" Ama drew back, clutching her royal robe. "Then we must call for her. Demand that she come."

"An invitation might be better. Sofia has her own mind." And she might not come if Ama sent the message. Obviously the two of them traveled in different circles. "Could you say that I have asked for her? That I am ill?"

That sounded stupid and overly dramatic, but I wanted to make this right for Gregorio before I left. The awkward boy with a great mind had won my heart.

And if I were honest with myself, so had his father.

***

The following morning, we had just finished class when Milo appeared at the door. He was dressed in black as usual. "What is it?" I stepped into the hall. "Are we going on a trip into town?" I had so much to do.

"No, Profesora. But Sofia has come to see how you are." Here Milo paused, confused.

Ama had acted quickly. "Give me five minutes, Milo. Then show her to my room, please."

"Of course, Profesora."

Did I imagine the hint of respect in his tone? I ran a hand over my forehead. Maybe this heat was making me delirious. "Early dismissal," I told Lexi and Gregorio, gathering up my notes and books. "Why don't you two have an early lunch?"

They looked at each other with the excitement students show when a snowstorm back home is about to cancel school. I hurried to my room, unlocked the door and set down my books. Then I paced. What would I say to Sofia? When we'd talked about Gregorio's future, she seemed to be in Marco's camp.

I didn't have long to wait. A knock came on the door and I

rushed to open it. Sofia bustled inside. "Whatever has happened to you, Christina?" Seeing me, she stopped. "But I expected to find you wasting away in your bed." Her eyes flicked to the smoothed pane, every bolster pillow in place.

"Sofia, you are so good to come. Please sit." I motioned to a chair and took one across from her.

Settling herself with her usual elegance, Sofia studied my room. "Couldn't they have done better than this? So old-fashioned."

I glanced around at the castle trappings that had become dear to me this summer. "Trust me, this is nicer than any hotel room I've ever known."

She sniffed. "Then don't expect me to visit you in America."

I burst into chuckles, imagining what she would say about my modest cottage. "Ama and I are appealing to you for help."

Her eyebrows disappeared into her dark curls. "You and Ama are plotting together?"

The words set me back. I gripped the carved arms of the chair. "Not plotting exactly. We are...hoping. We both wish the best for Gregorio's future."

"As do I," Sofia broke in. "After all, I'm his godmother and his aunt."

Her passionate defense made me bold. "Gregorio doesn't want to go to Harvard." Might as well lay it right out there.

"He doesn't?" Her jaw slackened in amazement. "But I thought he was eager to go to America."

I lifted a shoulder. "Maybe so. But not as a business student working to take over his father's vineyards. He wants to be a chef,

Sofia."

To my surprise, her lips slowly tilted into a Cheshire smile. "I always knew there was something. Something I wasn't seeing but feeling." She patted her ample bosom.

Now this was news to me. "You did?"

"Ah, yes." She sat back with satisfaction, crossing her legs and bobbing the toe of one bowed shoe. "The care he takes with sauces, not too thick or too thin. And always the freshest vegetables. One time he sent my salad back to Constanza because he said the lettuce was not fresh."

I chuckled. "Oh, you must love Gregorio if you noticed those details."

"Of course, I do," she huffed. "I want what is best for him." She nipped her lower lip between her teeth. "But I can see the problem. Marco has always had hopes for his son and they include a degree from Harvard to better manage those family vineyards."

Oh, this was so exasperating. "But can't he have different hopes? Can't he see that Gregorio could win world renown as a chef?" That might be a stretch but what was life if not to follow your dreams?

Sofia grew thoughtful. "Gregorio has told you that this is what he wants?"

"Oh yes, no question about that." I paused thinking about the sadness in his face recently. "I'm afraid sending that young man off to Harvard would be a big mistake. And he might not even be accepted, Sofia. Only a small percentage of the applicants make it. Gregorio's aspiration is much more reachable."

"I see." Rising, Sofia smoothed her summer sundress. Studded with sprigs of lavender, it did not come from a catalogue. "Then I must speak with Marco at once."

I followed her to the door. "Do you think Gregorio has a chance?"

Wearing a smug expression, Sofia turned. "Marco loves his son very much. Like most parents, he wants what is best. Granted, this will be a difficult decision. There's a lot at stake, but I think he will see reason."

"I understand that." Thinking back to this crazy summer which had started as a way to save Lexi from herself and ended with me scheming to protect my pupil, I nodded. "Yes, parents will do anything to save their children."

"And what about you?" When she turned, her full skirt rustled. I opened the door. "What do you mean?"

Sofia leaned closer, although no one appeared to be in the hall. "What about you and Marco?"

I stepped back. "Sofia, I don't know what you've heard but there is no 'me and Marco.'" The very idea was preposterous.

"Heard?" The pearl drops hanging from her ears quivered when she gave her head an impatient shake. "Don't be silly. I have eyes. I watched you two dancing at the party."

Oh, for heaven sakes. What was she talking about? My heart was beating wildly.

Twirling around with a cute little giggle, she skipped out into the hall. "Why don't you come with me?"

"Oh, no. This should be your personal conversation." Seeing

Marco again? I couldn't imagine it. All I wanted was to leave and go home.

"No, no." She waved me on. "Come. You will save me the worry of telling you everything we say."

She had a point. I did want to hear this in person. But the thought of facing Marco sent my heart into spasms.

***

Bolstered by Sofia's energy, I tried to be hopeful as she rapped on Marco's door.

"Come in!" he called out.

The tone of his voice made me turn to Sofia. "He sounds a little surly."

"We'll fix that," she whispered.

Wearing an impish smile, Sofia popped her head into the office. "Do you have time for a short visit?"

"I always have time for you, Sofia."

Grabbing my hand, she towed me along with her. Maybe this had been a bad idea.

Marco looked surprised to see me. "And for you too, Profesora." His tone softened. I relaxed a little.

Coming around the desk, he kissed his sister-in-law on both cheeks. "As usual, you look wonderful and fresh."

Sofia giggled while his eyes turned to me. Drawing in a breath, he said nothing and turned away. Reaching for the brass bell used to call the servants, he asked, "Would you ladies like something. Coffee? A mimosa, perhaps?"

Looking like she meant business, Sofia shook her head. "Not

for me."

"Profesora?" Marco's eyes seemed so impersonal, as if he'd erected a shield.

"Nothing, thank you." I was having second thoughts about coming here.

"The only thing I want," Sofia said, "is your undivided attention, Marco."

With a guarded look, he motioned to the chairs. "Then please sit down." Returning to his desk, Marco got comfortable. "So, what's up, as the Americans say?"

"I'm here to talk about Gregorio. My godchild."

"Is something wrong?" His eyes turned wary.

"Maybe." Sofia pursed her lips. It amazed me how she could tease him with a look, while standing her ground. "It's always been important to me that my son Alfonso be happy about his future. Don't you wish the same for Gregorio?"

"But of course."

Folding her hands in her lap, Sofia pinned Marco with a serious look. The mood had changed. "When we were younger, we all had our dreams, right? Certainly I thought I would marry the man of my dreams and live happily ever after."

"Vincenzo was a very good man. Perhaps too old for you, but your parents meant well. Hadn't they done the same for Bianca?" Here, Marco sighed. "We cannot blame our parents for decisions they made."

"Goals." Sofia stabbed the air with a manicured nail. "Our marriages were goals, Marco. You know that well."

Although I knew nothing about Sofia's marriage, she was now giving me a glimpse. One that made me feel great compassion for her. Was this the nature of marriage among royalty?

The lines on Marco's face deepened and I sensed what he might look like in his old age. How it pained me that I would not be there to smooth away his concerns and soften life's disappointments. "You're right," he finally said. "Perhaps Bianca may not have been my first choice, or I, hers."

But Sofia was not about to become mired in the past. "Bianca was young. Perfect for the mother of your children."

"She could be charming. So innocent and isolated from life's problems." A shadow crossed his handsome features. "I'd hoped that would change with motherhood and maturity."

"Let's not dwell on my poor sister." Sofia got back to business. "She did not like motherhood. I felt sorry for her because she could not appreciate that joy."

This conversation had turned into a walk down memory lane. Although it may be enlightening, I didn't see how dredging up painful memories could benefit Gregorio.

"If you could have had your dream, what would you have done?" Sofia waited. And so did I.

Marco played with his empty coffee cup.

"Marco?" Sofia was waiting.

Releasing a sigh, he finally looked up. "I would have gone on to school. You know that, Sofia. Oxford or perhaps Harvard."

Could Sofia hear the loss in his voice? The dream deferred?

Marco's sister-in-law gave a curt nod. "Exactly. You did not have your dream. I did not have mine. Do we want our children to reach this age and still feel the pang of loss?"

"No, of course not." Marco moved restlessly in his chair. His eyes swept me and Sofia. "I do not want that for Gregorio."

Maybe progress was being made. I wanted to cheer. Leaning forward, Sofia tapped a finger on his desk. "Our responsibilities do not have to be our children's fate."

My heart almost stopped when suspicion flickered over his face. "So you two have been talking?"

Her eyes veering to mine, she tilted her head as if to say *Maybe*. "What if we have, Marco? A problem is a problem, no matter who brings it to your attention."

"Is the situation that serious?" Beneath his golden tan, the King was looking a little pale.

"Oh, I think so." When Sofia bobbed her head, those pearls quivered. "A child that is forced to do something is not a happy child. But it is not too late to prove that you are a good father concerned for the happiness of your child. Not only his family heritage, but also his happiness. Look at the Windsor family. Do you think it was wise to arrange that marriage with Diana? How did that turn out?"

"Yes, of course you're right." He ran a hand over his forehead. "That will not happen. When the time comes, I will not force Gregorio into a loveless marriage."

"A career is like a love affair, Marco. What you do every day either makes you happy or miserable. Would you wish that on Gregorio?"

At that point, Marco darted me an incriminating look. I tried to look innocent but probably failed. Wasn't this what I had told him about teaching? I loved it... but my love for him counted more. I saw that now.

My love for Marco felt huge. So all-encompassing that losing the sight of him every day would feel far worse than the loss of a job. The thought rocked me.

Marco rose with an abrupt lurch. Our eyes followed him as he paced from one end of the office to the other, head bowed and hands behind his back. Finally, he circled back to us. "You have made your point. Perhaps I should talk to Gregorio."

"I think so." Sofia looked over at me. "Perhaps you should re-evaluate other areas of your life as well."

Oh mercy. I had to get out of here.

Sofia wasn't finished and Marco was definitely listening. "What will bring joy back to this castle? Whatever your decision is, soon Gregorio will be gone. Once people leave, you lose the opportunity to fix that relationship."

Tears clouded my vision. "Excuse me. I am late...for something." And with that I stumbled from the room.

***

The kittens were soft, furry balls as they clambered over me. Their delicate claws snagged on my shirt while they cuddled. That one bold, gray male scrambled to lick my chin, his tiny tongue making me giggle, although I sure didn't feel like laughing. Not after that scene with Sofia and Marco. A brisk ride on Tesoro seemed like a good idea after that painful but hopefully successful meeting. Sofia had done a wonderful job and I hoped that something good would come out of that for Gregorio.

Right now, I needed this distraction of the mother cat and her kittens. They were so tiny. Their whole life lay before them. Not in any hurry, I stretched out in the prickly hay, murmuring sweet nothings to those babies. I felt drained.

The sound of boots on the walkway made me freeze. Marco. Cupping my furry friends, I hunkered down. But Rudolfo must have given him a heads-up. Soon Marco's head appeared over the stall. "What are you doing, Profesora?" Not a man who asked permission, he opened the gate and entered. "What is this? New kittens?"

Dropping my eyes, I concentrated on the playful brood. "Paying a maternity visit. I love these little guys."

I had to smile as Marco tiptoed over very carefully to sit next to me in the straw. Alarmed, the mother began picking up her kittens to move them to another corner.

"She is afraid of me?" Marco watched them go.

"Maybe she knows you are a man who wants his way."

Was that necessary? The hurt look on his face made me regret my words. "Sorry."

"No, no." Picking up a piece of straw, he began to mindlessly shred it. "You are right. Are you always right, Profesora?"

Oh, he was so handsome sitting there with that rueful smile, the fading light burnishing his curls. "No. I am not always right. Look at that first day when I thought you were the stable boy."

His sadness lifted, as if he were remembering too. "Yes, you felt so good in my arms. I wondered." Marco gave me a devious side glance.

"You wondered what?" I waited.

He shrugged. "Well, of course I wanted you. You felt so right in my arms. And you'd been so brave, rolling through the thorn bush. All those sticks in your hair and scratches on your lovely hands." While I thought about "feeling right" in his arms, he began to play with my fingers. His touch was soft but the effect on me was electric. "I'm glad you came to see me today with Sofia."

"Really?" I could hardly breathe. One word was all I could manage. "Why?"

"She told me things I needed to hear. Christina, I want Gregorio to be happy. And if cooking will make him happy, then so be it. Let him be a cook." Leaving my fingers, he held up both hands in surrender.

"A chef," I interjected. No way did I want Gregorio's career brushed off as mere cooking. Hope rose in my heart. *Oh, Sofia. How can I thank you?*

"Yes, fine. A chef, wearing the white hat. Then I am fine with that. If he does not want Harvard, well, I will accept that." Indeed, he did look resigned. "I want my son to have a happy life. Do you think it is too late, Christina? Have I made a mess of things?"

His eyes were liquid when he lifted them to mine, as if he were tormented.

"No. It is not too late. Gregorio will be so happy. You'll see."

As he listened carefully, the tension in Marco's body eased. The gray kitten had wandered back to curl up next to me.

Reaching over, Marco petted the kitten. He could have such a gentle way about him. I almost felt those strokes on my own skin. But I had more work to do. "Before I leave, I'll do some research on the right school for him."

His hand stilled. "Oh, Christina. Those words make me so sad." And he did look miserable.

"Don't worry. We will find the right school for him. You and Gregorio can visit the campuses in the months ahead and see which program might be a good fit."

"But I want you to come too." His lower lip came out.

"I'm afraid there won't be time for that." A heavy sadness settled on my heart. "I'll be back home teaching by then."

For a long moment he studied me, this man that I loved. The man I would miss every day for the rest of my life. I knew that deep in my heart, felt it in my soul.

"Your leaving makes me so sad, Christina." And he stopped, considering. "I want you to stay."

How I cherished those words. But they didn't change the situation. "I wish I could. But school is starting." I'd come for this job and now the job was over.

"Marry me, Christina."

The words came so softly. I almost missed them. "What did you just say?"

Setting the kitten aside, he tugged me gently into his arms. I could not push him away. He nuzzled my forehead, his lips in my hair. "You make me crazy and happy all at the same time. Please stay. Marry me. You know we will be happy together."

"But that's madness." I wasn't crazy but his lips might bring me to that point.

"Is it?" With a slow smile, he cupped my chin in one hand and kissed me. The kiss was slow and delicious. The warmth of his hands on my neck set the rest of my body on fire.

Could madness somehow become my future? "But what about Lexi?"

I could feel his smile. "She has already told Gregorio that she hopes we will marry."

Now, that was a shock. "But her schooling?"

"She wants to go to school in the village with Gregorio. She thinks he will introduce her to some 'hot guys.' I think that's what he told me."

Sometimes a mother can be surprised.

"You have not had a good husband. Let me be your good husband. I promise, I will do everything to make you happy," he murmured while my head spun between kisses.

"That might be a big order," I murmured, "—making me happy."

"Yes, I know," he said, giving my nose a soft tap. "But I am the king. I can make things happen."

"Is that a personal promise?" Pulling away, I poked his chest with a finger and ended up flattening my palm on his thudding heart. "I don't want a promise from the king of Napolitano. I want a promise from Marco—the man I love."

Taking my shoulders, he nudged me back into the hay, so warm against my back. "I promise now and forever. And we will have fun making each other happy. This I promise." That roguish smile of his made my stomach quiver in anticipation.

"I love you so much, Christina. I will never be able to find the words." And he did looked bemused.

"Let me teach you," I suggested, loving the grin that lit up his face.

"Oh, please. Yes."

And there I was, ready to rush mindlessly into a thrilling future, when something occurred to me. A deal-breaker for sure. "But I probably can't have more children. I want all the cards on the table."

His lips pursed as he thought. "All right. That is fine. We will play cards together too." After another kiss that sealed the deal, he pulled back, all foolishness gone. "We already have Gregorio and Lexi. We don't need more children, hmm? But we should probably try a lot. Just a scientific experiment. Don't you think?"

When he wiggled a wicked brow, all rational thought fled. "Oh, yes. Yes." I clutched the fabric of his shirt in my hands.

"Then it shall be so." Marco fanned my hair over the prickly hay with his fingers. Delighted, the male kitten began playing with it. "And no more tight cornettos with your hair, please?"

I chuckled. "That's going to be a lot of work in the morning."

He twirled a curl around one finger. "Ah, I look forward to helping you, Queen Christina."

I sat up so fast, I nearly smashed into Marco's chin.

"What's wrong?" He sat up on his elbows. The kitten backed off with a tiny meow.

"Nothing. I just hadn't thought about that part. Crowns and all that. I wouldn't have to wear one of those heavy crowns, would I?"

The weight of my wandering mind made me sink back into the straw.

"Don't worry." With a sigh, Marco stretched out next to me. "You don't have to do anything you don't want to do."

"Okay then. That's a yes." I knew this man would make me laugh forever.

"And we must have the wedding soon." His eyes sparkled.

"So, you're a man in a hurry?" I played with the tab on his shirt.

"Yes. Strictly for the country." For a second his straight face had me fooled.

"You stinker."

Looking horrified, he sniffed the air.

"No, no. I am kidding. You are perfect." And I kissed him just so he'd know this was true.

Epilogue

Reena

Holding Christina's arms for balance, I crushed grapes under my feet. They felt squishy and weird, oozing through my toes. We kept hopping.

"My heels are starting to hurt," I admitted. "We've been at this for fifteen minutes. You're just tapping the grapes and I'm crushing them."

"You're right. This stomping stuff hurts. I don't want to bruise my feet." My friend laughed. Had I ever seen her this carefree?

A cool October breeze rustled the colorful fall leaves that stretched to the horizon like a crazy quilt. I could hardly believe that Christina lived here now. But how wonderful. I liked her new husband so much. Every once in a while, a welcome spray hit us from the fountain.

"We can stop." Christina slowed her pace. "Marco thought this might be fun. You know, a memorable visit for you. Harvesting the grapes is a big deal here."

"Yeah, I understand. Who knew a year ago that we would be crushing grapes for the harvest?"

Christina gave me a soft smile. "If we were back home, we'd be preparing for class or grading essays." She gave the crushed grapes another thump or two.

"Right, but I'm glad that we've moved on."

"I want to hear more about that when we're finished here." She stared down at our wine-stained calves.

Marco ambled over to the big wooden tub. "You look beautiful, Cara. And such a good worker."

When he talked to Christina like that, I felt I shouldn't be here. That look in his eyes as he took in his new bride sent my own tummy swirling. "So you guys do this every year?" I asked, just to remind them that I was still here.

"Yes, the harvest is very special for us. In the old days, we didn't have the presses to crush the grapes." He gave a cute shrug. "So what you're doing is symbolic. Acknowledging the past."

"Beautifully said." Christina gave him a smile and kept stomping, her dark blonde hair flying every which way.

"I like your hair, by the way." What a relief to discover she'd ditched the stern topknot.

"And so do I." Marco overheard us. "But now I must circulate. That is a new concept Christina has taught me. Circulating."

"Just a suggestion, Marco." Christina sent him a sweet grin. I had a feeling these two teased each other a lot.

"And maybe stop such hard crushing with your delicate...," he looked at me, "...feet."

Turning, he began talking to his sister-in-law Sofia, a neat lady who'd stopped by when I arrived from England.

"I wish I could have been here for the wedding," I managed to say between breaths. Although I'd tucked my skirt up in my waistband, it kept slipping.

"Everything happened so quickly." Propped on the edge of the oaken tub, Christina smiled that secret smile, no doubt reliving wonderful moments. Her wedding pictures brought tears to my eyes. Their love was so palpable. Lexi and Gregorio seemed to share in that joy.

"I'm happy for you. You've inspired me." But that pinch in my chest may have been a little jealousy.

She leaned closer. "Let's take a break so you can tell me about breaking up with Judd. And I want to hear more about England and your Aunt Penelope."

Marco had returned. Time to leave the grapes behind for some girl talk. Grabbing his hand, Christina stepped from the vat. I was next. A woman rushed forward with a warm, damp towel for each of us.

Sporting purple legs, we made our way to a table. Lexi was there to give me a big hug. "Aunt Reena, look at you! You're such a good sport."

I ruffled her hair. Although I wasn't biologically her aunt, I sure liked that title. She'd grown up over the summer. "Talk about a good sport, Lexi. You came all the way over here with your mom. That was pretty brave."

She rolled her eyes. "Like I had a choice. At first I was mad, but things got better. Gregorio and I are buds now." She nodded to her new brother, who smiled shyly. He was kind of quiet and still in that awkward teenage phase, but he clearly adored Christina and

Lexi.

Sitting down in a chair, I wiped my forehead with the towel before starting on my legs.

"When will these grapes be used for wine?" I asked Christina.

"Marco tells me they will begin to ferment immediately. But it will be years before this batch is wine."

"These grapes mean a lot to the family." Yesterday Marco had taken us out to his vineyards. Pride shone in his eyes. Christina had shared Gregorio's story and how Marco had reluctantly approved a change in the plans for his son's future.

"Yes, the vineyards and the olive trees. Gregorio has been talking to his father about those olives. Something to do with his future culinary studies."

One of the staff members passed by with wine and mimosas. Setting the towel aside, I snagged a mimosa and turned to Christina. "How about you?"

"Grape juice, please?" she asked the man. "But in a wine glass please, Alfredo."

"Of course, Your Majesty."

Christina shook her head as the man turned and walked away. "I just can't get used to that title."

"Mom, just tell 'em." Lexi spoke up. "I told the men to call me Lexi, not something royal."

I totally understood why Christina looked so uncomfortable. This was a huge leap for her. "Yes, sweetheart, but it's good to remember that we aren't royal," she said. "I happened to marry into the royals."

"No, you are the queen. Just ask my father." Gregorio spoke up and Christina's blush deepened.

"Come on. There's someone I want you to meet," he said to Lexi.

She bounced up and gave me a quick kiss. "See you at dinner, Aunt Reena."

Tossing her towel aside, Christina settled back in her chair. "Now tell me about Judd. You two had been engaged forever. What happened? I thought you might have a Christmas wedding."

That realization still hurt. Had I wasted three years? "Maybe that was the problem. We took each other for granted. At the end, I'm not sure the passion was there. Hate to admit it, but that's how it felt." My voice broke and Christina leaned over to squeeze my hand.

"Well, you've got to have that." She sat back. I loved the way Christina's eyes found Marco as he made his way through the crowd. "I think Judd was too quiet for you, Reena. But England. How did you end up there?"

An empty hole opened up inside. "I couldn't stay in Pittsburgh. Not after Judd and I broke it off. Cripes, everyone felt sorry for me. Mary Carmichael was already planning a shower for me. I felt terrible, giving her the news."

"That must have been miserable." Christina threw me a commiserating glance.

"I hated the pity." My temper flared, just thinking about it. "Anyway, over in England my Aunt Penelope fell and broke her hip. Because of my dad's stroke in the spring, my mother couldn't go over and help. I volunteered."

Reaching over, Christina squeezed my arm. "That's so you, Reena. Always so generous."

I wrinkled my nose. "Is that pity I hear in your voice?"

Christina giggled. "No. That is pure admiration."

"Turned out not to be so bad. Devon is beautiful." I'd leave it there.

"Devon. How wonderful! We can see each other more often. So you decided to stay a little longer?"

"Your good luck made me willing to take more chances. The man who took your position at school has a wife who also teaches English. They're new in town, so this was perfect. Why not explore some possibilities, as Emily Dickinson said."

Christina chuckled. "Ah, yes. 'I dwell in possibility.' Remember that quote? Well, you have no children, so you can make your own decisions."

"True, but there are risks with this. I'm renting out my condo, not putting it up for sale."

"Great idea. At some point, I'll have to go back and put my house on the market."

We'd finished with our legs. Christina rolled up her towel and a woman whisked it from her hand, along with mine. I could get used to this kind of service.

I gave the castle another glance. "Your digs aren't too shabby."

She shook her head. "Come on. You're staying in my old room. Dated, wouldn't you say? We're in the process of doing some redecorating. So, back to England. Any available men in Devon?"

I choked on my mimosa. "Napkin, please," I managed to get out.

Christina managed to hand me one. "Oh, I hoped you don't get all sticky from the orange juice." With all the fuss and dabbing at juice, I hoped Christina would forget where this conversation had left off.

But no luck. "Again," she said, waving her goblet of juice, "back to the men."

"Well, there are some." What more could I say without sending her to the Internet for details?

"Okay, any chemistry?" Christina wasn't letting up.

"Not sure. The Brits can be a bit different—different bordering on difficult." We both broke into laughter. How I wished I had Christina around to laugh with the way we used to.

"Sometimes the difficult men are the best, the most interesting." Christina's distant smile made me wonder if Marco had fit that description.

Alfredo had returned with the grape juice and she took a sip.

Christina's mother-in-law appeared and she waved the older woman over. Ama was a really strange bird, in my book.

"Ama, are you going to take a turn at crushing the grapes?" I asked.

She looked at me with horror. "Such a disgusting show."

Well, that shouldn't surprise me. This was a woman who shuffled around in long dresses. Who knew what her legs looked like under all those layers?

Ama glanced over at Christina's glass. "You are not drinking wine, my dear?"

"N-no." Suddenly Christina got all flustered. My antenna went up. What was this? "Um, my stomach's a little upset."

Ama's brows lifted. "I see. Some soda crackers perhaps? I will see what Constanza has." And with that she took off, skirts flapping.

I turned to my friend. "Hey, what was that about?"

Christina's blush got deeper. "Nothing."

I went through some numbers in my mind. They'd been married in early September and it was mid-October. Exciting possibilities twirled through my mind. I grabbed her hand. "Are you holding out on me?"

That silly smile told me I was right. "So, how far along?" This was downright amazing.

"Not far. I'm sure it's nothing. Maybe just early menopause. I've read about that." She gnawed the corner of her lips before breaking into an excited smile.

"Does he know?" I nodded to Marco who seemed to be headed back this way.

Her eyes widened. "No. Please don't say anything. I want to be more certain."

"What are you two talking about?" Marco arrived, leaning over the back of Christina's chair to give her a kiss. The man was one fine specimen. "Do you have secrets?"

The air had become very still, the splashing fountain the only sound.

Christina beamed a smile at him. "Maybe."

"Are you going to share your secret with me?" Marco was so cute the way he teased her, trailing a finger down her neck as if he couldn't resist touching her.

"Maybe?" Christina gave me a deer-in-the-headlight look.

Sitting next to her, Marco brought his lips close to her ear. My own ear tickled as I watched. "My mother went to get you some crackers. She thinks you might be pregnant." And he chuckled, as if this were the most outlandish thing in the world.

When Christina didn't laugh, Marco's jaw dropped. The air grew quiet and the world seemed to stop. I sat back, wishing I were somewhere else. This was such a personal moment.

"It's probably nothing," Christina said quietly.

"But you told me this was not possible. That this could not happen." Eyes wide, Marco pressed a hand to his heart. Geesh, was he going to have a heart attack?

Looking uncomfortable, Christina murmured, "I told you it probably wouldn't happen."

She looked to me for help, but what could I say?

"But you think maybe?" Hope shone in his eyes.

"I didn't mean to make this happen, Marco."

Hey, was she apologizing?

"No, no, cara mia. Whatever happens, I have everything already with you." Bringing her hand to his lips, Marco kissed it with such reverence that the gesture brought tears to my eyes. "But if you carry our child, I can't tell you how happy I would be."

Ama had returned. A woman of few words, she plopped a china plate on the wrought iron table. "Crackers. Nibble. Tiny bites."

Tucking her hands into her cuffs, she stood waiting with undisguised approval. "Wonderful, no?" She turned to me, as if this baby were a done deal.

"Yes, wonderful." Pushing up from the table, I winked at my friend. "And now I should go pack. Tomorrow I have to head back to England."

Who knew what awaited me at Devon? I'd left a bloody mess behind.

THE END

Be sure to sign up for Barbara's newsletter for an alert about other books in the *Romancing the Royals* series. Go to:

www.BarbaraLohrAuthor.com
www.facebook.com/barbaralohrauthor

Other Books by Barbara Lohr

Best Friends to Forever
Marry Me, Jackson
Steal My Heart, Trevor
Christmas with Dr. Darling

Man from Yesterday series
Coming Home to You
Always on His Mind
In His Eyes
Late Bloomer
Still Not Over You
Every Breath You Take
Christmas Dreams and Santa Schemes

Windy City Romance series
Finding Southern Comfort
Her Favorite Mistake
Her Favorite Honeymoon
Her Favorite Hot Doc
The Christmas Baby Bundle
Rescuing the Reluctant Groom
The Southern Comfort Christmas

About the Author

Barbara Lohr writes heartwarming contemporary romance. The *Best Friends to Forever* series is set in the Carolinas. Close friendships turn to attraction for Emily, Bryn, Josie and the men in their lives. This is a wholesome series that conveys all the emotions of sweet romance.

In her *Windy City Romance* series, the Kirkpatrick family and friends are based in Oak Park, Illinois, a suburb of Chicago. However, these adventurous girls take readers on exciting jaunts to Tuscany, Guatemala and Savannah. They travel wherever their hearts take them. This is a contemporary romance series. The *Man from Yesterday* series is set in Gull Harbor, Michigan, where the boy you left behind might be the man you want forever. The charming, small beach town actually exists but under another name.

Barbara lives in the South of the United States with her husband and a cat that insists he was Heathcliff in another life. Visit her Facebook page and be sure to sign up for her newsletter for new releases, great giveaways and a fun group of readers who enjoy Barbara's work. She loves to hear from her readers!

www.BarbaraLohrAuthor.com
www.facebook.com/Barbaralohrauthor
www.twitter.com/BarbaraJLohr

Made in the USA
Columbia, SC
14 June 2020